I0555526

LYING TRUTH

Edna Faust

Salem-Danvers Village Press

Salem-Danvers Village Press

Published by FGNA Publishing, a division of Faber Group North America. Faber Group North America is domesticated in the state of Delaware, in the United States of America. Completely virtual, not located anywhere.

Published by Salem-Danvers Village Press, an imprint by FGNA Publishing, which is a division of Faber Group North America.

First Salem-Danvers Village Press publishing/printing, June 2015.

First Edition; Paperback

Copyright © 2015 Edna Faust
Lying Truth

Unless otherwise noted, this book is printed in the United States of America, Great Britain, or Continental Europe.

The author retains this copyright unless noted otherwise.

Publication note:
This work is a creation of fiction. Any person indicated in this work of fiction is clearly an idea of the author. The people presented in this book are all fictitious, and do not exist. All areas of locations represented in this book are clearly fictitious and don't exist, even though they might exist. Nothing represented in this work of fiction is real, even though actual things might seem real. The author did however put some of his/her own entities into this book, but made so that they are different. **Some portions of this book are based on actual facts and actual life events, but certain names have been changed. Some portions of this book is non-fiction.** The publisher nor the author, or anybody affiliated with them are responsible for anything that occurs. This means that you may not file any legal action against us for something that occurs or occurred in your life.

No part of this book may ever be used or reproduced in any type of physical manner whatsoever without written and signed permission from the author and or publisher, except in the case of brief quotations embodied in articles and reviews, along with educational and research purposes. This book may be purchased for educational, research, personal use, business, or sales promotional use.

Copyright © 2015 Edna Faust
All rights reserved.

ISBN: 0692460942
ISBN-13: 978-0692460948

LYING TRUTH

Edna Faust

ACKNOWLEDGMENTS

There have been some instances of people who have encountered mysterious images and journeys of people getting away with anything they want. And so you suppose, there was a way that I would mention people in this area of acknowledgements, but why. Well, I will make this quick and simple, because I will only tell you, that something mysterious is going to occur, and you can never escape, but good luck.

Lying Truth
Edna Faust

LYING TRUTH

LYING TRUTH

Nothing Belongs Here

Contents

CHAPTER ONE

People always say the darndest things, at least what I've heard. Not only that, people can notice the stupidest things, but they also have developed a knack of narcissism. There have been many times in which a person might encounter such traits, but let's keep this simple, or so you think. For many reasons, you might think my story might end here, but it is just beginning. Alas, there might be more important things for you to do, but such activities might sway you to listen to my story, yet you will encounter nothing unusual, because I already expected you to encounter them before in your life, depending on your ability to have fun, or something like that, but try not to under estimate me, because I always win.

We begin in the small town of Winslow, South Dakota, where friends Amelia Walton, Erica Monansky,

Melissa Peters, and Elizabeth Ryan have known each other since birth. There is, however, another part of this story, that five years later, Allison Andrews and her family moved here to Winslow, South Dakota. But enough about that, and continue on to their childhood or something more interesting.

Eighteen years have now passed, and Amelia, Erica, Melissa, Elizabeth, and Allison are just starting their senior year of high school, at the prestigious school of Prep Stone Academy. Oh, yeah, all of them turned eighteen in August, which was one month before the start of the school year. One thing that I forgot to mention was that they all had lots of money, since their parents and ancestors struck it big with oil, diamonds, and gold. In the simple mind of something that could take long and hard years, these ancestors made it possible within one day, yet, I also forgot to mention that all five families knew each other and were business partners, but they moved on with their lives, ever since the stock market crash of 1929. Sure, they were immune from the crash, because they did not use bank accounts, nor did they believe in them, but they did have them, and only kept the minimal balance required to avoid unnecessary fees.

On the eve of the first day of school, the group meets up at a secret location, where they have been holding secret events, in which only certain people know. In the time that it takes them to discuss what they are doing, you probably will already be bored. So, in the epitome of the people, you have been excused from today's events. Dealing with something normal, the girls decide to take some action, but before that, it is the time to construct their details of the never-ending break up scene, which doesn't exist until it appears.

Appearing from behind is nothing, but it remains unseen. There is a noise heard by the girls. Irk, said Allison, something is happening. Nothing is happening, yet Allison believed she heard a noise. The power goes off, and soon the girls head to the basement to find the circuit break, only to find nothing but skeletons and a half naked man, from the waist up, with gorgeous abs. Knowing nothing, all five girls escape and head back home, so that they can rest for their first day of school tomorrow. Beginning tomorrow is a new chapter in their life, as it is seen as the last chapter of compulsory schooling for their entire lives. It is known that they are actually all smart and have excellent GPAs, also to be a perfect 5.0 on the IB scale, since all of them are gifted and too smart for everything. It seems obvious to dictate anything, yet, they find it meaningless, since it is useless in the real world.

Over the course of the years, the girls remained close. In seventh grade, they started their own clique or some unusual group that relates to a group. They were the most popular in school, and yes, this is still at the prestigious Prep Stone Academy in Winslow, South Dakota. Nothing is known of the group, but it is often shrouded in mystery, yet people have heard of it, often so have everyone else. No one can join, since it is exclusive to just the five girls, yet, sometimes there are crazy people who think membership is often. In order to get join, you must be invited, and they must like you. Once you have been selected, you will face numerous hazing activities, but it is not even hazing, because prospective members will do anything to join a selective group of girls just to become popular. Everything you thought you knew about high school and cliques remains a mystery, and since you probably already knew that, you should also know that the five girls are also the most popular at this school. Basically, they run this school, since they can, and since their parents donate a huge sum of money just to fund the school. If you think that might change, Prep Stone Academy already has an endowment of fifty billion dollars, yet alumni and certain other people keep funding it. It is known that the school does not need any more funding, but people just want to make sure it never goes bankrupt.

The mere thought of no funding by people to Prep Stone Academy would result in a systematic failure for the local economy, as well as decreasing property values. In other words, if the school collapses or is not funded, the entire economy will collapse in the entire state. Billionaires and millionaires send their children here to learn at the Prep Stone Academy. There is no requirement for the teachers to have an education degree or even a teaching certificate, since it is a private school. Prep Stone Academy was always treated as a college. The minimum requirement to teach is a master's degree in the chosen field. Sure, most teachers have PhDs in their fields, but they are well qualified and make above average salaries than other teachers in the field. Everything about this school is prestigious, yet it seems like a normal prep school for college. It has all the basic groups of a normal school, the jocks, the geeks, the band, the orchestra, the nerds, and the misfits. Altogether, there are three campuses, one for elementary, one for junior high, and one for senior high. Each campus is located less than five minutes away from each other.

From the very beginning, students learn how to

add, subtract, multiply, and divide in kindergarten. By the first grade they are learning pre-algebra in order to learn and build the foundations of math. Science is also learned early in the curriculum, as it will help the students understand about life. Each teacher, as I mentioned, teaches core subjects. That means, instead of spending all day in one class during elementary school, you will spend different amounts of times in different class rooms, just like middle school and high school. Everything is better this way, as it builds learning to a new level that will increase knowledge and help broaden the country to a more competitive level. One word of advice is that this school does not teach or believe in creationism because creationism does not teach anything. Creationism does not even exist. The entire universe is way older than ten thousand years old, yet people still believe it is this age. Dinosaurs did not live with humans, but certain people believe that dinosaurs did live with humans. Creationism does not explain anything because it is not true, and everything about it is wrong. The whole process was built on a lie by Moses on the basis of Adam and Eve, then Cain and Able, and possibly Noah and his Ark. There is no proof that Adam, Eve, Cain, and Able existed. There is a possibility that Noah existed, but how could you explain a flood that is forty days and forty nights. You can't have an even amount of days and nights, and if you did, it would have to occur in the middle of day. Forty days equals thirty-nine nights, and it does not mean eighty days.

Sure, you could probably scold me, but everything I say is the truth. I only speak of the truth. There is only truth, never any lies. It is highly impossible to doubt my claims, because every one of my claims is an actual fact.

Yet, there is a possibility that could happen in the course of all events. In the scenario that will cause everything to turn to stone, well, that is unlikely, but could be true if you had the proper tools, such as cement, but who needs cement when you have asphalt, which could contain tar. I am not going to torture you, and since you think I am, you must be mistaken or incompetent. Nothing will ever try to harm you, unless you harm it first, which have different meanings. If you harmed something but you think you did not harm something, you probably did harm something. Different species, kingdoms, geniuses, classes, and other groups live different. What one action to you is, well that action has a different meaning to the other. That is the way the chain of life is built. Everything has a meaning to the balance of life, and this is widely known and accepted, yet critics exist, and attempt to denounce everything.

There was, however, something that is simply wrong, which was the Warren Commission. In actuality, the mafia killed John Fitzgerald Kennedy, not Lee Harvey Oswald, who was a scapegoat. The same happened to JFK's brother, who was some sort of jerk towards the mafia, and who also thought gambling by a wire communication would abolish the mafia completely. There is something to learn from all of this, which is nothing sort of new, but it is that government should not overregulate anything. Overregulation is the reason why there is a catastrophic meltdown in the entire economy. Yes, I know that the Faberx Corporation (pronounced: Far-Burg) is the United States of America, and that everything I said could be in the past. But the real issue is that it takes time to overcome certain hurdles in life. There is something that would always want to change the topic, and it will attempt to block progress because it hates progress.

As it was certainly known, the five girls that I mentioned before, well, it is almost morning, and almost time for them to head to school. One hour remains until they have to wake up and head to Prep Stone Academy. The whole idea seems useless, just a bunch of garbage, and that is just what people want you to think. Believe it or not, there is still some thinking going on in your head. Your brain is still developing, yet you see it fit to undermine the society of a global index. In order for you to keep on going you must engage in your opinions and remove the obstacles. This might be difficult but it will have to happen, if you want to make it in this world. Yet, there remains an intricate mechanism that allows people to engage in the exact opposite behavior. Most religious people will describe this as the devil's work, but is that meaning actually accurate, or is it just an excuse because that is what they believe. And if you believe it is the devil's work, you are actually wrong and are grouped with the average people. Nothing can see the light of day if people believe that the devil wants to promote bad behavior. The devil does not promote bad behavior because there is no such thing as the devil. Instead, from an actual perspective, the brain causes behavior. Sure, bad spirits might exist, but it is actually the brain that can cause behavior, because of abnormalities that can occur within. There are many reasons why people will object to this, and it is primarily based upon their religious (Christian or Fundamentalist) beliefs. But believe me, fundamentalism is much worse than Christianity. Religion can't explain anything because it is an excuse for people to ignore the truth, and as a matter of fact, everything in the Book of Revelations already occurred, when Simon Peter wrote the damn story. The entire story of Genesis as well as the Rapture is false or could be proven to be fictitious because there is no evidence any of that ever happened. The whole idea is completely bonkers, and as you may suspect, there is something to be confused about. You still believe in the rapture as well as the book of revelations, which is complete nonsense. Simon Peter, if you ever heard of him, was the person who wrote. Everything that he wrote in the Book of Revelations was only meant for that era, the era of Emperor Nero. Ah, Emperor Nero, the abusive King of the Roman Empire, was the real identifier of 666. Of course, I could be wrong. John the Apostle could have written the book of revelation. In fact, there is still debate going on who wrote the damn book. Yet, there remains a true case of crazy people who believe everything in this apocalyptic book was meant for the future. If the book of revelation was meant for the future, why did nothing bad happen yet. The book of revelation was just a prediction to promote a probable story of emperor Nero attacking his enemies, and the possibility of the ultimate destruction of his demise. In other words, the entire book was just meant to be a form of entertainment. Whoever wrote it did not expect people to take it seriously, especially centuries later.

On a side note, I do know what you are thinking, and you believe it is blasphemous for me to say this, well, blasphemy was created by the organized religions back when humans first existed. Primates were probably the true inventor of the Gods, yet people still don't seem to grasp reality. Because you might say something controversial, other people might think I am very controversial, bigoted, or even an idiot, but I only speak the truth, as I have said before. One might think that the assassination of John F. Kennedy and his brother was just a coincidence, but let me tell you something that I already know, which is the actual truth. It is not a conspiracy theory because there is no such thing as a conspiracy theory. The word conspiracy was invented by idiots for idiots to dispute their enemies from their friends. You might recall I mentioned this before about the link between the president, the senator, and the mafia. Well, it goes like this, and what I mentioned before was only a brief look. John Fitzgerald Kennedy came to power with the help of the mafia. It was known that his father was connected with the mafia as well. Young John was probably not aware of his father's involvement with the mafia, and later he wanted fame. Young John came to power to the former White House do to his father's connections with the mafia. The father of John and Robert Kennedy did not want either to find out, but he knew that something could happen to him if he wasn't careful. As John grew older, he wanted more power. John wanted to outlaw the mafia with his brother, Robert. Well, one fateful day in Texas, John was shot and killed. Some expected it was Lee Harvey Oswald, but he was only a patsy, someone who was framed. The real killer was a member or members of the mafia, who killed him because of his policies towards them. The story stops there and picks up in 1968 when Robert decided to run for the president. The mafia did not want Robert to run for president so, while in Los Angeles, a lady in a polka dot dress, along with two other people, attempted to assassinate the brother of JFK. In reality, only one person fired the gun, which was Sirhan Sirhan, a Palestinian from Jordan, or something like that. Sirhan claimed that he was seduced by the lady in the polka dot dress. Some sources believe it was the work of the CIA back then. It could be retaliation from the CIA, or a hit ordered by the mafia, or it could be both. Anyway, before this, the father, Joseph Kennedy, suffered a severe stroke that left him paralyzed. He still had some ability to walk but later had to use a wheelchair. There was a rumor that Joseph Kennedy tried to warn both sons about to leave the mafia out of any prosecution, but that alleged advice failed to work. In the end, both brothers were assassinated, but there were more siblings, yet, these two brothers were the most infamous, who failed to recognize their involvement against the mafia would result in something unknown.

At the eerie side of town, you expected something like the mafia would make sense, well, stop thinking about the mafia and focus more on your education. There is a sign that you must pay attention, or you will fall behind. There is the possibility of a failed attempt at a dark school, yet, you won't know that unless you are told, but it won't be easy to find out. There remains something mysterious, something that could fatally link something unknown to the creation of everything else, to the extent of the politics of the never-ending drama of a forced outcast of the organism of the creature to be unknown. Yet, there lies a creative, but simple plan to overthrow this plan, in which what might tangle the fabric of time, so might say the demented people of the ignorant curiosity. There is something for everyone, but you might need to explain that to certain people with blonde hair, because I heard they are idiots, or fail to comprehend reality. Over the course of time, there might be a distraction, but some might find it tedious, to the extent that it has nothing to do with reality. Society can have several cultures, but the dominant culture often harasses every other cultures because of certain beliefs. There is something to say about this but some might dispute it, so it could be stated that no one is ever telling the truth. In the aftermath of something special, there is more to this story than explain, but at the cost of the society, people want to censor everything, for fear of the truth, which might contradict their findings. There is no shortcut in life, but if you have money, there could be a way out, and since you might say something, there could be nothing more useful than the sight of no significance. In the time that you read this, you will already figure out that there is something mysterious happening in this town of Winslow, South Dakota, yet there could be something connected, but who would ever believe other people, because of skepticism.

Alas, it is now time to start the day, where Amelia, Erica, Allison, Melissa, and Elizabeth are about to wake up and get ready for their first day of school. Staring down from the walkways of the heavens of the glorious revolution, there seemed to be a unanimous decision regarding the space and time control decision. Some people claim that time travel is impossible, but then there are others who said they are inventing a time machine. Let's get one thing straight, I am the original inventor of time travel, but I destroyed it because it would cause trouble. Enough about that, and let me tell you about something else. There is actually something different. The Roman Empire is not the same thing as the Holy Roman Empire. Surely, they sound similar, but they have to do with different eras. The Roman Empire did exist simultaneously as the Holy Roman Empire, but that was after it split into two different portions, the west and the east. People often think that they are the same, but the names are clearly misleading, as there was nothing holy about the Holy Roman Empire, which was not also Roman. Yes, I am talking about that Roman ideology, the one where Rome was the first official world government, but it must have done something right because it existed for many centuries.

There seems to be a lack of oversight into the way you think, and you might think this is the way the world operates, well, sometimes, but most of the time, nobody ever cares. People do not care who you are or what you do because they have other things, such as their own life to worry about. You are nothing special, and if you think you are, well, you are an idiot, and you deserve to go to rehab for narcissism. There is nothing that will help you now. As it stands, there is an influx of crazy people who want to destroy the world, yet, people who mention change are idiots. There is nothing that will ever determine the ideology of nothing because there is a reason where it might affect the reason of personal gain. In the interest of everyone, there seems to be a coincidental appearance of everything that relates to the overtone of society. Nothing ever convenes to the correct atmospheric pressure levels, yet, there seems to be an overconfident telling of the crazy people who fail to demonstrate the empire of a true death experience, something that might help explain the correct dictionary approval of the improper culture of a necessity level of the most terrible society. People can demonstrate the different approval of appreciations, but approval might request the opposite, so there is already a complication, but at the request of the board of directors, you might think otherwise.

The last thing you ever expected was to feel delusional, but aside from that, the opposite might happen. Let me explain some relative complex reasoning skills with you. There is a wormhole in the room next to you. You only find out about this wormhole because you see a flash of light from the hallway. When you enter the room, you see nothing, and you decide to ignore it. The next thing that you do is that you realize someone is watching you in your sleep, but you are hesitant to believe anything. When you wake up you see nothing, but you remain curious. You do not know what happened to you, but time travel is real, but I destroyed the first time machine. The wormhole is a lot dangerous than the regular time machine, because the wormhole could lead to your death, or you could never escape the wretched thing. Of course, the wormhole could take you to an alternate world or an alternate dimension where everything might fit your reality. This paradox could also make it appear that you are awake, while you are actually sleeping. There is something known as a controlled wormhole, where it is a manmade device, that is similar to a time machine. Yes, wormholes can be used for time travel also, but that is a different story. In the immediate aftermath of the destruction of a time traveling device you must make sure you have everything necessary to get back. That's why it is important to have backup devices to get back to your era, such as programmable time travel watches you saw in numerous television series and movies. Yet, nothing will remain a mystery, as there is something more than a society of regular people. In the abundance of a critical analysis, you have noticed something different, and as it became clearer, you determined that there was a new society, at least you could come to a conclusion that has yet to evolve. In the correct space of time, you might think of something evolutionary, yet nothing remains rural, or in that term, a type of crazy society that controls people. There is nothing that you will do that will harness your abilities to grow, and as a result, we have now entered a reason why your life must be controlled by the adjustment bureau. The reason is simple as it is necessary in society to control life. There is nothing more complex than free reasoning.

When you first heard about free reasoning, you think you have the ability to think without restrictions. Yet, people have failed to think responsibly, which was the case in the American Civil War, the First World War, the Second World War, and the French Revolution. There are many other cases of free reason where it had gone wrong. For instance, in the first world war, politicians thought they could use their own free will to do whatever they want, and this was the exact same thing for the second World War. Not only did their free will ruin the rest of society, but it also meant that certain people could never be trusted to think on their own. Not all people deserve to think freely, because some people develop a mentality that they believe is a one-for-all solution, or a solution that fits everything that needs to be fixed.

Destructive decisions just don't ruin free thinking but they also hurt the ability to think freely. Everything that you might think is carefully coordinated. Without coordination there would be mass chaos and mass destruction. Free will needs to be earned by showing you can act responsibly. Free will should be taken away when you cause destructive decisions, such as when you decide to start a war because you don't agree with the other side. For now, people will need to have their free will controlled, but not everyone needs to have their free will controlled. The only people who need to have their free will controlled is that of the ninety-nine and a half percent. The half of a percent understands the idea of free will. Sure, that is a lot of people, even at half a percent, but in order to get to the true population who understands the ideology of free will, you must divide that half a percent into fifty times, but wait, you have to divide that by 7.2, then by five, and finally by two, to get the actual answer. If you clearly understand that there is a meaning in life, then you also must understand that there is a meaning in the rest of society, because the basic principle of free will is to use it responsibly. You need to make clear choices that does not affect anyone else. You are not allowed to control the rest of society just because you see fit. The timing of granting free will is the precise moment when you must understand the culture as a whole. Without principle, there is no such thing as free will, and if chaos is allowed, well everything will have to be controlled and or punished, just because a single person ruined it for everyone else. There is no reason to ruin something for the rest of the world. Just because of your beliefs does not give you an excuse. There is no excuse for anything, and as it was used as abuse, sometimes, controlling the minds of people is necessary. As the rest of the world thinks differently, there is still that one section of the world who wants to bring on destruction, just because of their beliefs.

If destruction happens, free will shall never exist peacefully. Instead, people must have a pre-determined plan created for them. Without this plan, everyone will cause chaos and that would lead to the destruction of the society and culture of people.

In any case, you can believe what they tell you, well, there is a difference that could affect your entire lifestyle. Imagine the American Revolution of 1776. In 1776, the British Colonies of America finally had it with the British Government. You could say that, but in fact, the colonists hated the constant taxes from the British Parliament and also King George III, but the colonists never thought of becoming a separate entity before. In fact, they never wanted to separate from the British Empire. The colonists wanted to stay with the British Empire, but they also wanted representation in Parliament. Since they had no representation in Parliament, the colonists felt as they were being treated unfairly, due to the fact that there were no representatives from the British Colonies to represent the colonists in Parliament. Now, you thought that some ministers in parliament did sympathize with the colonists, well, there were only a select few. The reason for something that was the death of the colonies was due to the act of aggression by the British Empire, as stated by the colonists themselves. The British thought it was necessary, because they used the colonies as a reason to increase taxes on the colonists just to raise lost assets by previous wars. Even though the colonists rejected several new laws, the British Empire did not do anything. Some could say this meant that there was a lack of authority, but others could say the British Empire was lazy to impose laws on the colonists. In the days and weeks that passed, there was something new. On the third of July in 1776, the colonists finally declared some form of treasonous uprising called the declaration of independence. Now, whether the British Empire recognized it was not the point. The British Empire could care less about a piece of paper. Instead, the British thought it was quite amusing, but the war would not end there. It would continue on for years.

Without a doubt, the current constitution of the new United States of America was still incapable of fulfilling the necessary freedoms of society and culture. Instead, it took a lot of time just to think about how to propose the new constitution in 1787. There was a lack of competence within the Philadelphia Convention. Nobody knew what they were doing, and there were committees formed just to increase the awareness of the entire process. There was the Virginia Plan, the New Jersey Plan, Hamilton's Plan, Pinckney's Plan, and finally the Connecticut Compromise. Now, you probably already knew that the latter plan received the winning vote, but that is beside the point. The real issue was what was going to happen next. During the convention itself, many of the assigned delegates failed to show up, do to probably a lack of transportation, or some other excuse. There was a real issue. In the time that it could take to compose a new constitution, there was a major problem, which was, this was probably the first time that they had to think without the British Empire helping them. Now, the British Empire would never commit such an act back in that era, but it was do to the fact that they wanted to use the colonies just to collect revenues from their joint-stock companies. If anything is like what it is before, there remains something global. There was also a fight to reconstruct the constitution just to include the fundamental rights of basic liberties, such as freedom of speech, and other stuff like that. Well, some people wanted to re-write the constitution altogether, but others just wanted to add amendments. Regardless of the fact, these people were known as the Federalists and the Anti-Federalists. Now, these two terms might sound confusing, and they are, because they are the exact opposite of their real meanings.

Federalists promoted big government and were usually very wealthy individuals. Anti-Federalists hated big government and actually feared the idea of a monarchy. But, in fact, if you now reverse those two terms, and research intensively, you will find that both factions actually were the exact opposite. In fact, the name was a complete hijack. Yet, the British War does not end there, but picks up during the War of 1812, where the British storm the new capital of Washington D.C., in order to regain territory. The British soldiers thought it would be amusing to retake the former colonies as their own again. The British Empire burned downed buildings and started fires, but the new country of the United States of America fought back, and there was a new opponent in the long fought competition of imminent survival. People must understand that there remains something that could struggle to cooperate, but that advice might cause severe distress, such as the formation of something evil. In order to eliminate something from happening, there must be something to agitate to eliminate the future cause from ever catching on with the past. If nothing ever happens, there would never be an uprising in the first place, or so you believe. The competition never ends, as it is the result of something that never disappears. Sure, you thought it disappeared, but it came back. Let me give you an example, such as that of cancer.

Cancer, as you know, is very dangerous, and can kill you instantly or very slow. It determines on how fast it spreads. The faster it spreads, the worse you will become, and will result in anxiety, stress, and pain. The pain does not need to be physical, because it can be mental. You decide to go to the doctor and he tells you have cancer, well, the most common kind of cancer that is known is breast cancer. You could undergo something known as chemotherapy, which might help. If chemotherapy is successful, don't be surprise if your cancer resurfaces, which could be more powerful than before. Wait, you thought it disappeared, well, it does not fully disappear. Instead, a small cell remains, which is the size of a grain of sand. This is never detectable by any type of machine because it is such minute in size. Maybe in the future, this size of a cell could be detected, but now, it is still impossible. Anyway, in order to eliminate the threat fully, you must have the cancerous tissue removed. So, I will suggest you have all of your breast tissue removed once you find out you have breast cancer. You could also opt to have all of your breast tissue removed after your completion of chemotherapy or other treatment, if you sought some type of treatment. The most effective way to prevent cancer is to remove it by surgery, but it you are not early, you could die, so you must decide. Also, a lump does not always indicate it is malignant. A lump could mean anything, such as a pimple, which can be removed by applying ointment. I understand that surgery could be painful, but any type of cancer is dangerous to your health, yet people either seek radiation or chemotherapy, thinking it is the best possible option, but then, to their surprise, it appears years later. The cells were just lying dormant, waiting for an infection or a weakness in your immune system. Cancer can spread if not removed, and this is the reason why you must act now, if you think you have it, or else, you will be too late. In any case, preventing a growth might seem harmful, but it will be helpful. Do to the fact that something can destroy your body and your life, your response time is a must.

There is a reason for everything, and as you figure out, you will notice that there is a time that might hamper your decisions. If you have cancer, it can spread from your breast, to the liver, to the colon, to the pelvic area, the kidneys, and possibly the heart, if you act too late, which could also be the cause of a staph infection. Good hygiene is a must. Every time you finish doing something, always wash your hands, and yes for more than one second. You should wash your hands for at least half a minute without soap under lukewarm water or one minute with soap under lukewarm water. If you can handle the heat you can use hot water, if you don't easily burn. There seems to be a distinction between hygiene and disease. The better the hygiene you use, the less disease you will develop. You can develop an immunity against any disease if you follow certain health guidelines carefully, but this has nothing to do with Obsessive Compulsive Disorder, which is a form of an anxiety order. People with OCD of washing their hands usually fear of germs or contaminations, and they use it constantly when it is not even necessary. You should always wash your hands after you touch or finish something, because that object could be dirty or contaminated. Yet, people with OCD of hand washing will develop a fear, and that fear will impair their daily life. So, in reality, if it does not impair your daily life, you probably don't have a disorder, so you shouldn't worry about anything. Yet, no one wants to forget to complete something, so you must be careful.

There is a sense of instability, and that causes people to undermine the whole process. Instead of doing something completely irrelevant, there is something more than just a form letter, yes, that thing, which has no supervision, because it is just a rubberstamp. Everything could be a rubberstamp, but that is not what the whole idea is, yet, people fail to forget and would rather relinquish their basic constitutional rights and civil liberties just to promote better security. If you do this, you do not deserve any freedom, as you are promoting a police state. Yet, even police states grant you basic freedoms, but if you think security is the best option for everything and you oppose freedom, well my friend, you are a complete idiot and you deserve to do nothing. This means that you must change your ideology, and instead, you should promote the basic values, but never force some ideology on another person, because, if you channel the wrong person, you will be scolded, and you would of deserved that. For any reason, you must decide the most appropriate action, which might mean anything, so, there is something to recognize. At the most apparent act of meaning, you should entitle that the entirety of the focus of the series will never be the same again. For the most basic timing, you must achieve the goal of not doing anything that is offensive. Some people are easily offended, which will result in a public outcry. At some instances, people will demand for your job and you to be persecuted, yet, these people still fail to understand the basis of your principles, yet there is something better, which could be the abundance of a central party. There is the reason that could affect the entire situation, and this might force change, so the rest of society might reason with culture. On the other hand, no one will ever be perfect. There is always that pariah, outcast, or nobody who seems to want to start a riot, just to cause trouble and chaos. This will start nothing but it will not lead to any solution. There is the possibility it could help, but in reality, you must be crazy, if you think chaos and trouble improves society. To the rest of the people, there might be a time when there is the probability of increasing the cause of something good, yet, it has not arrived. To put something in place, no one will remember anything, yet people will need to know that there is a possibility that there is a coordinated effort to start the period of progression. Yet, the time still remains where aggression could overpower anything, due to the fact the people who support aggression are idiots and are greedy with power. There is never anything that will connect to the society and culture if aggression receives the majority of approval in the society in culture, but something could change that.

In the matter of minutes that you will realize that something is happening, you will finally find out that there is something wrong with your theories. You will notice something new that is hard to escape. You will find out that nothing was ever the same or would ease your process. There is an evil within, and you must decide the outcome, or you might go blind, meaning that you will develop amnesia, to the point where it was anterograde,

26

not retrograde, but it could be both. There is nothing worse than a disability, but the disabilities act has been abused many times by lawyers and people in motorized and non-motorized wheelchairs, just by measuring with a cane, so, it has come clear that people want money, and they devised a plan just to seek money, because they have nothing better to do. There is also the possibility that they are just scum. Other people might object to anything, but their reason is based on flawed logic. Sure, logic can help, but if your only assert opinions that are not well-founded, you will be the laughing stock of the centuries yet to gain critical attention. You must assert something that can be at least plausible, yet it must remain efficient enough to have the development of the entire community, so you must be able to handle critical acclaim, so, people must remain in the interests of no one.

When anything happens, there is always a bunch of garbage that people might relate with, yet, as the facts start to appear, it seems that everything was based on something but a single opinion. Anyone can assert something, yet, as something is necessary, it appears to be difficult to understand anything. As people might determine that there is an obvious objective, there might be something better. Instead of using opinion, you should use your brain and think, which might actually teach you something. There is nothing wrong with research. Research is being conducted in order to determine the history and probable cause of scenarios in everyday life and situations. If you object to this method, than there is actually something wrong with you. Research will grant the way of the future, and could be optimistic to your values, or you could have no opinion about anything. With certain objectives in critical acclaim there is something better than a regular timestamp with no meaning in life. There is no such thing as a conspiracy, or anything related to the opposite of that. Since anything can be related with each other, it is at the point in time where there is nothing actually happening. After all, this whole thing is just based on the focus of observation, and without observation, nothing else could ever be achievable, unless there is a reason to believe that a vacation can help determine the cause of all evil. Without anything really, you basically are useless to the entire society of your culture. You will never able to contribute anything to the rest of society. Everybody will consider you a nobody. Yet, if you achieve something, you might notice something drastic is happening in your life, which might cause a change in your entire lifestyle. You must be able to adapt to everyday surroundings, since there is no hope for useless people. You must blend in with the crowd, for you are the only person who can control your own destiny, that is, if you know how to use free will responsibly.

Some people have issues with responsibility, such as, they think they are above responsibility, and that no one can tell them what to do. If nothing ever gets done, well, you, my friend are going to have one messy living quarters. Next thing you will notice is that there is a big pile of garbage in your living space, and you keep thinking that it will go away automatically. Well, if you believe that, automatic trash cans built into the garbage itself has not been invented, and it will probably be a few centuries until someone will figure out how to trigger garbage into a trash can. This my friend is some type of crazy invention that you have created in your mind. You have not seen crazy until you finally met yourself. There is nothing more better than the possibility of now insects getting involved. Even if this invention ever came true, you still need to transport your garbage to the landfill. Better yet, instead, you should burn your garbage in a secluded area in the woods so that nothing will go wrong. If you do this, you should wear a gas mask and a bio hazard suit, since it is very dangerous. You should also buy the land just so you will have ownership over the entire land, and so you won't get into any trouble. The whole idea is completely nonsense, and it teaches you nothing, much to the contrary of certain people who object to everything people might believe. In any scenario, you must be willing to accept the society as the resting place of culture. You must be able to achieve accurate responsibility without harming society. Most people achieve responsibility but they also harm society, without knowing it, and this results in nothing but chaos. Some people are idiots, and others were born as idiots, meaning, they are closed-minded. To the rest of the people, there is always something that might happen, so in this stage, you must learn to cope with the rest of the world. You must enter reality and differentiate between fantasy and reality, because they are not the same, and if you think fantasy is reality, well, you probably need to seek mental health, do to it being abnormal behavior. Everything else will gradually enter, while you try to achieve the most probable scenario in society and culture. Because there is only one path, nothing else is achievable, unless you achieve an alternate path, which could be a trick.

There will always be a time that is right, to the extent that there is no guidance required. If this made sense, then I wouldn't need to explain. There could be complications, such as the usual consequences of inventing something. You will find never-ending relentlessness from different predators. Your predators are your enemies, who are the people or entities who want you to fail. Sure, they say they want to help you, but secretly, they are trying to sabotage your efforts. Now, sometimes this is a good thing, but if it is used incorrectly, the entire process will be extremely dangerous. There is nothing else that you can do, but there is the option of time travel, but I destroyed that option decades ago, in order to prevent the wrong person from changing the universe into an evil empire. There is the reason of the unknown that determines something that is never known, for the purpose is still known, and when it is known, there is a reaction to the no reaction process. In case people might ask, yes, the entire process is extremely confusing, which results in the majority of not recognizing the real properties, because they are in fact looking in the opposite direction of reality. The focus must lie within the process of nothing but the untrained eye, as it might seem false, but it is actually true.

During the exact moment, you might find something that is irreplaceable, so says your friends and family, yet it can be replaced if you had a time machine. After the process has begun, there is a tedious process until the end is near, which could take days, weeks, months, years, decades, or even centuries, depending on your specific scenario. If you are planning on something specific, it might take you longer, but undertaking something general can increase your length by an imminent amount of weight because it is still too many items involved. The middle of the process nears when people decide to finally take happen, which hardly ever happens, and can be the longest waiting period in your life. Once the middle process has started, it has to be stable for an unspecified amount of time, which will result in the end of the process once the middle process has been completed. There is nothing but complexity and simplicity within the entire process. This will have a determined effect on individual as well as group minds, since there is something to gain. Nothing is at the center of attention because the center of attention is never actually present, because it is always present, but you will never find it, since it is layered within the process of a never-ending committee effect. There is the reason why people might complicate things, since there is nothing occurring in any part of the process. The entire process is flawed, because it was meant to be flawed, and if in fact it is never flawed, there is the reason why there was the cause to determine the nothingness of the presence of the future to alter the past within the accurate amount of critical analysis, since everything is the complete opposite of the complete accurate with the benign consistency.

Since anything can determine anything, nothing can also determine anything, but nothing will ever complete the effect of the revival of the process. No one will ever design this process, because I have created it, and I own the designs, and I will never sell it to some corporation or head hunter. I will sell it myself, and I will license it, because it is my creation, yet many people are idiots, since idiots are idiots. There is the reason why the reason is irrelevant, since nothing will ever be the same, and since the creation is unknown to anyone. There is the result that nothing will result in anything. As the process is in the process, there is the process to finish, and this is where the story starts to begin, of how the whole process began.

CHAPTER TWO

Before something bad happens, we now go back to the year 2006, where Melissa, Allison, Erica, Amelia, and Elizabeth are now departing for school. Yet, you think that is what is going to happen, but before that, there was the incident that changed everything. Before long, there was no scandal, so, nothing could ever happen worth embarrassing. This was actually the first incident that occurred for the first time, ever since the town was founded, but it was not in the actual confines of the town of Winslow, since it was located deep within the woods.

It was like any other day, one that was always part of the plan. Alas, there was something wrong, and it could be felt. Amelia just got back from the spa, with Alison. The rest of the girls were not interested in going to the spa because they had to complete house work. So, on the way back from the spa, they went through the woods, then, they heard something. Out of the woods came something unfamiliar, something that was normal, it seemed a regular occurrence, so nothing is at the center of the meaning. From the tree behind them, there was a noise, a noise or screeching, that it made the wolves cried. The wolves were not seen, yet only their yells were heard, which seems pretty normal, if you are familiar on the subject. So, on the weak end, there is something that will happen, but in the strong end, everything will happen because it must happen, and then it will lead to the theory of nothing.

Nevertheless, Amelia and Alison continue to enter the woods, and they see nothing. Nothing ever happens in the woods, and so you think, but what do you know. Almost everything happens in the woods, because the woods is a magical place where strange stuff can happen. If you ever think about it, almost everyone who disappeared, well, they disappeared in the middle of nowhere, which is located in the middle of the woods. There is a price to pay if you ever take a shortcut into the woods. Sometimes, nothing will ever happen, but in reality, different noises are always heard in the woods. As a word of advice, the woods offer something that is vital to life, and without the woods, nothing will ever happen, as it is connected to the realm of living, along with the dimension of prosperity and guidance. You need these items in order to survive, as the place without them, well, would could your worst fears to come true. So, before you think that the woods is scary, well, that was the point, since it was necessary to develop the character of nothing but the less you might think. There is the obvious reason to know that nothing ever makes it out alive, and if it does, well, that is just chance or luck. You will need all the luck you can receive, because without it, you will never survive some sort of escape. For other purposes this is why no one who enters the woods ever exits, unless they are familiar with the territory, or, they run like a cheetah, while the latter could be possible, if you are high, but why do you care, that is something new.

Aside from the fact that there is wilderness all around you, you seem to lack something that is presently known, yet there is no known reason to realize that personality or trait, since it has been replaced. At the last end of the puzzle, something will happen to you, as it might tangle some genes to negotiate the deal of the century, which makes no sense at all. Everything is irrational, and you know it, so don't make an argument about it, since, nothing will ever help people survive the terrible plague of everything. This is the story of nothing, nothing that results in the incapable hero of rationality and morality, but to a certain amount of people, neither of those things are important. There is the reason why something might help, yet, the present is still unknown, since no one will know what will ever happen, but I do, because I presently know everything about this story. You probably might make it, but, on the other hand, I am not interested in learning about your true fate, so you might be ignored.

Anyone who ever decided to walk in these woods often had three possibilities, they were lost, they were dared, or they were just curious to find something. Of course, there is the fourth option, which was that they had something important to do there, like meet with someone, but otherwise, no other reason exists. There is a reason why no one ever enters the woods, and I have already explained it to you, so you must be more patient, as it will take time. Since there is nothing else better to do, everything else must be necessary, and as a way of life, you must understand the difficulties of how something seems fair, while other actions are never fair.

Rationality, will screw that, because it is a distraction for everything in existence, and it is the reason why people are always irrational. Yes, my friends, rationality is caused by irrationality, which also causes rationality, and that always decreases morality, which decreases ethics. Nothing will ever conform to society, because people are always irrational and rational, which means they think, since they are a prosecutor, they think they can prosecute and persecute anything. That is the real meaning of rationality and irrationality, people acting on a vendetta. Always remember nothing, because you must remember everything, and as that might not make sense at all, there is the reason to adopt nothing but nothing. On the course of something adventurous, you might find something, but it might be a mirage, because it is always a mirage, and the mirage is nothing good, since it is an evil organization controlled by people who want government to control everything. There is nothing wrong with government, but government must be limited in a way that it does not affect your daily life. Government should give you free healthcare, since insurance companies charge you too much. Government should provide anything that helps you, but government should never interfere by telling you what you should do. There is a reason why the United States of America fell in the 1980s, which was the result of government overregulation, which resulted in people starting a revolution, because the American people finally realized that the politicians were wrong about everything. The revolution finally collapsed when the Faberx Corporation bought out the entire nation and made it one of the best countries in the world. There was universal healthcare for anyone. There was no more cronyism. The entire New Deal programs were erased from history. Everything became better, and the Internal Revenue Service was abolished, along with the Income Tax, and all of those fifty states. Instead of fifty states, there were only thirteen, yes, thirteen, as in the thirteen colonies. The states were combined into larger states, and as a result, nothing was ever better. Of course, the states were now known as provinces, but each province consisted of a governor-general who is elected to represent the entire region in the national legislature, which is different but unique from before.

So, let me explain the new United States of America so you won't get confused. There was a revolution, which resulted in the deposition of the government. From there, a new government was created after the Faberx Corporation bought out the United States of America and its central government. After that, a new constitution was drafted, then written in under one month, which only took about two weeks. The executive branch consisted of the Faberx corporation. The legislative branch consisted of the national council and the national assembly, the latter being the lower house of parliament. And then there was the judicial branch, which followed civil law instead of common law. Within the executive branch, there was a cabinet, but there was also an elected representative from each region known as the governor-general. Now, each region, well, there was no such thing as regional or even municipal laws. There were only laws passed by the central government, which meant better oversight, and less criminalization. Everything else was regarded as normal, so as people put it, it was a better thing than anything. Well, you might think that the governor-general reports to the legislature, but it actually reports to the executive branch. The governor-general does give reports to the legislature, but in actuality, reports to the Faberx corporation. So, in reality, there are two cabinets in the executive branch, one that oversees all departments or ministries, and one that gives occasional updates about life.

Now, while that is interesting, I have successfully distracted you and pulled you away from the real story, which will now resume, or so you think, yet there is reason to believe that something will enter the universe. There is nothing else worthy of, except the unfortunate theory of anything, which is the same as nothing. If you ever encountered something like that, well, you have probably been conned, yet you will only realize it unless you realize it, which means you must always understand the reality of the alternate dimension theory. There is surely something that can occur from time to time, but this result is occasionally rare. From there, once you have entered the woods, you will notice that you have finally entered the alternate dimension of reality. There is the reason to believe that something might help you, but it is relatively unknown, so you must wait for something to develop. As people might say, anything is possible, well, the exact opposite is true, because of the alternate dimension theory. As a result, it will be known, because it will never be known, as the result of something that determines the overall goal of society.

As a notion of truth, Amelia and Alison finally enter the woods, after about an hour of walking through the enchanted forest, which is totally different from the woods, and is more dangerous. However, the woods is the most dangerous, as it is due to the alternate dimensions within, but sure, that is because the woods and the enchanted forest are the exact same thing, which means that once they entered the enchanted forest, they were already in the woods. Anyway, after Amelia and Alison entered the woods, they found themselves in unfamiliar territory, but they thought they have seen this place before. It was a place of imagination, perhaps the location of all dreams ever created. It could be that, but it could also be something very mysterious, and the result could be troubling, unless there was something that could alter the dimensions within the alternate mind of a paradox.

Walking in circles, which was exactly they were doing, for three hours, they thought they were going in circles, since they remembered familiar objects. Everything became so foreign that it was familiar, as if something told them to enter the woods. Everything else could not be explained, and as it might sound, well, there was a way out, but it was at the center of something impossible to imagine. After eight hours of nothing, it was finally dark, and Amelia finally saw some sort of light, and Alison followed. The light grew closer and closer, and it was apparent that something was happening, so as it might turn out, after a while, you thought it would be suspended animation, but that was only a possibility. Instead, it took nearly an hour just to finally see the light, but it disappeared, resulting in confusion. Then, a door opened, and both Amelia and Alison entered. Looking back, well, that what you were told to never to do, and as a result, they saw everything burning behind them, but then the door closed behind them, and they were safe, or so you might believe. In reality, they were still stuck, but they were inside of a building that was located within the woods, known as the HEPTAGON. Now, the HEPTAGON, well, it was located in the former state of Washington, in the current city of Seattle. As you might notice, you are wondering how one could be in Seattle when they were in South Dakota just half a day before. Well, the reason is that a paradox was opened, and it was in the display as the woods. The woods were known to be a spiritual place, but could also be evil.

It has now been three hours after Amelia and Alison have entered the HEPTAGON, and they hear animal sounds, and other types of sounds, but they realize it is just speakers trying to agitate them when they look up. After two more hours, they see a corridor and open the first door, which, luckily, led to the exit of the HEPTAGON, but now, there stuck in the middle of grasslands in Canada, so they went back in the door they came from, and well, they were back in Winslow, South Dakota. It was a strange experience for Amelia and Alison, and they would never talk about it again, or so you think, after they got home, only to find Erica, Melissa, and Elizabeth back at Amelia's place. The rest of the girls questioned Amelia and Alison, but they knew where they were the whole entire time, after they told them about their strange experience. It seems quite interesting, but since then, well, no one ever wants to remember it, except for Erica, Melissa, and Elizabeth, since they knew everything.

Back at the present, where it is the first day of being seniors at the prestigious Prep Stone Academy in Winslow, South Dakota, which results in something familiar, but the day is just beginning. There was this place, located in the high school, that some believed was mysterious, as it might sound creepy, but that was only a rumor. As people might figure out, sometimes rumors only exist to eradicate every single enemy in existence, or, just to have some fun. In some ways, there is some sort of mysterious agenda, that no one ever mentions, yet, as time flies by, there is the exact same problem. Nothing ever mentions the basic agenda of anything as there is never any agenda, just something that imitates the goal. For the reason to understand, there is nothing new about this, as nothing is the same as the exact physical form of the fortunate life of nothing more than a creature. There is nothing to debate about, as debating leads to nowhere, because there is always an argument on what people seem to fail to comprehend. Everything is at the center of attention, so there is something that must handle the situation. As there is something that takes away the peaceful process, no one ever seems to have acknowledged the critical acclaim of something more useless than a rock. If you can ever imagine what would happen, then there could be an uprising. Nothing is unusual about an uprising, as it seems pretty normal, and yes, they do exist, so, there is the question of what might happen. People might disappear, and some might die, so something is always important, which is absolutely nothing, because nothing is always important. The category where people might start to notice is something different, so there is a generalization that might cause

41

nothing to ever happen. People might determine the outcome of the reasonal dictation of something that might always occur, yet there is something that will always happen, as nothing will ever happen, due to the result of something that will cause the righteous movement of the never-ending loop, so as you might say, a rant is kind of unnecessary, but when you look at a rant, it only tries to explain reason, unless you are crazy, which makes you excited, so as a result, you must think of something else.

Some people might say, well, what does this have to do with this mysterious place, and I will say nothing, but that is exactly what I want you to think. In actuality, this rant describes what people have observed of the place, and what probably goes on. There are rumors about the certain activities, and the possible members. It could be a club, but why would there be a club. There is always the reason why people would interpret the unfounded explanation of something that never existed. So, in retrospect, nothing could be a possibility because everything is always a possibility. Since nothing might make sense, there is nothing else that may even make sense, as nothing is the result of anything, and there is no such thing as anything, but nothing always exists in abundance. The theory is that something might exist because it has to exist, which is quite irrational, and as something might reason, that is basically impossible. There is no such thing as something that might call the situation as something extraordinary, but what is, because people always have a misconception about anything, which is why this secret place must have something to hide.

This secret place is nothing special, because it is just a secret club, similar to something like something that people might hate because of exclusivity. There is nothing that makes sense about anything you believe, so people might answer it as a ridiculous question to determine the right amount of reason. There is nothing that will ever determine anything, as I might add again, or so you might think, because the club is only meant for seniors, and no one else. The price is simplistic, if you dare enter, but is invitation only. Handed down by class, year by year, this club is exclusively for seniors with high-ranking popularity in their class standings, so it is just some type of secret society, which is what certain people hate. Amelia, Alison, Erica, Melissa, and Elizabeth are all members of this society, as well as someone named Charles Hindson and Carlos Ryan, who is related to Elizabeth Ryan, and are in fact twins. The core values are not important, as they are all the same, so the most important factor is to control the entire school. There is nothing more perfect that will lead the crisis to a century of numerous attitudes at the center of attention. There is nothing that can expect to determine at the cause of something that might happen to the history of nothing that will happen, because it has yet to happen, and as the will of the people, there is the creation of nothing but anything. The premise is at most will always be at the center of attention.

Throughout the cause of nothing more than just a case, there is nothing more important than an education, but there is the reason to start your own business, at the cost of nothing other than the possibility of nothing ever happening. So, the case is to estimate the possibility to negotiate the deal that must be planned between both sides. There is the popular side, and then there are the subordinates, who might be more powerful or even lazier than the popular side. Negotiations will never be easy, and as there might seem some optimism, well everything can always change in a snap, so I will encourage you to enter into a relationship that causes no harm. In any stance, there will always be the theory of what might coordinate the possibility of never escaping, yet, there is the reason to accept nothing but they theory of everything, in order to become the understanding of the creation of something that might cause the interpretation of the opposite effect. In other words, nothing will ever be the same because it has always been the same.

But, that is not what this is about, because this is about something more sinister, something which might have a surprise ending. Yet, there is something more, and as it has the timing of an inadequate policy, well, there might be something to change. On the other hand, everything is unnecessary, and there is the reason to develop something that is unrelated to the exact opposite of the sphere, so something else might be necessary in order to tighten the deal.

Hey, said Melissa, there is a price to pay for everything, but I don't see a way out. Or, there could be something interesting, yet, I am still bored. Good thing class is about to start in a few minutes.

I wonder who we will meet, asked Erica.

There is something strange going on here, right everybody, questioned Amelia.

I feel as if something is going to happen, well, it might be useful to wait, Elizabeth stated.

Well, Alison believes that something could happen, but why do I always believe myself.

The girls go to their first class of the day,

44

advanced creative Latin, which turns out to be the highest foreign language class in the school. Well, since Latin is a requirement, they took it, but it was only required for two years of study, in high school. This was their fourth Latin class they took, in high school, and all other Latin classes were the same.

As a basic principle for rigorous learning, Latin is taught differently. Requirements might vary school by school or regionally. Yet, at Prep Stone Academy, Latin studies begin by first learning the ancient Latin script, which I forgot to mention was that foreign language studies begin at the first grade, so information can be absorbed more quickly. The ancient Latin script is first learned at first grade. Then, in grade three, classical Latin is learned. From there, at grade five, medieval Latin is learned. In grade six, there is a review of all Latin learned, then, in the final month, modern Latin is learned. Once in high seventh grade, modern Latin will be picked up to be resumed, due to the absence of school breaks. In eighth grade, Latin is a creative writing class. From ninth grade and forward, all Latin classes are a review, but most teach classical Latin, but prefer ancient Latin.

Amelia, Alison, Erica, Melissa, and Elizabeth prefer ancient Latin, because it is unique and has the least amounts of letters. Yet, no one cares what script is used. All Latin instructors at Prep Stone know all scripts.

Looking down at something, Alison stares at the floor, intentionally dropping her pen.

Wanting to help Alison, Patrick picks up the pen and hands it to her. While getting up, Patrick notices that Alison isn't wearing any panties, buy says nothing. Yet, this was something that Patrick wasn't expecting.

45

Patrick hands the pen to Alison.

Alison looks up and smiles, then crosses her legs.

The Latin instructor walks in and introduces himself as Mr. Rafael Santiago, a dual citizen of Spain and Montenegro. Mr. Santiago has a doctorate in Latin studies, a master's degree in European history, a master's degree in international relations, and a bachelor's degree in Latin and Italian Studies. However, Mr. Santiago is only twenty-seven, and this is his second year of teaching high school. Mr. Santiago explains his expectations, and urges his students to ask questions if necessary. At the end of class, he hands his students a question packet to be returned the next day.

Second period has arrived, and all five girls head to Experimental Biology, where they will learn about interesting things. Realizing nothing, well, there is nothing to realize, as it is a complete waste of time. The instructor arrives. Her name is Dr. Carlie Henderson. Carlie Henderson has a doctorate in medicine from the University of Paris, a master's degree in biology, a master's degree in virology and immunology, a bachelor's in immunology, and a bachelor's in zoology, and is only twenty-eight years old, who has been teaching high school for also two years.

Henderson explains everything about the class, giving her students a packet of information about everything that will occur over the entire year. The packet, well, it is single spaced and contains about five-hundred pages, which is bounded together by glue and string. In other words, it is basically an introduction to the course. Now is the time that everyone complains, but the girls are used to this type of coursework, and so are the rest of the

46

students. Everyone could just complain, but there is nothing to complain about, since nothing even exists for the consumption. After the packet is handed out, Carlie hands each student some sort of information questionnaire, which is the first assignment of the year, and is due the next day. With that, the class is over, and the girls head to the restroom just to talk.

Alison explains to Amelia, Melissa, Erica, and Elizabeth that she knew Patrick looked up her skirt, explaining that she did it on purpose to drop her pen. Amelia calls Patrick a crazy prick and then laughs hysterically. Melissa just finds it amusing that Patrick was an idiot. Elizabeth, well, she was just jealous because of the attention gained by Alison. Erica, well, she did that before and taught that to Patrick. They all talk in the restroom, explaining about everything they noticed, and then they exit to head to their next class.

All five girls go to third period, which for them is Advanced Calculus four, with Jack Jonathan. Jack Jonathan has a doctorate in statistics, a master's in math, a master's in engineering, and a bachelor's in physics, and is only twenty-six years old, who has been teaching high school for one year. Jack explains that this is his first year teaching here, but he looks at Amelia seductively, while Alison laughs quietly. This embarrasses Amelia, but she smiles at Jack, yet he moves to the chalk board to write down his office hours and other important information. Everything else, well he hands each student a fifteen-page packet to return the next day, well, only the required assignment.

Third period is now over, and it is now time for lunch, something that is overrated. For the reason that is lunch, well, it is just overrated, since nothing is ever good, or so you say. Well, this is not a normal school, as you should already know. Breakfast can consist of anything fancy, such as caviar, eggs benedict, or something special. Lunch, well, that is extra fancy. At lunch, there is a sushi bar, international delicacies, seafood, whole milk, soda, and other items. There is nothing other than whole milk, since it is the best, and because the other types of milk, such as skim and one-percent are either laced with sugar or is a pathetic solution of water. Two-percent milk, well, that reduces the fat by increasing sugar. The substitute milks made of plants are not even real milk, since they are a solution of forced processing. Real soda is served, and not that diet crap, since diet is cancerous. There is never any processed foods at this cafeteria. Everything is fresh, where all foods are strictly cooked on school grounds. Nothing is ever from the government. Nothing is prepared by the government. The government meal program was always providing a lack of nutrition, since it was based on bad data and junk science, by irrelevant people. You can still get a slice of pizza, but it will be very thin, like in Venice, Italy. Everybody at this school enjoys the meals, and it is probably the best that anyone ever tasted. So, there is nothing crazier than the time to go back to class, where there is a notion to strike a deal with the center of attention, at the conclusion of school.

Amelia talks to Alison.

Alison talks to Erica.

Everyone soon starts a conversation.

Amelia, Alison, Erica, Melissa, and Elizabeth all start to eat their lunches. Soon, everyone starts to gossip. It is probably the best gossip anyone has ever discussed.

Who gets nothing, about the time of the proximity of attention, said an unidentified person.

No one even knew what that person was saying.

No one even wanted to know, because that person is probably crazy.

Nothing is ever supposed to engage anything. In the aftermath of something special, well, there is never anything special since it is just fiction.

No one needs to know anything. Everything is always at the center of attention.

The physical attractiveness of your body is nothing new, well, maybe, but forget that.

Move on to something else.

There is more stuff that might be interesting than crap.

There is something to learn, and it could help people to identify the background.

Others might misinterpret something for the exact opposite.

There is nothing wrong, and as people might believe the exact opposite, nothing will ever remain the same. The same might apply to other people but why would they care, since the world is nothing new.

Go jump off a bridge.

You will never jump off a bridge.

People are so cruel, replied Elizabeth.

There is something better to do than engineer comments like that, said Erica.

The rest of the people are idiots, indicated Amelia. Everything is an idiot, because they are all idiots, proclaimed Alison.

The very nature of their habits remain a mystery.

Amelia replied, since all of their radical ideas mentioned never attended the real meaning of society.

For the next fifteen minutes, Alison went on a crazy rant, indicating nothing but craziness.

I can't wait. There is too much information. Everything is happening so quickly. Nothing is going to happen. I will not stay here for the rest of my life.

There is nothing that will make me. I will never participate in something that is chaotic.

Nothing is chaotic.

Sex is never chaotic.

There is no such thing as virginity.

Virginity was invented by organized religion.

Organized religion is bad for society.

Everything is at the same place as it had before.

Nothing needs to change. Everything needs to change. I would not do anything to change the day.

There is nothing that you can do to me that will help you.

Everything will always determine the course of your environment because nothing is at the will of the environment. There is the reason why you must stay home. You must stay home in order to do your chores.

Look around.

There is nothing to see.

Everything is broken, as it was nothing but trouble.

There is nothing to see.

People need to enter the exact realm of society.

At the last minute, there is nothing that will help you, so help your life.

Everything about you is an ignorant piece of shit.

Namaste, an idiotic meaning in life. That is what hippies like to say. Some say it during yoga. Well, Namaste yourself. You can go dig a hole for yourself. That is nothing. Namaste means absolutely nothing.

If you want to go to yoga, just focus on yoga. Yoga is so useless, that it is about the same as Pilates.

Yoga and Pilates, they are exactly the same but are from different cultures.

Who the fuck cares, because I know they are both useless.

People use yoga as an excuse for happiness and sex. Ah, sex, a useless thing that people might want to restrict your activities.

Well, they can go fuck themselves.

There is nothing wrong with premarital sex. Nothing is wrong with it. People who are opposed to it are prudes, who are people who hate everything about sex, meaning they want to ban it, because they believe it is bad for society and culture. These people believe sex is a bad word. There is nothing wrong with sex. Sex is good for you. Remember, there is no such thing as virginity or virgins. Nothing of that even exists. The only reason why it is a word is because of organized reason. Those two words are just fictitious.

Mention nothing about anything. There is nothing about anything.

Anything is nothing and nothing is everything, so there is nothing to see, as nothing even exists.

There is no case to action.

Nothing of that type exists.

I want to determine your life, or so you might think, but you might want to do something differently.

Consider yourself a loser, someone who is a poser, and has nothing.

Once you consider everything, you decided to act as someone who you impersonate.

Nothing will cause nothing.

There is a lack of evidence for something to ever happen. People might happen to notice about anything, but that is just an excuse for people to be determined at nothing personal. There is no right from wrong. Everything exists in an open place. Every piece of that open place is nothing but your imagination.

You can go screw yourself. When I mean now, I mean it, because you are a useless piece of crap.

I can't believe you even exist.

You must be useless in society because you were never meant to be. There is no hope for you.

Nothing will help you.

You need to find something quick, or you might be considered the worst piece of crap in the history of the world. You better decide on how to live your life. You will never be happy, never, because you will encounter nothing in your life. Everything about you is the same.

No one could care less, and that is what people will think of you.

You will always have a minimum wage job. You will stay in the same place for the rest of your life.

Nothing will encounter your life. Everything will pass you by. You will never enter college because you already dropped out of middle school.

You thought it was hard, but guess what, there are more successful middle school dropouts than you.

School is not hard because it is meant to be a

learning experience. Everything about school might sound hard, but that is just the way it was meant to be.

Stop whining.

People need to make quick decisions.

As a matter of fact, I enjoy sex.

Sure, call me a nymph, but I enjoy sex because it is great.

Stop thinking that prostitution is degrading. Nothing is degrading. Degrading is just another word invented by the entire organized religions of society.

Organized religions must be stopped by having influence in government.

Organized religion is bad for society.

Don't force your ideology unto me, because I am not the same as you.

You are not my boss.

You do not own me.

I own my own body.

I am my own boss. You need to stop it and let people make up their own minds. There is nothing wrong with feminism. If you want a woman to have equal rights as a man, well, I suggest you grow a pair.

Yeah, that's right, you should grow a penis. You want to be treated the same as a man, well, now, you will be. The only thing wrong with feminism is when you demand entitlement for everything. Entitlement is some sort of politically correct word, invented by radical fascists.

Feminism is also some sort of politically correct ideology, since people think it is meant as something that is correct in society.

Well, you know what I say to that, fuck that, fuck this, fuck everything that is politically correct.

Political correctness can go fuck itself.

Entitlement can go fuck itself.

Feminism can go fuck itself.

No one tells me what to do, because I determine my society.

Society does not need to conform to anything. There is nothing wrong with society.

People need to understand that there is nothing wrong with them.

If people tell you to avoid sex, well, you might develop a mental disorder that ends up hurting you when you have intercourse.

Society needs to understand nothing. There is nothing to worry about. You must determine the rest of society for yourself. In the exact same time, you might encounter something, but that is just something new. You need to remove the single ideal that is nothing else but the rest of the world. In the designed theory of something, well, that is just garbage, something that probably doesn't even exist. People will always screw you. They will always be misled.

Society is the meaning of nothing.

Nothing is at the top of the world, since nothing is good.

Something that is good is meant to be bad, as nothing means what is supposed to be. You might think the exact opposite, but what will that teach you. You are an ignorant fool that deserves nothing.

You constantly complain.

You always feel entitled to everything.

You must learn to fit in, but you feel you want everything.

You can't have everything, so I suggest you work for it, so help the members of society. Cosplay you say, well, what do you know about dressing in costumes. You think you are going to a comic book convention, well, guess again.

Nothing will help you.

You were meant to be screwed.

You will have a tough life.

Well, now, there is nothing more to say. Since I am finished, well, there is nothing more to talk about. Nothing more, because I am done with you.

Alison finished her rant. She finished her lunch, and she now heads to the girl's restroom, where she will use it. Everyone else, well, there is nothing to see here. Everything that you know is not available.

Fourth period is just around the corner.

Engineering Physics, something that might sound crazy, as it is crazy. Soon, the five girls head to their physics class. The teacher arrives, looking sexy, fit, and handsome. He is gorgeous, exclaimed a student.

Another student wanted to marry him.

His name, well, it is John Carter, who holds a doctorate in mechanical engineering, a master's degree in aerospace engineering, a master's degree in astrophysics, and a dual bachelor's degree in engineering and biochemistry. John Carter is only twenty-seven years old and has been teaching for two years. Yet, he is one of the smartest of the faculty, since he received million dollar grants for the school. His background and personal life, well, that is still mysterious, as the previous teacher of this class decided to retire for no reason.

Anyway, Mr. Carter introduces himself to the class, and gives the student a packet of paper with words.

Physical evidence of something that matters is something that never matters. As the people might comprehend, no case even exists, as nothing is evident to the course of nature. People might say that Alison is crazy, but there is no reason for that assumption. As a matter of fact, nothing of that nature even exists in reality. For a few to say that the matter was never resolved, well, certain people have no clue about due process.

Around the time of particular accounts, nothing ever exists, since nothing needs to exists.

Again and again.

The time is closing to an end.

People have their crazy theories of the world.

Alison is here, and so is Amelia.

Elizabeth, Erica, and Melissa never left.

The case is unclear, but why is it unclear, to the extent of political madness. There is no reason to wait, no reason to disclose any information, but nothing exists in the nature of policy change.

Critical adaptation, the nature of something that must occur overnight, is nonsense.

There is nothing more irritating than people.

People are idiots.

People need to shut the fuck up.

At no time is correct for anything .

Everything is junk science, so people are idiots.

Not all people are idiots, since some are smarter than normal. Consider nothing, because nothing is everywhere, and nothing will lead to the adjustment of a better society. There is nothing left but an equal society.

Everything is unfair, but being unfair might mean equality.

Across the pond.

Through the wind.

There is a place to wander.

People might say, that nothing is there.

The roads are filled with color. People might fill the tank. Everything is so sweet. There is nothing that can be destroyed. People are dismayed. There is a problem. There is a solution. People will forget the idea of a century. Not everything will survive. There is a call for action. Everyone believes in nothing. No one will ever survive. There is the thing that nothing is the true existence. People are the way to enter the creation of a center of attention.

Motivation is key.

Nothing will work better.

You will see this as you explore the center of the universe. People are at the edge of their seats. Nothing will survive. Everything will survive. There is no reason to live, as people are killing people. No one has the reason to kill, yet it is the reason to be unknown, as a way of disaster. There is the reason that there is no reason. People, well, people are the basic forms of life for nothing but producing and consuming. Nothing ever exists for the rest of society, and as a reason for the thing to encourage you, that is something with no meaning defined in the dictionary.

Everyone survives.

Everyone must survive, in order to prosper.

There is a way out.

The skies are filled with rainbows.

The grass is blue.

The sky is green.

Everything is the exact opposite.

You think you are dreaming, but it is something else.

There is a mirage, something that is bad, a thing that might be the end of the world. You must see past this mirage. You must fight this urge, as it is a way to encounter the discomfort of a society. Everything is irrelevant as it is never relevant to the opposite effect. The whole notion of everything being precisely as a matter of a coincidence is a fallacy. Everything is a fallacy, making everything the reason that you had the exact view of your reasoning. Nothing is meant for survival, because nothing needs to exist. Everything needs to die off, since the rest of society is in the case of a mental patient. People might find out, that nothing is at the mercy of anything. There is nothing that can ever help you, since the mirage has taken over your mind. There is a reason why you must encourage freedom to defeat security. Security is a lie. Security never protects anything. Security will lead to a police state, and it will lead to the destruction of society. People might fight, but there are always radical people who think security is the best concept in society. Those who prefer security do not need freedom, because they need their basic rights taken away. Security will lead to your death, and it is the basis of something more sinister. Everything about security is a fraud, as it was meant to control society.

In the aftermath, nothing will ever survive, as it was meant to be nothing. The call to action needs to exist in a timely manner, or something bad might happen. In the reason of a mental breakdown, there is no real reason to disclose certain information. Everything is at the center of attention. Everything needs to be resolved. Everything needs to be correct. Security must be wiped out, in order to promote freedom. Freedom must replace security. Freedom is better than security. Freedom is never misleading. There is no truth but the truth. Security promotes propaganda. There is a reason why propaganda exists, because people promote security. There needs to be a way to end the security debate. People must realize that sometimes they are irrational because they lack the skills to understand the importance of freedom.

There is the reason for freedom, the case for something uniform in nature, as everything is in the middle of a debate, yet nothing is at the center of attention. People will evolve. People will realize. People will finally know that freedom is better than security but this will take some time.

At the forefront of nothing is the reason why something must be nothing. As the reason is the notification of the truth behind the critical study of the theory of nothing but the exact opposite. The world is an unknown place, filled with the reason why people might want to escape. Provide that information to Marcus Garvey, the person who wanted all blacks to return to Africa, in order to protest treatment. Not many blacks joined, as it was a disappointment to society. Not everyone who was black was actually from Africa.

As there was the reason to understand right from wrong, there was the reason to identify with the past. People always make crazy assumptions, and this might be why there is a lapse in judgment. Everything can reason to the extent of a possibility, to the theory that nothing is the reason why it ever existed. For everything to survive,

nothing must survive, so there must be a reason why
nothing always escapes everything. Nothing ever dies, so
there is a flawed reason to determine the cause of death.
People will retaliate, and it might be unclear, yet the point
is obvious, kill the traitor.

Sure, kill the traitor.

The traitor is a deserter.

The deserter is an idiot.

Everything is at nothing.

These reasons are flawed and promote security.
Security means nothing but overregulation. You need to
understand that freedom is better. Freedom will promote
everything. The police state must be eradicated. Security
must be eradicated. People must comprehend the ability to
render the system obsolete. People must understand the
difference between good and bad. There is no other way
out.

Security is bad.

Freedom is good.

The police state promotes violence.

Violence leads to more security.

Security will harm the rest of society as a means of
control. Security must be stopped.

Security will ruin everything. There is no reason
for security to ever exist. The core values of security have
already been stated. Nothing will determine the course of
all action. There will be a debate, yet this debate will not
mean anything, unless something is resolved.

Something must be done.

Freedom has escaped people before.

Nothing will create the reason, but it must
promote.

It must promote freedom.

Security is a threat. Security must be stopped. There is no reason to support security.

Security is a lie.

The cake is a lie.

Everything is a lie.

Freedom is never a lie.

The end could be near. People must realize, that nothing is near. As there is no reason to fear. There is everything to fear. Everything is at the center of attention. Everything is at the call to action. People must realize that something might hinder the growth of society.

Everything is the reason to determine nothing. Life will lead to nothing important. There is no reason to live. There is no reason to die. Everything must die. Immortality is a gift, but only a select people are immortal.

Immortality is a curse.

Immortals can die but they must choose to die, when they want to die.

Immortals have seen the world, and they have traveled the world.

Immortals can give up their immortality but they rather choose to die. Choosing something is difficult, as it never makes any sense. There are some who say that nothing is ever correct, but people will need to remember that everything is the reason for nothing. Nothing must have a reason. Society must render security obsolete. There is a reason to understand something that is near death.

In the future, there is nothing but insanity.

Insanity is nothing.

People will not correct anything.

There is a reason to get upset.

Immortality is nothing new. No one can demand immortality, as it is a special gift. There are basic qualifications, and only a select few exist. You must be accepting a pact to survive for eternity. You must evolve. You must be willing to travel the world for eons. You can stay in one place, but that is after your journey of traveling has been completed. Once completed, well, you still retain your immortality, but you can retire traveling the world. You must create world peace. You must create war. You must promote security and war, along with freedom at the same time. You must be willing to have multiple beliefs. You must be willing to develop a strategy that will be beneficial to you and the rest of the world. You must be willing to endure eons of criticisms. You must have a plan that will help you devise the exact location of everything. You must be able to persuade people, in order to secure the rest of society.

Immortality is no joke, as it is the way that the world used to operate. Nothing will ever mean anything. There is nothing that will help you. Nothing will give you immortality. Immortality will not just appear out of nowhere. Immortality is only for certain people. Immortals can blend in, but they are always humans. Immortals have a reason to live, in order to determine the course of life. Immortals control the society, and they are trusted people. Immortals know the difference between right and wrong. Immortals are ancient, and they were trained from the start of human civilization. Immortals have ancient degrees, and they are well qualified. Immortals know what is going on, and they know everything.

Determine the course of action. Return to your

classes. Learn, as you must be educated. There is a reason to promote the reason of the rest of the world. Nothing will determine the precise moment, but you must be willing to accept certain challenges in order to face life itself. The world is continuing to evolve, and it will evolve until there is no reason to determine the course of an infinite action.

CHAPTER THREE

Sitting through any class might be boring, but the bell rings, and it is now time for an advanced writing class. Sigh, that is over, and it is now time for a history class. Yet, seventh period arrives, the last class of the day, resulting in an economic class, something that is dreadful to listen to. Amelia, Alison, Melissa, Elizabeth, and Erica have just completed their first day of their senior year in high school, but something is going to happen soon, which will be in a few seconds when all of them walk down a hallway and see a flash of light, leading to something magnificent, yet impossible, according to some of those skeptics.

A mysterious portal appears.

It resembles a flash of light.

All five girls walk up to it, not realizing what could happen to them. It might be a sign. There could be a reason for this to be happening. No one will ever know, unless they have traveled.

They enter the portal.

It sucks them in.

Everything is flashing before their eyes.

They are traveling faster than the speed of light.

No one will know.

They stop traveling, and the portal spits them out, revealing something strange but almost familiar. It could be the past or even the future. They have to walk to find out. This universe feels different because it is different. Everything is different.

There is a sign that reads the MPAA, and everywhere you go, it's either that or the RIAA.

This must mean something.

Something bad might happen.

The girls might be in trouble, or even worse, the world.

What would happen next?

Could it be?

No!

Something must be happening, but what?

There is something to think about. Just as you might think otherwise, it does matter. Nothing is the same, nor will it ever be the same. There is nothing central to the rest of society. Even if people refused to identify the indication of something so minute that nothing will ever happen. The course for everyone to imagine is nothing but the lack of seriousness by the questions involved. Nothing is at present danger because everything is dangerous, so there might be something happening to the rest of the world. Nothing might remember the situation of everything. There is nothing weaker than the seriousness of nothing. People will never evolve, as there is a reason to escape reality. Certain indications will lead you to nowhere, or something else might happen.

People must remember, that something is happening, so you might just remember that something is going to happen soon. Something is going to happen. Something should happen. Something needs to happen. Nothing is the reason for everything. There is the reason why nothing is the very first indication that something will remember nothing because that is in fact incapable of ever happening. There is no theory of what might happen. As indicated, something might seem normal, but how is it normal, since it has nothing more than the imagination of a single-minded organism. There is nothing that can stop it, since nothing has ever happened. People might seem obnoxious but that reason only applies to extroverts.

There is no reason to indicate anything, since everything is at the center of attention. Every time you might determine something is correct it is actually incorrect because nothing has real value. There is no reason to be determined in order to determine the outcome of something relevant to the irrational fear of nothing irrational. Everything is a delinquent attention seeker, so there is nothing to remember, as everything contains the meaning of nothing, so help your soul. Amelia exits first, followed by Melissa, Erica, Elizabeth, and Alison last.

This dimension is different than anything they ever saw. That's because it is different. It is actually an alternate future, where the former MPAA and Hollywood studios, and the RIAA succeeded in taking over the federal government of the United States of America. This is a very dark day in American History. The MPAA does not promote freedom, and in fact, they oppose everything about file sharing. The same applies with the RIAA.

They support draconian laws, filled with security instead of freedom. Information is good, but it must not be prevented. Internet censorship will be widespread. It is clear that there might be something that must be done, or else, the end might be near. The people might retaliate. People might already been retaliating. There must be a reason why this is happening, so there is the reason why something is at the reason of disposal. Unless, there could be something, but it must be related in order to determine the history of something that must be completed, but there must be something.

Weakness is nothing new, as that what the MPAA and RIAA wants. They promote internet censorship, something that is the reason why creativity is not able to thrive around the world. They need to stay out of peoples' lives, because they are against freedom and they are just terribly, plain people, who are against all types of freedom. Nothing will please them but the reason to restriction to promote censorship everywhere. There is a way out, something that is capable that will influence the mind. Nothing is clear, but it is a possibility, so there is the reason to promote something other than the time where it was irritable.

When government restricts freedom, independent research websites appear, attempting to promote freedom, by revealing the corrupted politicians, people, organizations, and governments involves. These websites are good for society. When everything is fine, these websites shutdown temporarily because they know they are not needed until something draconian happens. WikiLeaks, a website of such nature, promotes freedom, equality, and personal liberty, by revealing the corrupt people and organizations who want to censor everything. WikiLeaks does not like corruption, as corruption promotes security. Security must be stopped.

It all began in 2010, in some future alternate dimensional universe, when the MPAA decided to sleep with the former FBI. The MPAA decided that they hated this website called Teraload, an online file sharing service. Like it all not, Teraload was a legitimate business. It was a Hong Kong based business. Teraload offered free services as well as fremium, meaning that accounts started as free, and if you wanted more space, you had to pay a price. Well, starting in 2010 of that year, the MPAA decided they had enough of Teraload because it promoted free speech and file sharing. The MPAA took a stance against freedom and file sharing. They urged that file sharing was harming their industry by preventing money going to their clients.

The MPAA wanted Teraload to be eradicated from the internet, and in 2012 the former FBI decided to raid the mansion of the founder, known as Timothy Mestor, who lived a flamboyant lifestyle in New Zealand. The former FBI, known for their unpatriotic attacks against businesses and laws around the world, well, they faced some backlash from the international community. There was the certain questions that arose during the raid itself. The raid was illegal because the former FBI does not have jurisdiction over the sovereign nation of New Zealand. The FBI misled the authorities of New Zealand, claiming a crime was committed, when really, no crime was ever committed. The FBI wanted to extradite the founder, Timothy Mestor, to the United States, all because of alleged copyright infringement. The FBI later added the former RICO Act charges onto the indictment against the founder of the site. Copyright infringement itself is not an extraditable offense, so, they FBI just added those bogus charges to the indictment.

If you looked at the case more closely, you will notice nothing criminal was happening. The FBI claimed it as the TERA Conspiracy, but that was just a hoax. There was no basis for the indictment itself. The case lacked merit and was baseless on all counts. There was also the matter of jurisdiction. Timothy Mestor did not break any law, as he had dual citizenship from Germany and Finland. In 2009, Mr. Mestor moved to New Zealand, where he and his family gained residency one year later. The jurisdiction matter does not stop there, as Teraload was a foreign corporation based in China, and it had no physical presence in the United States of America. The only reason why the reason why it was possibly shutdown was because there were servers in the United States of America, but that still lacks merit and is baseless on all possible grounds. Since it was a foreign company as well as a foreign website, with no physical presence in the United States of America, there was never any basis for the arrest and indictment of the founder, Timothy Mestor. Timothy Mestor and his staff even followed the former DMCA treaty and the former PRO-IP Act. He, his website, and his staff was protected by safe harbor conditions. Even though he followed the guidelines of a foreign law not subject to another sovereign nation, he still was indicted one day after PIPA and SOPA was denied a hearing in the former Congress. It now made perfect sense, revenge.

Easily, the United States Government thought extradition would be a breeze, but the courts in New Zealand demanded answers. The FBI never gave answers, as they believed they were justified. The FBI seized all assets from Timothy Mestor, even though they had no jurisdiction. The courts deemed the raid and seizure of assets illegal, then another court deemed the raid legal but the seizure of assets as illegal. Later, the FBI wanted bail to be revoked, but there was no proof of any violations. Another year passed, and the MPAA studios decided to sue Teraload and its founder. This lawsuit was later frozen for six months. It is now 2015, and the United States Government just stole all of Timothy Mestor's assets by claiming civil asset forfeiture, with a rubberstamp granted by a judge to fails to follow the law. The United States Government believed that New Zealand would easily grant a rubberstamp extradition, but it has been three years, because the government of New Zealand wanted an explanation about every possible detail into the alleged criminal acts.

There was, however, one thing wrong with the entire case, which was, Mr. Mestor was not a citizen of the United States of America, nor has he ever traveled there. He has also never committed any type of criminal act in the United States of America, because he never went there. The FBI and the United States Government knows this, but they refuse to accept this, because they believe that U.S. Domestic law supersedes the law in New Zealand. New Zealand, a sovereign nation, have their own laws, their own policies, and their own constitution. The United

States Government just violated New Zealand law and the New Zealand constitution, as well as international law. The United States Government can't arrest a foreign person who resides in a sovereign nation outside of its boundaries. In fact, no sovereign nation can ever do that, since it is a violation of sovereign status of a sovereign nation.

There will be a decision about an unrelated extradition decision early in May or mid-May of 2015. Timothy Mestor could be deported to Finland or Germany, because of a traffic conviction not disclosed on his residency form, which he claims was a misunderstanding by his advisors. The month after that, June 2015, is possibly another extradition, but to the United States of America, but this will be an uphill battle for the United States of America. If Mestor is deported to either European country, it would make it possibly harder to have him extradited to the United States of America. If Mestor urges the judge in New Zealand to postpone the extradition hearing after the end of November, well, it would be also harder for him to be extradited to the United States of America. At the end of November, Mestor will become a citizen of New Zealand, under the country's investment program.

Now there, now you have it, but that is just the beginning. So, the five girls are still in this mysterious place of the year 2015. They are facing something new. They have just arrived at an alternate dimension, in which the former United States of America exists. If something isn't done now, there could possibly be an alteration in history, as well as the space-time continuum. That would be impossible to fix.

Judicial review, something that is important, as the matter that relates to everything else. In the matter of any opinion, if it is accepted, then there will be a delay in the process, which might be good, if you ever thought about the situation. Hollywood took over the government, and as you already know, they want to censor your freedom of speech. Censorship is bad, not only for the society, but also for innovation. Censorship prevents innovation, but Hollywood hates that for other people. Hollywood only wants innovation for themselves and no one else. Hypocrisy, well, you probably already knew that. It is the extent of something that might seem fine, but it is a double standard. Never is everything in mind, and if you are a hypocrite, then you support narcissism to the point that hypocrisy doesn't even exist. Nothing will be more entertaining than your decision to reprimand the rest of society, but why do you care. There is something special that might interest you, yet, you have never envisioned a society with freedom. You just imagined a society with massive security, that supports big government, some sort of Big Brother that wants to control your life.

There is nothing more sinister than that. Sinister, well, there is something that might determine the price of something without the merits of the things that change the way life is, but there is nothing similar to the type of life that is the same of the exact opposite of how someone lives their life. So, help, the passage, by not doing anything, in order to do something. There is the reason that might be determined to outlandish the entire system because of the basis of something relevant to the rest of society. And, you say, there might be a connection to all of this crazy information. You might think that something is possible, well, at the end of the immediate birth, of the death, well, something will never happen, because it will happen in the early future, which is immediate after the fact. Nothing is strange about this, so you might say, and as there is no evidence to support everything, as evidence was destroyed. Nothing is up to par, as the United States Government encouraged the deletion of all evidence related to the Mestor case, and the MPAA along with the RIAA refused to grant access to anybody, because they are promoted by greed.

In the aftermath, well, there is never any aftermath, as this is a basis for nothing other than the crazy person in the idiotic shill paid by greed. The MPAA and RIAA are both professional shill organizations to discourage innovation, only because they want to keep all the rights to your innovative content. This isn't surprising, as people have been fighting it, to the extent that nothing is superior, but at the time that there might be something, which might be nothing, well, that case is clearly strange, and will need to be determined by idiots and nothing else, as everyone is considered an idiot, according to the former United States Government. There is something more interesting to this, in which that something might be interested to be stranded. You might be stranded, but why should you ever care. You don't need to do anything, and as something might happen to occur, well, that is just chance. Chance is nothing new, as there is a reason to not motivate yourself, to the idea that motivation lacks skill and judgment, but motivation also means work and responsibility, so you might have a chance to live your life. Sure, you want to live your life, because it might represent freedom, success, and free will. Well, according to the former United States Government, all of that stuff is against the law. Freedom is not illegal. Success is not illegal. Achievement is not illegal. The former United States Government, the MPAA, and the RIAA only targeted Mestor because of his success. Mestor complied with the law. Teraload complied with the law. Employees at Teraload worked hard to remove every possible infringing material uploaded to its servers, yet, the government refused to acknowledge this, because of something known as corruption and abuse, which is nothing new in government.

Companies like former websites known as YouTube, Dropbox, Google, and the late Teraload are all protected by the safe harbor provisions of the DMCA. Well, when the MPAA took over the government, they repealed those safe harbor provisions, in order to promote the destruction of freedom and innovation. Internet Service Providers are not liable for hosting third party content, but ever since the MPAA usurping power, well, it made it responsible. The ISP is not liable for infringing content because the third party users, known as account holders post the stuff. The account holders have to agree to the terms of service. The terms of service always indicates that the account holder owns the content. If the account holder violates the terms of service, well, then the account is suspended, revoked, or put on notice.

Nothing might be immune, because everything is controlled by the former Hollywood now. When the Faberx Corporation bought out the United States of America and its national government, the Faberx Corporation put the MPAA, the RIAA, and Hollywood in its place by revoking their status of organizations. But, somehow, somewhere, there were certain people who were angry, and they found a way to create a time machine, in order to invent an alternate dimension, in which freedom is censored. Censorship is their goal, and they have made it loud and clear. They must be in denial, since they believe censorship promotes innovation. Such agendas that promote suppression of freedom is bad for society, but also hinders every part of the society. Innovation is good, and as a matter of fact, it helps the rest of the world. Censorship does not help the consumer because it eliminates the necessary freedom to do anything. The MPAA and the other industries that promote censorship must be stopped.

But why did the people at the MPAA invent this alternate dimension in which Amelia, Alison, Erica, Melissa, and Elizabeth are all stuck in now. Well, I already told you, but the bigger answer was that they were just angry about what happened. They wanted to control the world by promoting censorship everywhere, even if it was not within their jurisdiction. The MPAA, RIAA, and Hollywood were just lobbying groups who wanted to take all royalties away from the rest of people and society. They promote greed, and nothing more or less, because they wanted everything to promote censorship. People must stand up to their government and demand that the lobbying industry never control the government, or something bad might happen to the rest of the world, regarding freedom.

When the Faberx Corporation, a multinational pharmaceutical research company, bought out the country and the government in 1986, they already knew the dangers of the copyright and lobbying industry, so they banned all lobbying organization. The Faberx Corporation basically rewrote the entire constitution written in 1787, and replaced it with a system that promoted more freedom than anything else. Of course, there were some opposition to this, but that was so minute, people laughed at those crazy opponents. The opponents wanted something to do, in order to eliminate freedom from the place of the earth. Under this new constitution, actual boundaries were placed. The boundaries only fell in within the jurisdiction of the former fifty states, however, there were now only forty-eight states, since Hawaii and Alaska became their own countries. But wait, these forty-eight states were divided into thirteen different regions. The state system was completely abolished. Still, I think I told you this already, but there was basically still a governor in each region, but with limited power, who only really represented the constituents in the executive branch of government.

The real power came from the new federal government of the United States of America. There was now a parliament, and not a Congress. The entire judicial system now relied on civil law, which is the best law of all, because it is the dominant type of law practiced around the world. Parliament did not have unlimited powers, and they could not write terrible laws. All legislation must be read, by every single person in the parliament. Failure to read the bill would result it in being barred until it was read. This was another reason why the Hollywood shills hated the new government, and they did not like anything about it. One thing for sure, they hated freedom, and they feared less censorship when the Faberx Corporation bought out this country. So, now, you will say something else, but there is nothing else, as you might think. There is actually more information.

The United States Government could no longer exerts its criminal bullying power against other sovereign nations. This made the MPAA, the RIAA, and Hollywood even angrier. The rest of the world, well, they were finally happy, when the Faberx Corporation bought out the United States of America and its centralized government. The countries and the people of those countries finally realized that the horrible conditions exerted and imposed by the former country and government was finally gone. They were relieved, since it was a major victory. People celebrated everywhere with the downfall of the United States of America and its government. There were parties around the world for months. Every country celebrated. People from around the world were happy, as they didn't have to listen to a bully country anymore. They were just excited with everything, as it was the best thing anyone has ever heard. There were always the opponents, but they were hated by everyone. No one liked the opponents, as the opponents promoted censorship openly. These opponents hated everything about the new country and government, and as you might think, they started a secret organization in order to promote mass censorship. They built a secret lair, then they created time-traveling devices. They made it possible that freedom was eliminated. Some might say that this is impossible, but if you are in politics, well, it just became possible.

So, how did the MPAA, the RIAA, and the rest of Hollywood gain power, well, it was too simple. They each sponsored a candidate, and in fact multiple candidates, one for each of the 435 districts in the former lower house of

Congress known as the House of Representatives. They did the same for the Senate, and the Whitehouse. Each candidate won their seat, but not by telling the truth, but by lying. The only branch that supported freedom was basically the judiciary, which was afraid now of every politician they encountered.

After the elections, and the swearing ins of the new politicians, time flew by, and the people who elected them finally realized something bad was happening. People started riots, and there were now massive protests everywhere. Countries around the world condemned the new policies of the United States of America. People protested everywhere, because of the new laws that made no sense, which also supported censorship. Countries started to impose sanctions on the United States of America, but the new Congress and Government did not care, since the new politicians believed they were promoting innovation by killing freedom. Freedom everywhere in the once great country was being diminished every single day. The riots were everywhere. People were being arrested for trying to promote freedom. The new government now designed androids that resembled actual humans, in order to arrest people. This new technology promoted a draconian government that wanted to know everything about your life.

There were some of the luckiest people, who were actually billionaires, who escaped this country before the elections, as they knew what was happening. These billionaires knew what was happening because they knew that these new politicians were androids. The billionaires sensed something once the android spoke. They noticed the eyes never moving. Each of the billionaires escaped to different parts of the world. Some went to New Zealand, and others went to Australia. The rest of the billionaires went to Europe. They went to foreign countries to seek citizenship by an investment program. After they invested money in the countries, they renounced their United States citizenship. They did not want to, but they had to, because they did not want any part of a totalitarian government that supported censorship

Within a year of the new government, five states already seceded, realizing that they did not want to support censorship. Florida was first, followed by South Dakota, North Dakota, Alaska, and then Hawaii. The federal government did not recognize this act of regression by the five states, as they deemed it treasonous. But the states also never recognized these federal politicians in Congress.

In retrospect, these states tried to prevent these new political androids from taking power, but they failed after Hollywood imprisoned them within their own states. These states still seceded, but they would no longer remain loyal to the union, all because of the dangerous direction of the new government.

Florida became an independent country of sovereign nation status under Spanish rule. Florida was now a commonwealth of the nation of Spain, so, it felt right, or so it did. Well, Hollywood didn't like this, so they bombed Spain, but after that incident, Spain bombed Hollywood. This war waged on, because Hollywood wanted everything to themselves. The country was a mess with Hollywood in control, as people might believe, yet, Florida did not want to be part of a dangerous new government that eliminated freedom and promoted censorship. The state known as Florida became known as the Florida commonwealth. Florida knew that they had to do something to escape the wraths of the new government of Hollywood, so they employed nearly two million engineers, construction workers, and other people to separate Florida from the landmass of North America. This was no easy task, as they had to have very powerful machines. This separation from a landmass would also mean that Florida would need to have a higher elevation, to prevent sinking.

So the workers worked, in unison, first by separating Florida from Alabama, then from Georgia. This was no easy task, as they also needed specialized water vehicles, about nearly half a million pulling the state in a southeast directions for about one hundred miles. But first, the vehicles had to move the state south for fifty miles. Everything needed to happen in unison, as it did, but before any of that ever happened, the state of Florida, as it was, had to be elevated. Construction started below the surface of Florida. Specialized construction workers connected billions of pounds of cement underwater. This was a special type of cement. To make sure the bond never broke, it was welded with titanium alloys, zinc, and platinum. Hook attachments were also connected. These hook attachments would make it possible to move the landmass of Florida away from the massive landmass of North America.

Construction started in 1987, a year after the new Hollywood government seized power by promoting propaganda, just to win. But this 1987 was not the same 1987, because this 1987, as you recall, is an alternate dimension created by Hollywood. As you might see, it is totally different, because in this 1987, the Faberx

Corporation, and all other businesses that support freedom, are considered information terrorism organizations, all thanks to this new draconian government enacted by Hollywood.

After a few years, it was now the year 1991, and the construction workers just finished welding the new materials under the bottom of the oceans unto Florida. It was now time to move Florida south fifty miles, then another hundred miles to the southeast. Altogether, the new Florida would be located near the Caribbean Islands. It took a mere month just to move the entire landmass to its new location.

The new sovereign nation of Florida was now elevated far more than ever, which was on average 350 meters, and the lowest point was half of that. The new Florida could now build underground transit systems, making it irresistible to the rest of the world. Cities were rebuilt, making buildings closer together, so that motor vehicles were never necessary. This made life easier for the people of New Florida. Yes, the new Florida was known as New Florida, as people liked the name better, even though the formal name was the Florida Commonwealth of the Spanish Empire, and the Florida Commonwealth for informal usage. Life was good, and people of the New Florida enjoyed every aspect of it. The Hollywood government considered this treasonous, but they could do nothing, as it was out of their jurisdiction.

Fast forward to the current year of 2015, where the Hollywood government is more ruthless than ever. There could be a way out, but it appears to be impossible. People are afraid of Hollywood and fear of being persecuted. Hollywood might kill you, or they might even make you disappear by kidnapping you so that no one will ever find out about the real truth. This might seem irrational, but Hollywood is nothing new to mass censorship, as it is its greatest weapon.

Months after Florida successfully moved to its new location, South Dakota, North Dakota, Alaska, and Hawaii followed suit. South Dakota and North Dakota formed a new landmass known as the Dakota Empire. The Dakota Empire was still landlocked to the North American landmass, but all they did was built a border surrounding their new nation. Alaska, well, they did the same thing as Florida, by moving west, but became an administrative division of the Great Russian Federation. Hawaii, well, they moved closer to Japan, and they did the same thing as Florida, in order to raise their elevation. Hawaii became known as the Polynesian Kingdom, which made sense, as it used to be its own monarchy.

After everything might make sense, Hollywood was even angrier, angry about the new border fence of the Dakota Empire, angry about Alaska, and angry about Hawaii. Hollywood revolted and demanded something to be done. After all, Hollywood believed freedom was a threat to the rest of society. So, now, everything was better, but that was actually false. Hollywood bombed every state that never seceded, and as something that might make sense, they did it to prevent freedom from ever happening. As something might take notice, there is a clear violation of international law. The new United States of America under the control of Hollywood is now isolated by every other nation. Sanctions have been passed, but Hollywood doesn't care. Hollywood is the only business allowed to exist in the United States of America.

Hollywood is the only business making money. Hollywood does not exist outside of the North American continent anymore. Hollywood is the United States of America. Hollywood sells everything in the United States of America. Hollywood does not do any business outside the United States of America. Hollywood still makes trillions of dollars every single year. Hollywood does not care about outsiders. Hollywood is the evil empire that supports greed and censorship. Hollywood must be stopped. There is a clear indication that Hollywood will never give up. Hollywood must be eliminated from the universe. All censorship must be eliminated, in order to secure a more prosperous goal of living in society. Without freedom, well, there is never any type of hope. Freedom promotes growth. Censorship promotes greed and propaganda.

There is a way out, but something must be done soon. If something is not done, there will be chaos everywhere. People will parish. There will be mass incarcerations. Nothing will ever be free again. The rest of the world must attack Hollywood, or something bad will be imminent. In something that is related, bad things have already happened. Bad things will continue to happen. Androids have already taken over the government under the control of Hollywood. Something else could happen. People must respond to opponents. The opposition is everywhere, but they have to hide constantly, do to being trampled on by the Hollywood Government. Hollywood is everywhere. Hollywood is the media. Hollywood is the reason why people are angry. There is a reason you must fight back. Failure to defeat Hollywood is not an option, as failure might lead to chaos. People will doubt you, and you will fall from the center of the world into a never-ending pit of the ground. Yes, if you fail, you might end up in a giant crater, which could lead to your death. Nothing will help you there and then, as it might cause even more chaos, so as it might be, you have no other choice but to fight the Hollywood machine. You must understand that if you do nothing, Hollywood will just gain more power over the government. The government is Hollywood, and it must be stopped.

Something must be done now, or terrorism might happen forever. State-sponsored terrorism is nothing new, as the former United States, before 1986, alleged that certain countries supported terrorism. There was never any proof to support this claim. Now, as you look back, the new Hollywood government now sponsors terrorism, as they see freedom as a threat. About every other country now recognizes the United States of America as a country of state-sponsored terrorism. Everything is now making sense, as it should, because in order to promote censorship, the government must promote chaos by eliminating freedom and the basic civil liberties. Middle eastern countries still treat their people better than the new Hollywood government in this alternate dimension. The rest of the world wants to defeat this new Hollywood government, but this Hollywood government has some of the best weapons defense systems in the world.

There must be another way to defeat this government and it must be done soon. There is time to plan and time to strategized, but it must be done quickly. Sure, some mistakes might be made, but it is a risk that might be required to happen. Nothing is perfect. The Islamic Republic of Iran does not exist anymore, ever since they found out that Hollywood became the new government of the United States of America. The Ayatollah resigned, and a new government was formed, promoting unlimited amounts of democracy. When the Hollywood government found out about this, they were angry that a country could change so drastically. Times are changing, and it will be a matter of days, weeks, months, or even years until something bad happens. Something needs to happen now, and in the matter of time, it might happen to be the most appropriate amount of time.

As terrorism was imminent, well, in the real dimension it was eradicated, but in this alternate dimension, the rest of the terrorism organizations are afraid of the Hollywood government. In fact, the world-wide terror organizations no longer exists, because they decided to eliminate their organizations from existence. The Islamic State, once a revered terror caliphate that everyone feared, now they have decided to launch their own military in order to eliminate terror from the rest of the world. The threat is known as the Hollywood government. The Hollywood government is big brother, and they will never rest. In order to defeat the Hollywood government, something will need to happen, which might result in something good for the rest of the world. There is the reason to consider that any plan will backfire, so there is the reason to respond to any action. Nothing is responsible for the greater good, as something might be misleading everything, so the rest of society must be prepared for anything.

Throughout the world, terrorism is a major problem, but only because of the Hollywood government. The Hollywood government developed androids and other drones. The majority of the politicians are androids because all of them are androids in Congress. The Hollywood government also made androids for military purposes, in order to start wars. These wars were unwarranted, and the other countries never posed a threat, but the Hollywood government supports unreasonable actions everywhere, even though if it is not within their jurisdiction. The world is in chaos as predicted before, and something worse might happen. In the United States of America alone, the Hollywood government sponsors terrorism everywhere. Everywhere you go, the Hollywood government terrorizes the people of the United States of America. This is the far worse event of any magnitude that has ever happened. For reasons of safety, this is just inappropriate to act this way, but the Hollywood government has succeeded in everything, or so you might think.

Chaos everywhere, well, that is nothing new. The Hollywood government invented new crimes, most of them unjust, but people fear for their lives. New apartments are now required to have video cameras and webcams that are on for the entire day and night. These cameras are plugged in to the electronic system of the entire power system, so they are on forever. The Hollywood government just made voyeurism legal. The androids want to watch you, everything you do. The Hollywood government also outlawed sex. If you have sex, and the Hollywood government finds out, well, they will make you have public sex, even if you feel uncomfortable. After that, they will give you the death penalty. The death penalty of course is the gallows. This government will stop at nothing. Resisting the Hollywood government was also a new crime. Resistance groups were outlawed. Everything was outlawed. It would soon be found out that real humans could not go out in public. If a real human was caught in public, you would be jailed, then hanged. This was something that was a threat to the Hollywood government, the thinking by humans.

These new laws were not only unjust, but they also made no sense. The media from around the world thought the laws were harsh and made no sense. People might seem crazy, but nobody thought anything like this would ever happen. The mere risk is something that has never happened. You might think of something that is correct, but that is not how it is supposed to work. Everything is responsible for at least the smallest scenario. If something is irrelevant, something must be done, yet, it is the sense that Hollywood might feel threatened from the smallest incident.

Something that isn't necessary, well, that would mean something will happen soon. There might be a revolution. Everything will change in the near future. There is a necessary evil that has already arrived, but at this time, the plan is still in developments. Things will change, as things are always changing. Nothing will remain the same forever, well, unless you are stubborn as fuck, as well as being hard-headed and anal, so yeah, some people hate change, as it poses a threat to their ideology of censorship. Censorship will get you nowhere, and it makes no sense at all, as there might be reasons for some related evidence to be determined. There is nothing more serious of an offense like censorship. Promoting censorship means that you are afraid. You are afraid of freedom. You do not want a revolution. The revolution is bad because it promotes freedom and civil liberties. You are afraid of civil liberties, and you hide behind a curtain, hoping no one will ever find you. You hope that something will not remove censorship, and you hope nothing will ever change. You believe in the ideology of censorship, as you think freedom is a threat that will harm the people and the society. You have no regard for human life, and you are an idiot. You believe restricting information should always be used. You want to block everything at your own will, but there is nothing that you can do to help to achieve your dream. Your new problem is to find you a sponsor. Luckily, you find one, which is in fact an evil organization. This organization takes advantage of you, then they kill you and turn you into one of their androids. You thought you could trust anyone to support censorship, but you were wrong. You are now dead. The evil organization turned you into an android. After that, they considered you an error and a mistake, so they dump you in the landfill, then set you on fire. You are now extremely dead. Nothing will help you now as you are unable to respond to anything.

After your demise, well, the evil organization took over the government and placed restrictions on everything it could, in order to eliminate freedom of any type. This evil organization, as you already know, became the future of the United States of America, the Hollywood government. You were betrayed, and you couldn't do anything. The Hollywood government had your same ideology and goals, but thought you were a threat to their plans. Nothing will ever recover, as it was meant to represent nothing.

Everything to the Hollywood government is about

money. Money is the only thing they care about. Money is the reason why the Hollywood government operates. Money must be eliminated from the Hollywood government. The Hollywood government constantly abused their powers, by abusing and complaining about everything they could. They did this before they took over the United States Government. They are afraid of technology. They are afraid of innovation, and everything else that might eliminate money. They promote greed, as they see it as the only possible route. Money isn't everything, as there is more than money. People need to understand that money or currency will never disappear. The Hollywood government acts in a manner in which every penny counts, but they are charging outrageous prices. These prices are unaffordable for some people. Why should you pay nearly two hundred dollars just for an animated movie, well, the answer is greed and money laundering. Everything is about organized crime to the Hollywood government. The Hollywood government is an organized criminal organization, and has always been, since they became too powerful in government activities. Their abuse of power is nothing new. They believe in denial. They complain about the smallest of things. They complain that they are the true owners of everyone's content. Nothing is the same, as they made it possible to abuse their powers. The Hollywood government is the reason why there is constant corruption. The Hollywood government should be avoided at all costs. Everything related to the Hollywood government involves nothing but abuse. This type of abuse will lead to chaos and a lack of freedom. Censorship will be widespread. Something must be done in order to eliminate this threat of the

Hollywood government.

Reasons for your safety are nothing new. You must be aware about your surroundings. Chaos is presently everywhere. Chaos is good, according to the Hollywood government. Revolution is bad, as the Hollywood government sees freedom as a threat to their business model. Their business model is obsolete and must change, but this will never happen. They will always be about greed and abuse of power. That is what they promote, and they know it, but they don't care.

The Hollywood government doesn't care about anyone, and as it might seem, there is the reason why they think they are in control. People around the world hate the Hollywood government, and they never even liked Hollywood. Hollywood must be reformed, or it might hinder the growth of society. Hindering the growth of society will cause chaos. Everything will cause chaos that is promoted by the Hollywood government because it promotes censorship. Censorship must be stopped because it is a threat to society and freedom. The Hollywood government is a threat to society, and they must be stopped, because nothing good will happen, since they abuse their power.

There is an understanding of a democracy. Democracy is nothing new, but a democracy is not a form of government. Democracy is an idea, an idea that sounds good, but its ideology can be abused. The people who abuse democracy only abuse it in order to seek corruption and fame. Nothing is possible if corruption is widespread. Corruption can lead to chaos. Everything can lead to chaos, but something more sinister is the fact that there is nothing more sinister. Democracy can be sinister, because sometimes it is unfair. The principles of democracy will be abused by certain people in power, because, well, they believe power will lead them to a higher power. Democracy is meant to equalize the society in a culture, and is not a form of political power. Democracy can be a dangerous word, but at times, it might lead to violence. Democracy is never easy to deal with, as there are a myriad of problems that constitute abuses of power by the government officials. Anyone can determine the possibility to answer the question, but as something might reflect that situation, there is a theory in mind to control the rest of society.

People must change their ways of thinking. People must evolve. The Hollywood government is watching your every move. You might think you can escape, but can you, or you might be delusional. Nothing will be imminent because everything is imminent. There is the reason why something should happen. Anything can happen, but why it must happen is the actual reason. The reason for the Hollywood government is because of jealousy and time traveling.

Time travel is useful, but left in the wrong hands, it can be detrimental to the rest of society. There is something to think about when you might happen to encounter such as the Hollywood government. Nothing is clear about the Hollywood government. Their agenda supports corruption, greed, censorship, and depriving people of freedom. They are the number one supporter of terrorism, which they have achieved in doing so in other countries. The Hollywood is not vulnerable because their soldiers are androids, artificial humans who were developed by the Hollywood government, in order to promote censorship. The time for change is now, and it is necessary to defeat them, for the time is the most useful attempt to defeat them. There is a way to defeat the Hollywood government, and it is the best chance there is to have a winning chance. Change is going to happen. Change must happen. The time of change is here. The reason to change is the reason to prosper. Nothing good can come from censorship.

Before any attempts are made, nothing is yet known. With the exception of the threat, there is something else to consider. The only way to eliminate the threat from ever happening is time traveling. People must go back in time to the past to prevent Hollywood from taking over the entire country and government. Luckily, there is a fighting chance. Amelia, Alison, Erica, Melissa, and Elizabeth have reluctantly agreed after entering a wormhole. There is something to learn from this, never trust a wormhole, since it can lead you anywhere, perhaps a dark dimension that promotes censorship.

At last, you finally might have a chance to consider all the possibilities. People might attempt to stop this time traveling journey, and there is a way to prevent stuff like this from happening. Many times, people have difficulty understanding the reason to accept the decision of a natural theme of a difficult task. There is a reason to forget. There is a reason to remember. People will remember and they will never forget, for this, there is the reason why people fail to understand the ideology of a failed policy.

Nothing is imminent, as everything is imminent, so in time, there might be something wrong with society as a whole. In the time that you have been distracted, you might realize something, which could mean the difference between survival and death. You do not want death, as death makes it impossible to grasp. There is a trap, and this trap is somewhere in time.

CHAPTER FOUR

Amelia, Alison, Elizabeth, Erica, and Melissa wait in a dim lighted hallway. They still haven't gone anywhere since they arrived. They are waiting for a sign, or something like it. All there is, well, there are signs everywhere. Everything is in ruins. What lies ahead is something unknown. Something bad has happened. The girls move forward, where they find a note on a desk. Then, they do outside, so see what has happened, not realizing where they truly are.

To whoever reads this, something bad has already happened. The Hollywood government has launched wars on the entire North American landmass, causing chaos, death, and mass suicide. There is a chance that something good might happen. Recently, it was revealed, that the European Union has developed a nuclear weapon that will wipe out the entire North American landmass. All people who were in Canada and escaped to the British Empire. The people in Mexico and Central America moved further south, to the middle of South America. The only people left are located in the now occupied United States of America.

There have been rumors floating around that the Dakota Empire was attacked severely by the Hollywood governments. These reports are true, but there are some survivors who continue to fight in an underground resistance group. The Dakota Empire has built a top-secret underground bunker that has the necessary supplies for about ten years. This bunkers is also equipped with state of the art defense systems.

Everywhere you pass, there are burning buildings. Everything around you has almost collapsed. Entire cities have fallen. All thanks to the Hollywood government. They perceived freedom as a threat, and believed people should be censored for eternity. The Hollywood government has lost legitimacy, and in all likelihood, they are still holding on.

To whoever you are, you need to know that you might be this country's last hope. The Dakotas built a border fence. Hawaii and Alaska escaped as far as they could. Florida became a floating island that is way above sea level now. There is not much good news, as I am writing this, the Hollywood government has found out about the European Union's plan to bomb the entire North American landmass. The Hollywood government has decided to attack immediately. If you ever go to the European Union again, you might see cities in shambles, falling apart, with people starving. The Hollywood government cares about no one, since they only care about censorship, greed, corruption, and politics. Their goal is to make everyone miserable, in order to eliminate freedom.

Hopefully, whoever you are, you might stand a fighting chance. You must train. Without your training, you will be unable to proceed to defeating the enemy, the Hollywood government. If you are successful in your training, you might be able to defeat the Hollywood government. After your training, you must travel back in time to defeat the Hollywood machine from gaining influence. You must travel back in time to the year 1986 to defeat the Hollywood machine. The Hollywood machine consists of the MPAA, the RIAA, the copyright lobby, and the studios. This must be done in order to return the time back to normal. The Hollywood machine has created a dangerous society, in which they promote propaganda and censorship in order to promote propaganda by eliminating freedom. They do this in order to gain influence over your beliefs. They want to control your mind, and this must be stopped, or something more extreme might happen, like the end of the world.

From the very start of your training, you will have exactly one year to prepare. You will train in a secret underground bunker that no one knows about. It is so classified that no one is supposed to know about it. The Hollywood government doesn't even know about. This bunker is located in the now deserted commonwealth of Canada. Everything in this bunker is state of the art with the most advanced features. It is luxurious and might be the most beautiful place you have ever been to. The name of the bunker is the HEPTAGON, and it is owned by the Faberx Corporation, who moved to Canada after Hollywood took over the government, fearing for safety. It is exactly one-trillion square feet, which is almost thirty-six thousand square miles, which could translate to almost twenty-three million acres.

Lastly, you can save this planet by helping us defeat this terroristic government. The Hollywood government has used chemical gases amongst the people. Beware, you could be poisoned. Androids could be anywhere, so be careful. In order to enter the HEPTAGON, you must enter a building with a green eye. The green eye represents a secret resistance movement. From there, you must follow a blue line until it ends, then you must enter the silver

door to your right. After that, you will pass through several corridors.
Continue going straight, until you see stairs. When you see the stairs,
walk down them, and you will find yourself inside the secret bunker
known as the HEPTAGON. Currently, you are located near the
Canadian border. The building with the green eye is just some type of
border crossing between Canada and the Dakota Empire that has
been abandoned. To this date, it has been abandoned since the wars
started, over twenty years ago. Don't worry about defeating the
Hollywood government now, as soldiers are trying to defeat the
Hollywood government now. I have no idea how long I can make it,
but I might be at the HEPTAGON myself. There is a chance that
I might be killed, but if I make it, I might be able to help you. By
the way, no one knows where you will be going.

Good luck,
Rafael Santiago

    Clearly stricken with disbelief about everything
that is happening around them, the girls finally decide to
exit the building. They know who Rafael Santiago is,
which is their Latin instructor from school. Clearly,
something must be happening, so they follow the
directions until they arrive at the building with the green
eye.
    Thinking something bad might happen, Alison
decides to go out first, followed by Amelia, Elizabeth,
Melissa, and finally, Erica. There is a chance they could be
caught, but that is a risk that must be taken. This is no easy
task of what they are doing. It is the most dangerous
situation the girls have ever faced before in their entire
lives. If everything goes as planned, there might be a

change in history, but the training is only the beginning of the hurdle.

Everything is just about to begin. One year from today, they will be ready to fight. Fight the Hollywood government, fight till the end, and fight to their defeat. They will learn the craft of martial arts, the art of logic, the way of the tiger, and the way of advanced weaponry. This is no easy task, as it is a requirement to defeat the enemy. The enemy as we know it is the Hollywood government, and we must defeat them at all costs. There is no other way, they must be defeated. Failure is never an option. Investment is a key issue. There will be days when it gets difficult, and there is the times of backing down and giving up, but nothing has been done yet. It is at the current situation that the end of the world is near, that the threat has been made public, and that the focus of the threat is to eliminate freedom. Freedom, as we know it, has already been trampled on. This government is totalitarian, and there has never been a fair election since. Those that ran against the Hollywood government were jailed, killed, fined, and even forced to disappear. The call to action must be made, as time is running out, and before you know it, censorship will be the ultimate weapon against society.

Continuing along, the girls walk side-by-side, in order to avoid any possible harm. There is a chance that can be made clear, but things are not clear. Things are way out of proportion and have been for the last few decades, or you might think. When you think about this, everything could just be about jealousy, or it could be that something did not go in favor of the Hollywood machine. The Hollywood created this mess, the wars, the chaos, the censorship, the propaganda, and this alternate dimension. When the portal appeared to the girls in their dimension, it froze their dimension, effectively freezing time as we know it. Their dimension, the time from which they were at school, was the time that was threatened. This caused everything to change. The alternate dimension merged with the real dimension, effectively creating something that wiped out everything that was good. Freedom died on that day, making censorship and propaganda, along with terrorism, the number one goal in the rest of society. For many people, this meant a sign of defeat, as their freedom was trampled on. Their privacy was eliminated. The Hollywood government made privacy illegal, as they considered it a threat to their industry. There was no way out. There seems to be but it is difficult to operate in a location when everything is in chaos. People become stressed, resulting in depression and mania. People have a tendency to run wild, naked, with no one even noticing them. They have become obvious to everything. Everything has gone mad, as there seems to be a mental disorder. Chaos can cause crazy stuff to happen, including mental disorders. This is the reason why it must be stopped, or there could be something that will never happen again. Chaos is the root of all evil.

Reflecting on the past is nothing new, as it might trample upon your life. This is the reason why the girls are training. They are training in order to defeat the Hollywood machine. The Hollywood machine is the mirage. The mirage is something that tricks you, as it is real, but in reality, it is a secret society with a cloaking utility. Their cloaking utility hides their location, but the mirage used to be good, until they got involved in corruption and politics. Something went wrong somewhere, and it possibly made something go haywire. People can be irrational at times, but it must be made clear, as there is something to think about. Before the situation, there might be something to hide, but there could also be something that is known that it is hidden in society. The reason why something must be done is that the mirage is the same thing as the Hollywood machine, because they are the Hollywood machine, making them the Hollywood government, the government that promotes and sponsors global terrorism, propaganda, hatred, corruption, and mass censorship. The reason is known, and that is the reason why people are fighting the enemy, in order to restore order, peace, and law. Law has been trampled on, and so has everything else. Everything must return to its rightful place, and the Faberx Corporation must be the power to eliminate the threat of global threats.

Moving on, as they saw it, the girls saw fires, rubble, smoke, and damaged buildings everywhere. They had to cover their faces, as smoke was thick with fog. The ozone has been polluted by everything that has happened. This place is nor safe for anyone. Bodies everywhere, the entire city looked like a morgue, and a dangerous one at that. Disease was imminent if you were not careful. Bacteria and viruses could escape and invade your entire body. The whole situation was just a massive cry for humanitarian aid.

Finding the building with the green eye was no easy task, as the girls had to walk miles of road, filled with disease and other pollution. Everything was not what it seemed. The girls reluctantly volunteered, as they were forced to, since they were the first people to see the portal enter their dimension. They had no other choice but to volunteer, since the portal chose them, for a particular reason. There might be something to explain, as how did their Latin instructor become the one to write the letter. The Latin instructor, Rafael Santiago, could have been tracking the portal, as he was an avid fan and supporter of time travel. Rafael Santiago also liked the idea of traveling to other dimensions, but so was every other instructor that they had, or so you thought. Mainly, it is believed to be that four of their current instructors were fans and supporters of time travel and creating alternate dimensions. In fact, it could easily be proven that they helped each other to create these time traveling devices at very young ages, all at the same time, because all of them were actually childhood friends, or so you thought. There is something good for this, as they only did it for education, as they used it to get their college degrees in each of their respected fields.

Something must be known, yet, there is a reason for good. There is also a reason to support good things. The instructors never even helped the Hollywood machine, as they hated Hollywood themselves. Rafael Santiago could have tracked this portal down to the alternate dimension, as he has made special glasses that could see anything, and so did the three other instructors. There is nothing more to know, but Rafael could have seen the five girls enter the dimension, but when they saw it, it was already visible. When Rafael saw it, the portal was not there, but he saw it when they entered the portal. Rafael has already been to this alternate dimension, as he had wrote the note. He might have returned to the current dimension just to teach school, but he decided that he hated the alternate dimension, after he visited it and saw what was happening. Everything was widespread. There was nothing that could eliminate the problem of a global threat, until he found something. Rafael and his friends, the three other instructors, found this three years ago, and they kept it a secret, but they could be surprised that it even appeared.

Three years ago, they explored the entire Dakota Empire. The four instructors saw damage everywhere, robots and android rampaging the streets, and fires that resembled ash. Fog was everywhere, resulting in a pollution so thick, nothing could escape its reach. This was very startling to the four instructors, as they knew they had to hide. They found the building with the green eye first. All four instructors ran straight inside of the building with the green eye, and then followed the path, as it was indicated as an escape route by the abandoned Canadian government. For one year, each of them trained, where they learned the importance of defeating the Hollywood government. They knew that they needed back up, but that could mean another few years of waiting. Training occurred at the HEPTAGON, where the five girls are headed to, and yet, something might happen soon. Before long, a year had passed, and they had to all teach.

As a result, after returning to the actual dimension of reality, the four instructors created an indicator watch, along with an indicator program to sense time travel and alternate dimension pop-ups. This watch and program would reveal when an alternate dimension, a wormhole, or a time traveling device was activated or revealed. Three years later, well, actually almost three years, because the instructors explored the Dakota Empire again, and it showed it has changed drastically with more violence and pollution, and they stayed at the HEPTAGON, where they thought of a plan.

Summer break was almost over, and the instructors soon had to teach again, but this time, Rafael left a note, indicating something bad, asking for help. Rafael then left the alternate dimension, and arrived one week before the beginning of the current school year of 2006-2007. So after time traveling into the distant future of an alternate dimension, the instructors time traveled to the past, which is actually the present. Some could say that when the portal appeared on the first day of the school year, it could be a coincidence, or it could be a sign that was triggered by accident. The way that it is actually seen, is that, an anomaly happened, meaning the Hollywood government was messing with the space-time continuum, so yeah, it was a coincidence, but there is more. As indicated, not only did Rafael noticed the portal, but the three other instructors were notified as well. All four instructors had a meeting, and then they used their watches to travel to the alternate dimension, ten minutes after the girls decided to enter it, which from there is something intriguing.

Now, as it appears, the girls finally made it to the building with the green eye. They follow the directions of the note, where it takes too long, about nearly an hour, because it is so massive of a building. An hour passes, and the girls finally sees a sign indicating that they had arrived at the HEPTAGON. All they had to do was to wait for instructions, or something else, like a sign. Who knows, maybe help could be on the way, but the four instructors knew a shortcut, in which they could bypass the building with the green eye. The instructors found out that they could use a portal to transport them to the HEPTAGON. And so, the instructors arrived five hours before the girls. The instructors then made instructions for the girls, indicating their duties to train.

After five minutes, after the girls arrived at the massive place known as the HEPTAGON, they found the instructions or directions on a desk, which was the in the lobby. The girls were in the HEPTAGON for five minutes, and they found the instructions, as the lobby had the sign indicating they had just entered the HEPTAGON. In other words, the sign was in the lobby, where the lobby is the entrance and exit for pedestrians of the Dakota Empire.

While reading the instructions, it occurred that something is missing, but that is just a feeling. There could be a coincidence, yet it is meant as something but offering something else. That is just a mystery, but nothing is clear, as it just might be something else, like anxiety, mood, or even some mental disorder. Whatever it is, it surely must be controlled, yet it is still a mystery.

The note is divided into five sections, the introduction, the daily routine, the active training, the focus of the war, and the conclusion.

Good Afternoon,
Amelia, Alison, Elizabeth, Erica, and Elizabeth

Introduction

You are wondering why you are here, and you all have a right to know. For three years, me, dr. Carlie Henderson, dr. Jack Jonathan, and dr. John Carter have all known about this alternate dimension. All of you have actually travelled to the future, to the year 2015, where the Hollywood government still continues to torture people. The Hollywood government promotes censorship, and they have started unwarranted wars. Since they took over the United States of America, society has become dangerous, rifled with chaos, disease, and a lack of freedom.

All four of us has traveled here before, as it was probably mentioned already. The last time we came here was over summer break. However, as you all know, summer break started in June 2006. School started in September 2006. So, when we came here, it was actually nine years later. When you saw the flash of light, we were alerted to the scenario, as we held a meeting. I saw all of you enter into a portal reluctantly. All of you had no idea what it was, but you entered it anyway.

If you are wondering how I and three of your other instructors got here before you, well, we avoided traveling hours by using teleportation straight to the HEPTAGON. Right now, you are all located in a deep underground facility known as the HEPTAGON. The HEPTAGON is a state of the art facility with several truck bays. It is in fact a training facility, as well as a research facility. The HEPTAGON has living quarters and everything else that a home might resemble, including the amenities and features of a luxury resort. All of you will be training for one year. When you have completed training, all of you will travel back in time to the year 1986 to defeat the Hollywood machine, before they can launch a bid to take over the government.

Daily Routine

All of you will have the same exact daily routine. Keeping on time is of vital importance in order to eliminate the Hollywood threat. Failure to maintain the routine will result in a strategic weakness. Therefore, each of you will follow the routine detailed below.

Starting at 0500 hours am, you will wake up, and get ready for physical exercise.

Around 0530 hours am, you will be at the fitness center ready to exercise.

At 0700 hours am, you will have free time, until 0945 hours am, were you can do anything you want.

At 1000 hours am, you will report for weapons and defense training, in the training center, and you will be here until 1300 hours pm.

At 1315 hours pm until 1400 hours pm, you will eat lunch in the cafeteria.

Around 1415 hours pm, you will have free time, until 1700 hours pm. You can do anything you want.

Beginning at 1715 hours pm, you must report to the fitness center again, to exercise and train, until 2000 hours pm.

Between 2015 hours pm and 2100 hours pm, you will eat dinner in the cafeteria.

At 2101 hours pm, you will have free time, until 2345 pm. During this time, it is encouraged that you start sleeping in your rooms, so you will feel less sleepy when you wake up.

Around 0000 hours am until 0500 hours am, you will be under curfew in your rooms. You are encouraged to go to sleep during this time, but when you wake up, you might still feel tired.

Active Training

Active training can be described as physical fitness, exercise, and weapons training. During active training, you will encounter physical obstacles. Active training consists of three main components, which are physical fitness, personal training, and weapons training. Of these three, they are all important.

Physical fitness includes but is not limited to exercise, swimming, running, jogging, using the gym, and sports. These activities will all be completed in the state of the art fitness center. Without this training, you will be incapable of completing your mission.

Personal training is done at your own free time. Personal training includes physical fitness as well as weapons training. During your free time, it is advised that you complete your personal training so that you are better ready to defeat the enemy, the Hollywood machine.

Weapons training is one of the most important steps in active training. Without weapons training, you will be unable to use the weapons. These weapons are highly advanced and feature state of the art technology. The Hollywood machine or government does not even have these types of weapons. You will learn the features as well as the backups associated with them. You will train with and without armor.

The goal of active training is to prepare you to enter the past. You will be training to stop an alternate dimension from ever happening. The reason why active training is important is because it teaches you lessons as well as the importance of certain duties. You will be training to prevent evil. You will be training to return society back to normal. You are helping society to regenerate and to bring an end to chaos, censorship, and propaganda. You will help restore freedom everywhere. You might think this as too much, but it is vital everywhere.

Focus of the War

The war started by the Hollywood machine caused chaos. If you don't already know, the Faberx Corporation, a pharmaceutical research company, bought out the United States of America and its national government in the year 1986 because the United States of America was collapsing, do to massive wars, censorship, and chaos. The Faberx Corporation established a new system of government, eliminating the old constitution, replacing it with one that supported more freedom. The states were divided into regions called states, and these states now had limited power. There were thirteen regions established by the Faberx Corporation, consisting of different areas. Each region had their own representative in the executive branch, known as the governor-general. Now, the governor-general was an elected official for the legislature, but actually reported to the executive branch. Each governor-general reported statistics, such as crime, demographics, and issues to the executive branch. The governor-general was the elected people of each region, and each was a member of the cabinet system created by the Faberx Corporation.

There were no regional, municipal, or state laws. All laws originated from the central government. The Faberx Corporation was the executive branch, with two cabinets. The legislative branch consisted of two chambers or houses. The judicial branch relied upon civil law. All laws were replaced with civil law.

Since the Faberx Corporation bought out the country and government, everybody was happy, because of more freedom. Crime was effectively reduced to minimal incidents, and nobody had any issues. People started to be polite. Society also changed to better adapt to people. It was really a utopian society, where everyone was happy. However, there were some entities who hated this new found freedom, the MPAA, the RIAA, and Hollywood. These entities included people and businesses who hated the ideology of freedom. They promoted censorship as much as they could. They wanted to promote propaganda, chaos, and terrorism. Freedom was not very important, as it was deemed a threat.

In 1987, members of the Hollywood machine went back in time to the year 1984, in order to promote their new agenda. They somehow were able to make androids. These androids would replace the politicians of the former Congress. It only took them two years to win over the people. But, there was something left out. You see, the Hollywood machine invented these androids to defeat the current government of 1984 and beyond. They used these androids to run for political offices and other government positions. When it was finally time to campaign, these androids promoted more freedom than ever before. The future politicians promised less government and more freedom, eliminating censorship, and especially promoting the individual as something important. But if you look further, you will notice that this entire plan was all a lie. Once the androids actually got in office, the members of the Hollywood machine changed the programming of the android, effectively making them switch sides. It was a huge win for the Hollywood machine, as all politicians were replaced with these androids. The Hollywood machine was the Hollywood government, indicating something drastic has happened.

Once everything happened for the Hollywood government, it was time to change the goals. Beginning in 1987, the Hollywood machine became the new government. The androids started passing new laws that promoted censorship, wars, and terrorism. This was a programming change by the internal features of the android, and once each android got into office, they reversed course, and it could never be changed back. Once in office, the android would be responsible for promoting everything against freedom. This could normally be changed, but it was disabled once the android got into office. The most important thing you have to consider, is that, if you ever face these androids, you must consider them extremely dangerous, as they have super human strength.

Conclusion

Finally, your goal is not only to restore order, but to also promote freedom. There is something else you should know. In 2003, a person by the name of Timothy Mestor started a file sharing business. In 2012, the Hollywood government wanted him extradited to the United States of America from New Zealand. So far, the government of New Zealand has objected to that, and the Hollywood government was upset. Timothy Mestor was on the board of directors for the Faberx Corporation, in both dimensions. So, even if Hollywood never seized control of the government and the country, Teraload would exist either way. Another aspect was the creation of WikiLeaks, a website that supports open government and transparency, which would exist either way. The Hollywood government also tried to extradite Jeremy Hutcherson from the British Empire to the United States of America. This extradition attempt also failed, as he is still in the British Empire. Jeremy is also a member of the board of directors of the Faberx Corporation.

Either way you choose, freedom is still the best thing in the world. A draconian government that supports censorship, propaganda, and terrorism, along with war, and unjust laws, is a government that suppresses the people of the society. You must end this madness, by helping us defeat the Hollywood machine in the past. Now, enjoy your day off. You can get settled in.

Each of you will have your own rooms. Your rooms have state of the art technology, with the best and most luxurious amenities money can afford. Everything in this facility is extremely expensive, but is also built to last. Some things are unbreakable. There are also features that relate to security, such as biometric doors and specialty showers that will eliminate radiation.

Lastly, on the desk in front of you, each of you will find directions, as well as an envelope marked with your name. This envelope contains your key, which is also a master key to the entire facility. This key is a key card, with state of the art technology built in. Each of you will have your own room. Remember, this is serious. Now, again, have fun on your first day, because your training starts early tomorrow morning.

Good luck,
Your instructors

The instructions indicated an importance of defeating the Hollywood machine in the past. An indication of something happening, there was something else happening. There was a sense of guidance. Nothing else could happen. There might be as cast of light, yet, there is the reason to anticipate something else. Anticipation as we know it is something that you must wait for. The object will never disappear, but there is always the idea that something might happen to it, so as there might be something related, there is nothing to worry about. As many people think, there is the reason that nothing could correlate with anything, but anything else is possible.

Insanity is something else, as it might assume to contradict the notion of being sane. There will often be something that might attach itself to the rest of the body, but this is the reason why something might not happen.

The reason is that the mirage might prevent this from happening. The mirage as you know is the Hollywood machine, which became the Hollywood government. Nothing is more corrupt and evil than the Hollywood government. Something must be done to prevent them from achieving a nuclear weapon. If the Hollywood government has a nuclear weapon, well, then, the end of the world as we might know it is imminent. There will be a limited number of people left. Survivors would be limited, and as a result, there would be a lack of food and shelter. Supplies would be destroyed. Everything else will be scattered in faraway places that no one has ever visited before. People will develop new diseases, and those infected will become parasites to the rest of society.

These people who become parasites were initiated by parasites. Nothing will be better. Parasites are parasites, and these organisms are something that will destroy your life. You might think you are immune, but are you. There is the reason to think that there is a way out, but when is that even possible. There is a lack of criticism, as people become more dependent on nuisance programs that prevents you from making more money. These programs help nothing, but all they do is to encourage you to spend, spend, spend, and to never do anything else. You are a fool to use these welfare programs, but some people actually need it to survive, but then there are the people who don't want to give it up, because they feel they won't be complete. In fact, these people don't want to do anything but take money. They are using the program as their only source of income, and then there are the people who are idiots, due to the fact that something might happen, yet something will never happen. People need to remember that there is something that is in the middle that has been compromised and that there is another way out. There is the opportunity to survive. You must realize that something new is happening, and you must grasp this notion of how to survive without public assistance. Public assistance is not supposed to be a permanent thing because it is only supposed to last for a short period of time.

There is nothing that can stop you, as it might be determined that something is in a midlife crisis. As you might know something that is relative to the Hollywood government, you might need to explain it to your superiors, as they might be forced to obey the Hollywood machine. Your superior might even be an android, so you must think carefully, and as it might change something, nothing is going to be the same. The Hollywood government is an evil empire, as you might already know, and they will never give up. The only way to defeat them is to eliminate them from existence in the past. If you travel back to the past before they had any political influence, you could prevent this chaos from ever happening. You will time travel to the past, and you must defeat this Hollywood machine, but you must go further than 1987. You must time travel to the past of the year 1984, because that is when the Hollywood machine started to campaign to take over the government, and to prevent the Faberx Corporation from buying the country and government. The country was already in shambles during 1984, and it was getting closer to a train wreck that would fall into foreclosure and default.

Debts could no longer be paid. People were angry at the government for failing to negotiate with other countries. There was a lack of trade with other nations. The idiotic or stupid United States Congress enacted trade embargoes on almost anything that originated from Europe and Asia. The cause of this chaos started not in 1984, but in 1928, six months before the stock market crash. Everything was normal, but then, in 1929, the stock market crashed. This thing, which people called the Great Depression, became something as a great harm to society. Society was being sent to misery, as everybody started to lose money, yet, some people were smart enough to keep all of their money in their homes, inside of vaults. Regardless of the fact, the stock market crash was the least of the worries, since the President at the time was Franklin Roosevelt, who reportedly suffered from Polio, but actually suffered from an illness that mimicked the disease.

Unfortunately, Roosevelt made very horrible decisions, by implementing a ration for everyone. No one could buy unlimited food and beverages, resulting in people becoming enraged with anger. People demanded change. Proponents of the policy maintained that it was required, but by 1930, there was a drought, forcing farms to buy more dirt. This drought would later cause severe dust storms in the years to come. In the later years, it would affect crops, as well as an increase in smaller rations. The rations were the worst part of the Great Depression, depicting something that represented a new era. As the Great Depression ended, new programs called the New Deal were instituted, but there were many opponents. The focus of the New Deal was to implement a policy so that the Great Depression never happened again, well, it was just a waste of money.

Still hurting from the Great Depression, rations

started to appear again, as the Dust Bowl created a lack of agriculture. The reason for this is because the Government at the time demanded an unlimited amount of crops be planted and grown, so that people will have enough food. Well, there was this thing called a drought, and then there was something known as the wind, or atmospheric pressure, which picked up the excess dirt and crops from the earth. This was something bad. It could be called a dust storm or even a tornado, yet, it was not a hurricane, because there was never any rain. If it was a hurricane or a tropical storm, or even a monsoon, the damage would be more severe.

Starting in 1941, the Japanese Empire attacked something known as Pearl Harbor, yet, this is when the people of the United States would suffer the most. The rations never ended. Martial law was enforced, and people had to stay inside, effectively closing everything. The government of the United States soon declared war on Japan. This was not the end, but only the beginning of a lost cause. People became even angrier than before. No one could escape this war, as everyone could be considered an enemy, as this was considered normal back in the day. People started to accuse other people of being communists, but this was nothing new, as it was common during the Red Scare as well as the first war. There was a fear of hope, a fear of safety, and a fear of retaliation. There was an unjust order instituted by Roosevelt, interning all people of Japanese descent in prison camps. People became even angrier, and Japan had enough. Just as you think it would end, there was still more to come. There would be daily attacks against anyone. If you opposed the war, you were considered a communists, and you could be imprisoned. There was a lack of civil liberties, since the government thought freedom was a waste of time, and then, there was finally the death of Roosevelt, which made people happier, but it was not the end.

After Roosevelt died, there was the ruthless tyrant who took over, known as Harry Truman, who supported war and more attacks. Truman clearly hated international law, as he attacked sovereign nations with nuclear weapons. People were angry about this, and it happened to be something that would haunt the rest of society. The war was finally over, but everything after that caused a severe threat of the world to the rest of society. Because of the result of the war, Russia and Germany became oppressive nations, as it was the result by the win of the United States Government. This win by the United States Government trampled upon independent sovereign nations, yet, there was finally the Cold War, which would later cause the collapse of the United States of America, and in the end, nothing would be clear.

Around 1947, about two years after the war ended, the next war would start, but it was a war of weapons and mass destruction, as it was unnecessary. It was caused by the intervention and win by the United States Government. By 1961, there was a trade embargo against Cuba, which resulted in chaos. By 1973, there was another crisis, but this time, it affected oil, and there was a repeat of the same type six years later, in 1979. Yet, politicians in Congress, as well as the weak executive branch, ignored everything as normal. Now, in 1983, one year before something bad will happen, something drastic happened. In the last week of October 1983, the United States

Government invaded Grenada, which lasted nearly two months. The United States was already in deep financial troubles because of wars and programs. Yet, this invasion caused the government to fall off the edge.

Finally, one month after the celebration of the new year, the United States of America and the government defaulted. The government could no longer pay off their debts and people started to worry, causing a financial breakdown, and then there was the implementation of rations. For two years, no one knew what to do. The government itself felt that it could escape bankruptcy, and believed it could pay off debts, but that was impossible, since other nations refused to lend money to them, do to previous defaults.

Around March 1986, the Faberx Corporation finally bought out the country and the government, and this was unexpected, as the Faberx Corporation bought out all remaining debts. For two nears, the Congress was trying to figure out how to make money for the government and the country, but they never considered selling. People started to cheer. Within months of the purchase, everything was back to normal, but there were the opponents, also known as the Hollywood machine, because it was them who supported the wars and the lack of money, and they wanted censorship. Censorship was always present, but it would end.

As a result, this was the reason why the Hollywood machine sought revenge. People might this is just coincidental, but sometimes they are in denial. Denial can always occur when people don't want to believe in anything about the truth, yet, there clearly lies a difference. People can make up lies and half-truths, along with fallacies, that clearly disproves their theories, but these people still think their theories were clearly proven, pointing out that the evidence supports no such thing. People always seem to contradict their theories for just about anything. There is nothing that can help them because they are just idiots. These people must be delusional since something is wrong with their statements. As they grow closer, something must be common, yet, nothing has ever encouraged people to tell the truth, and instead, there is something else. Something else resembles something that is clearly defined but is a hoax, yet there is nothing available to analyze the sources. In all accounts, there is something that contradicts everything you might say, but this scenario is the reason why there might be something wrong with the universe. The universe is a place ere you don't want to screw up, because if you do, well something might happen to you and your relatives.

There is a way out, but this must be determined by everything else, as it might be necessary to determine the cause of all evil. It could also determine the cause of all good, as it might actually change the course of history. There is a reason that might ascertain to the public, as early as never, and as close as the next solar system, but this is nothing but torture. The thing behind something else is something else, as it might be mentioned in nothing else but everything else. There is no other reason to support anything, as nothing is at the precise level of something else. There is clearly a flaw present, as it might be determined that it has to be flawed, since that is the goal of the theory. Nothing can ever help, and because of this, it might be best to determine no course of action. Leave everything alone, and it might be determined to help the rest of the world. The world is something that you must respect, as it might be determined to have a close encounter. Nothing will ever be determined to help nothing, as they are the opposites of the rest of everything.

There seems to be something that is always irrelevant in nature, something that makes no sense to be alive. This is the reason why it might be the cause for action to determine the eligibility to determine a reverse survival group of nothing more than a complete nonsense of everything else. This will help something that might be determined to solve the problem of world hunger, but the other way to solve world hunger is to feed the people by donating food directly to their houses, and not some organization. Everything else is necessary because it is never necessary, and as people start to determine something that is in the physical realm of something, well, that might be something that might be determined for something else. At the realm of survival, there is no survival, because everyone will die, and as a result, everything will be lost, so the cause of action or course of action, whatever you choose, is always weak for anything related to nothing or something. There is never any excuse for anything.

Goals will be drawn, and it must be determined to take action for nothing, as there is nothing related to the theory of something that might happen to the theory of something else. For the rest of the world, all hope is lost, and nothing will be determined. The rest of the time, there might be something that will change, so there is nothing to worry about, but the reason to determine everything else is the reason to determine the scope of relating the existence to the theory of something that might not ever happen, so believe what you want, and hopefully, nothing will be determined to haunt your soul, because you will find out the hard way. Nothing is at the rate of what it used to be, and this might occur for the thing of the past. Nothing will be of great value, and you must realize that there is the reason why you must give up in order to succeed, and by doing this, you can succeed, but you first have to realize is that everything is a trick, and you will always lose, so you might have to cheat, which is not wrong, but please, never plagiarize, because that is wrong. Always cite your sources and consider the work of other authors, as you might think that something is defined. Luckily, plagiarism is only frowned upon in the academic community. Parodies just mock the situation and are considered humorous criticism. There is the reason why people might think something is useful, and this might be discouraged, so, determine the effectiveness of something that might be regarded as something that relates to the precise cause of action. You might be able to determine something that is relevant to nothing other than the rest of the world, where everything is at the reason of insanity.

Precisely, that might seem possible, but why is it that you are crazy, and since that could be a problem, you should be left alone, and it is the reason why you might have to determine that nothing will be related to the rest of the world. There is something wrong, and this is because of the crazy events that might happen now. It could also correspond to the events happening now, and as you determine something to be useful, there is a better, more environmental way, that will help you to determine the right action.

Well, screw the environment, and the

environmentalists, because they are such idiots. Sure, they might show concern, but all they do is trample on your freedoms and rights to consume. They think fishing is bad, and that seafood, as well as everything else living in the ocean should stay there. Well, people like to eat food from the ocean. Food from the ocean is good for your health, and is considered part of a good diet. These environmentalists also think research is bad. The environmentalists also believe everyone should only eat fruits, vegetables, and grains, well, that will not help you, as they fail to comprehend the value of meat. Meat is of importance to the vital systems of organs. Now, there is nothing wrong with just eating vegan or vegetarian, but only do so if it is a part of your culture. Don't be a vegan just to be healthy, as that is a foolish decision. The only thing that environmentalists should care about is pollution. Pollution is something that has been explained before, and it will be explained again. Pollution is bad for the environment, as it can cause a variety of problems. Sure, pollution can cause global warming or climate change, but that is only a small part.

Climate change or global warming, whatever you call it, is caused be time and evolution. Pollution only has a minute effect, as it does have one, but nothing that will change overnight. Pollution is constant fog, smog, smoke, and anything that effects the visible sky. The visible sky is the portion of the sky that you see when you are outside. Overtime, pollution might have an effect, but only if it is not controlled. Pollution does not even need to exist, as it is not important to the environment. The majority of the pollution is created by people and factories, by producing toxic fumes, and this is the reason why people become ill.

Pollution does not cause the climate to change, and it does not cause a difference in weather. Pollution just hurts environment. The thing that hurts the environment is the sun. The rays of the sun heat the planet, and this causes the planet to produce conditions that weaken the entire atmosphere, by creating toxins that cause immediate change to the climate. This is nothing new, as it might be explained further, to determine relevance.

Long, long, ago, there was a time when planets did not exist in this universe. Objects containing metal and other elements decided to torture the empty space, by colliding everywhere. Soon, there were incidents everywhere. These objects created new objects, and everything changed, so there would be an environment. Sometime later, well, these objects that were formed by the original objects, well, they now had an environment, but the only life that could exist was organisms. The surface of these objects were still too hot for animals and mammals to survive on them. Billions of years later, and it is now the time of those wretched dinosaurs. There were never any humans or other primates living with dinosaurs, as primates arrived sixty-three million years later. Dinosaurs ruled the world, but they were the only creatures to be predators of each other. Dinosaurs were in fact humans for their times, as they dominated everything. Other mammals and animals existed, but they did not have as much fun as the dinosaurs. After all, dinosaurs were the dominant creatures, and so, it was the reason why they are important.

So, there is the possibility that something happened, and there is, but it is something important. There was an incident that wiped out the entire dinosaur population, and it was called the asteroid incident. Dinosaurs had nowhere to hide, and most of them could never escape. If they did escape, well, they would eventually die off, becoming extinct. There cells would later help to create something else, which was deemed as something that would mean absolutely nothing.

With regard to something, dinosaurs became extinct, but during the beginning of the universe, something glorious happened, the creation of cells and life. The objects known as asteroids, comets, and all other space debris made of elements, well, they were the original creators of all life. These objects were made from rock, ice, and metal. When bright rays from stars projected their energy unto these asteroids, radiation was produced, but during this process, the radiation activated specialized particles, which caused life to be created once the asteroids crashed into one another, but it was a very slow process, that took billions of years. The first forms of life were tiny organisms, which lived in radiated water, as the water was created by radiation, do to the radiation and energy projected by the stars. Since this happened, it was the creator of life. These minute organisms created the rest of the creatures throughout the rest of the world, over a certain of an evolutionary timeline.

Overtime, these organisms would mix with minerals, in order to produce the first type of creatures. These creatures were created by the combination of minerals, compounds, and the minute organisms. By this process, mammals and animals were created, but after the creation of other organisms, because mammals and animals, along with reptiles were created by this process. After the first organisms were created, more advanced organisms were created, through the process of evolution and radiation. Something to consider that is important, is that, this is the exact process of how life first came to be. There was no Adam and Eve, because that was created by frauds and people who didn't understand life.

After a while, radiation decreased to a suitable level, which is when the tiny organisms created the mammals, animals, reptiles, amphibians, and other creatures. Their molecules would evolve overtime, and would help create more life, including everything that you see today. Life as we know it is something special. There are some objectors to this process, and these objectors claim that everything is the equivalent to ten thousand years old, which is impossible. These people are known as creationists, and they because that God invented everything, well let me tell you the truth about God. As a whole, God is the basis of everything.

In the beginning, it is prescribed as God creating the first humans, the universe, and everything else. Well, there is one thing wrong with that theory. The universe was created by something called the Big Bang Theory, which caused meteors and asteroids to collide with each other. These events created the planets and the rest of the universe. This event would later cause life to be created, leading to evolution and other events, and would determine the future. Dinosaurs did not create God, because God was created by the first form of humans, between two million and five hundred thousand years ago. It was in fact, cavemen, who invented God. When the cavemen invented God, they didn't actually know what they were doing. Cavemen thanked some mysterious being that didn't exist. For example, when cavemen first discovered, you could say that a caveman bowed down on their knees and talked to some invisible being. This is where God would later be defined. God was a creation by cavemen to thank and worship for a specific item or event that occurred. The cavemen didn't know what to do, so they thanked something. This is the true meaning of God, but others object to this notion because of beliefs.

Throughout history and evolution, God has grown to a different meaning, and by meaning, it is known as organized religion. Religion and organized religion was created by crazy people who believed in a prophecy that something bad will happen. They created a story saying that God will appear as a person, well, God appearing as a person is possible, but God was created by cavemen to give thanks for mysterious events and circumstances that happened. Besides, there is no one who has ever seen God. As a result, God was never actually part of life until humans existed, so, in part, you could say that God only existed for creative imagination. Nevertheless, people took God as a serious matter. Religion evolved and created organized religion. Religion also created corruption in government, politics, and business, as well as an abuse in power. People believed they were cursed because of God, and that God was killing them. Everything was deemed an act of God. Well, an act of God is something mysterious that happened, but people don't know what caused that event to happen, making it a sign that it was sent here for help or consequence. People might always subscribe to this act of God. But, the act of God, for most of the time, is caused by atmospheric pressure, from the sun or the moon, which further causes climate change. This climate change can change weather immediately, making it seem like a mysterious occurrence.

Of course, this is the correct explanation, but people still believe it is something else. And, to them, science does not make sense, as science is regarded as propaganda and nonsense. Science, in fact, describes everything about life, and how evolution first got started. Science is the reason why everything exists, and is the reason why life has evolved to a complex matter of environment. Science explains everything. The reason why people think God created everything is that because it existed in the earliest of human times.

So, as we dig deeper, we find that the earliest humans believed that God was in everything. The earliest humans didn't know what to call this. The word known as God and other translated meaning, is a recent word, but it is an ancient meaning, but not prehistoric. So, in that notion, God could be anything, meaning that anyone could be God. Humans believed that plants could be God, that animals could be God, and that everything with a spirit was a God. As we know this, it was a very early belief of animalism and polytheism. To build on that, there is nothing wrong with that meaning. However, objectors believe that there is only one God, a being that sees and reflect everything around the world. This is something known as monotheism, were God is depicted as the creator of everything, and that creationism is the reason why life actually exists. This is the reason why monotheism can reflect actual science and evolution as blasphemy and propaganda.

Evolution is not propaganda, and it is not blasphemy. Evolution is the truth about life, and it reflects the society as a whole, so it is in fact real. Objectors will always object because they know nothing but creationism. Creationism as a whole reflects something that is impossible, a thing by idiots who support propaganda and censorship. Censorship is the meaning of propaganda. Polytheism, as it is known, is the belief of believing in more than one God. For the term of God, well, it can be anything and anyone. Polytheists have claimed that God exists in every animal and every plant, as they believe everything is always is watching the world. There is nothing wrong with this belief, but it actually makes sense, however, the reflection of God in plants and animals reflects the idea of individual energy and radiation. Radiation and energy from any source makes it seem like that there is a spiritual being everywhere, which is the reason why something might be active for some particular reason. Objectors will claim that energy and radiation have no basis, and that God exists everywhere, well, have they ever seen God. The idea is that God resembles a spiritual being, but ghosts do exists, as well as evil and good spirits. The thing is, is that God could appear as anything, but that could mean you are experiencing hallucinations.

Energy and radiation explains everything about spirits, and they are always watching over you. Energy and radiation exist everywhere, but they can also make you hallucinate and feel delusional, if you act in a certain way, so you must always act normal. In the theory of everything else, well, there is nothing else to consider, and as a result, there might be something that will occur to the best of your knowledge, which, in time, will cause severe trauma. Trauma could be described as evil energy, but energy is always different. The price that you are willing to pay reflects on everything else.

To be precise, there could be something that made sense, but it is in fact, the opposite, so there is a good possibility that nothing else will ever happen. There is no such thing as something related to anything. Besides the fact, the entire universe acts in unison with each other, and all forms of energy realize that something is happening. In reality, it is a form of evolution, but in imagination and make believe world, well it is considered propaganda.

Then there was the result of what happened after the instructions . The girls read the instructions, then they took their room keys to their rooms, for the next year. Who knows, maybe they will meet someone new. This underground facility is too large anyways. No one knows where it is, and it could take up certain parts of Canada, or it could all be in exactly one place, still making it one of the largest buildings in the world, surpassing any previous record.

CHAPTER FIVE

During this whole crisis, well, nothing was ever normal, and the girls were waiting to start their training. It was only the first day, but it was a day to figure out the entire building, a time when they could relax and do whatever they wanted. It was a time when everything was in harmony, and a time where people could be people. Things can happen, and things are always happening, because everything has to evolve.

As things evolved, it is only a matter of time until the process begins. This process will continue for an eternity, and it will help explain the reasons why everything has to evolve, yet it is part of life. It remains as the most coincidental thing that there is always a reason to determine the purpose of anything, yet, the reason always remains unclear, so there is no knowing of what will ever happen. No one might ever find out about the truth, and no one might ever find out the reality of life. People must maintain their figures, and there needs to be uniformity, were everything is simplistic. Right now, everything is far too complex, and people hardly understand anything. As for the rest of society, well, many are idiots who fail to comprehend the process, or they just believe in something else. The reason remains unknowns, as it could be the issues of the past, yet it would mean a larger problem, something that will never make any sense at all. Something must be done, and something will be done, as all hope might relate to everything but the help. There is no reason to cause war, but that is what happened when Hollywood hijacked the entire country and the government, for fear of freedom, but they did this in the past, thereby creating an alternate universe.

As you already know, this alternate universe relies on censorship to eliminate freedom and civil liberties. Freedom is considered a threat and it is met with propaganda. At every possible obstacle, there is a built in mechanism were the Hollywood machine defends censorship. Censorship is considered good for the society, according to the Hollywood machine, and it is considered necessary in order to promote their policies. Their policies make no sense, not even in communist or socialist countries. Their logic is flawed, and it needs to change, but it never will, so, in time, there will always be a reason to disregard their rule of law. Everything is lost, and more will be lost if something is not fixed. There needs to be a decision, in which there is a correct path to determine the right cause of action. Of course, there is the way of the past, the way that got us nowhere. Right now, the way of the past still exists, all thanks to the Hollywood machine.

People always must keep their friends close, but their enemies closer. This notion needs to happen, as enemies need to be watched like a vulture. There is no other way to watch them, as they are considered the people who support censorship. Friends can help, and they can do this by watching the enemies. You hire your friends to observe your enemies, as your enemies might not know who your friends are. Your enemies might also be preoccupied doing something unrelated, but try not to get caught. In fact, just hire a licensed investigator. You will be safer, and you should not have any problems.

In the last thing, well, it might never end, so you might consider doing something that will help you. You might find something that is irrelevant, but this is only a stepping stone, something that might seem quick to judge, but it will help you in the end. You must focus, and you can do this with the process of evolution. As something might make sense, it is clear that something is happening now.

Waiting for something, there is silence and patience. The girls are waiting for the elevator, so that they can head to their rooms. They are all excited to fight to save the world, yet, there is no clue if their school exists anymore. Waiting for the elevator is something that must be done, and it is only a matter of time until training will begin. At last, the elevator finally arrives, and it recognizes their facial features, automatically selecting the correct floor level. The elevator takes them to the second floor, were they will live for the next year. They exit the elevator, and each of them unlock their door. What they find next, well, it is a surprise, because they are amazed at what they see. Everything in each of their room is magnificent, with beauty and luxury. They each check each other's room. For now, they can rest or do whatever they want, but tomorrow is the dawn of a new day. Tomorrow means something is already happening, because tomorrow is the beginning of advanced training to defeat the Hollywood machine, the reason because of propaganda, censorship, corruption, terrorism, and a widespread amount of government abuse. Tomorrow means the beginning of everything new.

There is a reason for this insanity, as it does make sense, so something is related to the exact point in the passing goal of nothing other than the mind of a fish. The negotiations must be started, and it appears as something is related to the rest of the world, and as it nears, something is at the point of no return. To propose something that is relevant means something is not relevant, as it might seem normal, but the rest of the meaning has something to hide. Hiding something is nothing new, as it represents something to be found.

Hiding at its best is the spiritual world. The spiritual world is filled with energy and nirvana, and everyone and anything who has seen it knows what it is. Yet, there remains a crucial story about this spiritual world, in which that something must be triggered to open it. You see, the only creatures who can actually see the spiritual world every time are non-humans, because these creatures have a special sense of hearing and sight, with regard to everything else.

Humans can only see the spiritual world by taking certain substances, such as ecstasy or THC, which produces hallucinations. Not all hallucinations that humans see are part of the spiritual world are aligned with the spiritual world. If you see a talking zebra, or something similar to that, well, you are not in the spiritual world, and instead, you are just too high on substances. The spiritual world is invisible, and it is the same as the visible world, but the spiritual world holds special sounds, sounds that are silent to the majority of humans. These sounds are proof that something exists, and they form the energy around the rest of the world. These sounds are a form of inter-communication, between the species and plants, in order to help each other to survive. No one can simply enter the spiritual world, as it is protected. Only a few beings actually know about it, and they will never tell you the exact location. The spiritual world is hidden because it is the real world, but no one is supposed to know about the spiritual world. When people speak of a spiritual world, well, they think of something known as heaven. Well, heaven does exist, but it is not the same as you might think.

In reality, heaven is another word for the atmosphere. Yes, there is an invisible layer in the atmosphere where all dead creatures exist, well, sort of. The thing is, there is no sort of thing that exist like this. There is no invisible layer in the atmosphere that contain angels or demons. The atmosphere is the sky. The angels and maybe some demons are actually located in the spiritual world, and not the sky. The location of the spiritual world is in another dimension, something that represents life and achievements. This dimension that is the spiritual world is far more connected than anything else, and is well suited for people to survive. It can be a form of relaxation, or a place to think. The spiritual world contains the necessary environment that will rehabilitate your entire mind and body, and at the least, will help you realize goals.

So, as you might think, how does anyone or anything enter this spiritual world. Well, it is impossible to enter without certain magical traits, but the spiritual world you might encounter is only a small world compared to the actual spiritual world. This means that the spiritual world that you see is only a small copy. The actual spiritual world, which likely was mentioned before, exists in an alternate dimension, where guardians protect and control the environment and the rest of society. Again, this alternate dimension is nothing new, as it is extremely complicated to locate. Within the actual world that creatures and plants actually live in, well, there is another dimension. This other dimension is the location of the actual spiritual world. It is hidden in order to protect society, the world, and the environment.

Everyone who actually tries to locate this alternate dimension finds themselves in a tricky situation, as they know they could disappear for eternity. If they find it, they might be trapped, but most of the time, they feel happy. The spiritual world always make people feel happy, and as a result, the explorers never want to return to the world in which humans live on. In the aftermath, yes, these explorers have actually returned, but in reality, they miss the spiritual world, as it is better and has more appeal.

With regard to anything, as we look further, there is a reason to find out what is happening in the real dimension, which is the dimension were creatures reside. Amelia, Alison, Elizabeth, Erica, and Melissa all look at each other's rooms, and like it was mentioned before, they are amazed. Tomorrow starts a new day, something that will help them achieve something. This is the time when things happen.

First, as you think you might know, everything that you could ever imagine is in fact in an entire room. Everything you want is here. There is no other luxurious amenities that could surpass this experience. It is filled with charm, atmosphere, and uniqueness, across all lines. No one could ever imagine, as something is always hindering the process. The day that you arrive at such a place is the day that you will feel left behind, because everything that you knew was a dream. Your dreams can come true, and it is important that you get what you want, as it might be vital to your success. There is something to think about, and this experience is not one of them, because you need to feel the warmth of a luxurious apartment.

Each individual room is filled with a fifty inch built-in television in the wall. There is a parlor, a bathroom, a laundry area, a kitchen, another bathroom, a bedroom, and a living room area. Each room is different, but the average size is about five thousand square feet. As for the shower area, well, there is another surprise, which is that the shower is a separate room, with a virtual television. One bathroom is just reserved for the shower. The other bathroom has everything else. The shower room is partly a built in sauna.

Before you think about it, there might be something else, but it just gets better and better, or you might believe something else. The reason might be clear, as you might be jealous, so you must decide to determine the richness of everything else. This place is magnificent. No one has seen anything like it before. There is no exception to anything, as it is related to everything else. People might determine some malignant aspect of something, but the proof will never exist, since it is invisible, because no evidence ever exists. There is the reason to do nothing, and as it might suffice, well, there is a thing that could help, but nothing is the same. The rooms were colorful, filled with bountiful items. The most expensive things you could ever imagine is present in this facility. It is something that could be a dream, but this is not a dream, since this is reality, and reality is not kind to people. The rest of the stuff, as you might imagine, well, it could be something from the past, but the past is something that you should consider seriously, since it might eventually change. Change is nothing like it was before, and oh, I forgot to mention that there are two closets in each room, both which are walk-ins, filled with necessary clothes, shoes, multiple dressers, and everything else. These closets are their own separate spaces, so you can add that to the list of amenities, and in such cases, nothing still changes.

The girls go to their separate rooms. Meanwhile, as you might imagine something particular, nothing actually is going to happen to you. Amelia decides to take a shower. She undresses and takes off her tiny pink panties off, followed by her boots, her skirt, her blouse, and then her bra. Now completely naked, she decides to take a shower. The water is warm, and it tingles her body. Amelia uses soap and spreads it all over her wet, hot steamy body. Amelia is gorgeous, as she is one of the best people who fits the description of a perfect body for a woman. Something that you think is something is nothing, but there is nothing but consideration.

Soap, oozing down her body, as no one would ever expect it. It is a sight that was meant to be glorious, something that resembles freedom. It is something that you could never expect to do in your life. Amelia finishes taking a shower, and gets dressed, but decides to go commando, since she is used to it. No bra and no panties, but everything else, and this makes her happy, as everyone wants to be happy. No one never wants to be sad or angry. That would mean something is wrong, as it was indicated to other people. Anyway, Amelia puts on a skirt and a top, and decides to lie down in bed. Maybe sometime later, she will decide to do something, but now, she decides to rest, as she has been walking for too long, which is far long more exercise than you have done in a year. The focus is not what happens, but what you do with your life, and sure, you probably have heard this before, well, people will keep telling it to you forever and ever, in order to brainwash you. There is something else to think about, and it should help you determine the true value of your life.

At the midpoint in life, you probably already did something, but as you grow older, you must also know that you are not going anywhere. Yet, again, if you do nothing, well, nothing will go anywhere. You will be stuck in a hell hole for all I care, but you can seek to escape, but you must achieve something so great that it will kill the trance. The trance is everywhere, and it has been placed upon you in order to brainwash your soul. You are stuck for eternity, yet you never knew it. For everything else, well, there is something to consider, but you must entertain the rest of the world, so help your mind. Now there, you should be luck you are receiving attention, because there are doubters who think you are not worthy of anything.

Still laying down on her bed, somehow Amelia dreams about having sex with Patrick. Fantasies being granted. Something else dreamy. A world of seduction, that causes change, which somehow reflects nothing. There is nothing else involved. Amelia's body thrusting up and down, for the sake up just wanting it. She climaxes as she experiences nothing but pleasure. It could be the best time of her life, yet, this is nothing compared to everything else. People won't do anything as they might tend to do something else. But, as Amelia fulfils some fantasy, it is something crazy, as she might have been jealous when Patrick saw Alison's shit when bending down to retrieve the pencil. The thing is, Amelia is kind of crazy when it comes to boys, yet she has no interest in Patrick or anyone else. As something might be an excuse, there is surely a way to determine the course of action. Amelia is some sort of chick that resembles addiction and seduction. I mean, all of the girls are hot with gorgeous bodies, and resemble the most prettiest in society, so, by all means, this is nothing irrelevant to the rest of the world. Everyone knows that seduction is part of the society that you live in, and you must always be fulfilled. There is nothing else but misery.

Amelia likes this feeling, as she keeps thrusting up and down on top of Patrick. She is dominant, where Patrick is submissive. Amelia enjoys what is happening, as she is waiting to climax. Amelia will achieving her goal of orgasmic activity until she is satisfied. This will go on for a while, and it will continue until something happens. The time is ripe for answers, and the satisfaction will be fulfilled. There is something else, and it must be determined to happen at a time when there is of importance to nothing. Causing something to happen might never happen, as it is a sign. This sign will mean nothing unless it is the meaning of the rest of society. There might be something happening because there is something that is currently happening. There is the way, to cope with a problem, but the problem is to understand the difficulty of life, with society at risk, and the possibility of an ordained function that will ruin the rest of cultural independence. There needs to be a solution, but the solution is actually the problem, where the problem is nothing but existence itself. Moral grounds are high, and it surely must be a mistake to think that something will solve a serious problem.

Beside the chamber, there lies something mysterious, and this will lead to something important, a sign or theory that might be misguided, so something that might remain with nothing but a lack of importance. Nothing needs to happen, as it is not necessary. There is a reason why certain stuff might be happening now, but that is something different, so you must decide on your opinion. Well, that is complete and utter bull, and no, nothing is ever related. Philosophy is not hogwash, as you could be an idiot yourself.

Thirty minutes have passed, and Amelia has finally achieved her maximum pleasure possible. She is happy but also tired. She rolls over to her side of the bed and finally rests for the night, but that is not actually what happened. That was only a dream, something she felt for no reason. It could mean something, but it is only sex. In reality, Amelia was just pleasuring herself the entire time. No one was ever in her room. Yet, the time has surpassed abnormal lengths, as it is now past midnight. As it might make sense, something else could happen, and it will make sense to determine the exact cause of something unrelated to the opposite effect of a nightmare, which might determine the entire process to achieve the best possible outcome. No one is able to accept something that they can decline, so it is only a matter of time until something can oppose everything in existence.

Meanwhile, Alison and Melissa have lost tracked of time, and have decided to fall asleep on each other, naked, and making no sense at all. They don't care about being naked, as it is no big deal. While Alison and Melissa are in Alison's room, Erica and Elizabeth are fast asleep in their own rooms. There is nothing else to know about, except that something will never happen.

The next day would arrive soon. It is filled with something known as charm, which you should be familiar with, and without it, well, that could ruin your life for a lack of atmosphere. Everything happens for a reason, and there will be some days that might have a reason to self-destruct, but that time might mean the difference between life and death, so you might think, and as everyone starts to listen, it is still in the infancy, so there is still time to learn from your mistakes. It is only a matter of time until there is a reason for the sanity to describe the reason for everything unknown. There is no room left for sane people, since it is a matter of critical analysis, which some people lack. There is something that can replace anything but your experimental designs. This is not the focus now, but instead, you must decide if you are willing to accept the theory of revolution, or something that might reflect off of your personality. To think of something makes no difference in life, but everything else might be missing. As for the reason, well, there are plenty, and they don't need to make sense at all, since nothing needs to make sense.

Before you know it, something will happen every second of your life. It might not make sense because it is never supposed to make sense. Reality is different from free will, and everything and everyone is set on a pre-determined goal, but this goal can be altered, but only in a way when it is deemed necessary by the forces of nature. Nature is something that you don't want to mess with, as it can destroy your life by altering the past with deceit and nonsense. So, when you decide to encourage something, you must be able to understand the complete goal of something, notwithstanding the possible penalties that are masked from visibility. Everything will always happen for a reason, so stay patient.

CHAPTER SIX

The next day arrived, and it is already filled with chaos and everything, so it might mean something, but it is not ready for the girls to wake up, since they still have half an hour. That might be short, but in any sense, it is still important to neuro activity in the brain. Anything can happen at any time, yet, it is the focus of the control center of the body. Yeah, I heard of the heart, but that just regulates your organs in order to live. The brain is the real thing that controls everything, as it determines what happens. Without the brain, then, you will be in a comatose state, unresponsive, or feel unable to do anything, because you can't do anything. The brain provides connections to the rest of the body in order to transmit information to survive the life of a normal creature. Not everything might have a brain, but it is necessary to live.

Without a doubt, there seems to be something happening to the rest of society, as to whether their knowledge is escaping, becoming stupider, or something else. People must make choices, but not all choices are equal. If you lack the smarts, you might make a dumb and idiotic choice, and people are surprise when they make a mistake. So, do yourself a favor, and try to determine the difference between good and idiotic natures, or you might face consequences.

With one minute left to go, it is almost time to wake up, in order to begin the first day of training. It probably was a very hard day in the end, but people ended up dreaming and sleeping together, so there might be a time to look back and determine it was nice. One minute later, the alarm clock rings in each room, but no one remembers setting it, so it might as well be a ghost or even a mystery. That's because the alarm clock is controlled by an automated system computer, as it is programmed to recognize people and their sleeping habits.

Quickly, the girls wake up and put on whatever they can find, but no underwear or bra. After a while, it is time to report to the fitness center, to exercise or what not. The girls head to the fitness center were they all take the elevator to the ground floor. There, they find something, but no one appears, so they must wait for something. Minutes later, a voice speaks into a loud speaker. It is an automated computer voice that says "all must undress in order to do and complete the first exercise, which are athletic swimming, then yoga." One at a time, they all take off what they were wearing, and all looked at each other, smiling cheerfully. So, let the games begin, the voice stated, were all of you must swim until time has been called. This will take as long as I deem it necessary, proclaimed the speaker. Knowing that something is happening, well, something is starting to happen.

During the removal of their clothing the girls did not feel embarrass, as they each saw each other naked before, and they like it. In fact, they each participated in some crazy event, but who cares. This was not the first time they had to be naked together, as it is necessary in some physical events. There is nothing that will be determined by this outcome, yet there is nothing that will ever create wind. This event is harmless, as it might be useful to the creation of something more beneficial in life concerning peace.

Nakedness, a bunch of people naked. Full-frontal nudity, nothing new, and this means nothing. Jumping for joy, the girls dive in one by one, and the voice says to start swimming. The girls start to swim. Second by second, and minute by minute, the girls swim until the voice wants them to stop. They can feel that the water is cold as shit, but not too cold, as it warms slightly as they swim, to a comfortable lukewarm temperature. Feeling the water between their thighs, the girls feel sensual pleasure, pleasure that makes them aroused or think about sex, something that is common in their age group, but this is nothing new, so pipe down. A breeze slides up their vaginas, making it feel as wind is present. It is a very sensual, yet comfortable feeling. Swimming seems carefree, yet, there remains the sexuality.

Everything is being as normal as possible, so there might be something happening, and as a matter of fact, there remains something to achieve. The goal of the swimming exercise is to build endurance in the ass muscles, something that will help you gain strength to lean over. As they continue to swim, the experience gets kind of sensual and even sexual, but there is an end in sight. After half an hour of swimming the voice tells the girls to get out and go to the automated dryers. The girls get out of the pool, soaking naked, with nothing on, and they follow an automated line generated by the computer to take them to the dryers. The girls arrive at the dryers, where they suddenly turn on, to the loudness of a jet engine. It takes nearly thirty seconds to finish the process.

From there, the voice tells the girls to head to another part of the fitness center, where they will all participate in naked yoga, something that is sensual. The girls arrive at the other part of the fitness center, where they will participate in the experience of yoga. The voice greets them, and explains to them to sit down with their legs in a kneeling style, yet it is actually bent on their knees. The girls bend down on their knees, and the voice tells them to switch to child's pose, one of the most basic fundamentals of yoga. Each girl listens, and as they listen, an automated built in projected television begins to turn on. There is now some person telling the girls how to do yoga, and each of them follows the steps in order to complete each pose. At some point, they might face difficulty, but now, their vaginas are still exposed, so it is still time to participate in this sensualizing experience with no clothes. Nothing is more important than exercise, and it is simply to create a physical force between you and nirvana. The simple situation is that it is time to stimulate the pubic area, and in order to do this, it is required to open up the Hyman, by which that blood will not exist. To the point of something natural, this is common place, as it is an exceptional experience.

At last, the yoga class is finished, and the girls are instructed to take a shower. Heading to the shower, the girls walk stark naked, while sweaty, and their pelvic area wet and moist from all the endurance they faced. So, as of now, they are taking a shower, and they decide to take a group shower, while each of them pleasure each other. Water dripping down, making it feel like a sensual experience, to the point of no return. There remains something special. Soap is dripping down their bodies, as if like it was foreign invaders. Touching each other continuously, they find each other g-spots, making their each of their clitoris start to climax and orgasm. Now is the time of no return, and they can't stop now, so they simply continue until they are satisfied. They pleasure each other until the desired outcome is reached.

There is a reason why this is happening, as it is a very sensual experience. They must remain calm and think lightly, in order to adjust to this form of appreciation. The timing is critical but not necessary, and as it is ready, there will be something new present. There is a reason why this stuff happen and they understand the consequences.

At last, they finally reach their climax, where each of them feels relieved. They continue to shower together and then they rinse off. From there, the voice tells the girls to go to the locker room where they will be dried off by the automated dryers again. After being dried off the voice tells them to get dressed with the appropriate clothing from the locker room closet, a pair of black-laced panties, a sheer black laced bra, a pair of trousers, a black tank top, and water shoes. From there the voice indicates that free time has begun, and implies them to work out or do something.

Free time has begun, and the girls decide to go to the spa, or something that might look like a spa, but is a bikini waxing place. A robot tells them to strip naked in front of each other, and they comply. The robot then takes them to one room, where it will now remove any pubic hair on their bodies with a specialized laser. The robot applies the laser and removes all pubic hair that it sees, and as a result, the feeling tickles their bodies, as it is a laser. The laser is more efficient than the old-fashioned way, in which wax strips are used. The robot finishes the job and tells the girls to go to the sauna to remove any unwanted fluids from their body. It takes twenty minutes to complete the process at the sauna, and then the robot tells the girls to go to the massage room to have an acupuncture massage, where the robot will massage the girls with a specialized laser while also applying acupuncture techniques on certain points on the body. The girls lie down on their stomachs, ass up, and the robot applies its methods on the girls, making it tickle more. It only took ten minutes, and the process is complete. The robot now tells the girl to lay down on their backs, where it will clean the entire front side of their body with water in order to remove any unwanted material from their body. This technique is used in order to remove any remaining area in the pubic or pelvic area. The robot is finally complete and it is only has been forty-five minutes. The robot tells the girls to get dress and to do whatever they want, so they get dressed and decide to go eat breakfast in the cafeteria, and they hope the food is good.

After arriving at the cafeteria, it is quiet, as there is

a robot cooking the food. Okay, so these aren't the typical robots you might think of. These robots are actually human androids, and they are the good ones, not the evil ones created by the Hollywood machine. These robots or androids, or whatever you like to call them have no feelings or emotions, but they just obey the procedures and guidelines of their jobs. They don't get paid because they don't need the money. The Faberx Corporation saves a bunch of money because of these androids, and androids are not humans, but they are not metal, because they are artificial creatures. Sure, these androids can participate in sex, everyday human activities, eating, and everything else a human does, but they don't get attached. With that in mind, there is nothing to worry about, as this facility is hidden underground in the middle of somewhere in Canada. All help is not loss, and the girls decides to eat a gourmet breakfast filled with caviar, eggs benedict, hash browns, capers, waffles, pancakes, crepes, and everything else. It is surely a great experience, and it will only get better.

Thirty minute passes, and the girls finish their breakfast. There is still about an hour of free time left, and so the girls go back to the fitness center to do something. What will be done, and something should be done. There is a mess outside, or in case, something unpredictable might happen. As the girls wander the fitness center, they go to the swimming pool. Since they don't want to get their clothes wet, they jump in naked. Feeling the same experience as before, or it could be the same, the girls feel a sigh of relief, or something that might never happen again. It is a sign that might regulate anything, but there is a simple task to hamper the rest of the day. There seems to be something related to the rest of the world, and as it might make sense, it should be a reminder that anything can happen, so in this manner, there is a reason to understand that another world does exist, just as you might make sense. People, people, and more people, that is what people are, and this is nothing more than a rant, something that is meant to sound unfortunate, yet the realization is appropriate.

Nothing is being done now as it is still free time, and there is finally something that has to happen, for any sake, there is a reason to think of nothing. Back and forth, side by side, the girls are focusing on their training, yet it might be impossible to know, so as it might sound coincidental, there is a reason to understand nothing. There is a reason to understand anything, and yet there is a reason to fulfill the prophecy, a thing that might never actually happen. For now, the girls sit in the pool, doing nothing but thinking. There is a reason for this as there is a reason for anything, and as it never makes sense, it is possible that something always happens every second. So, it is a period of announcement in which there might be a delay, so the rest of the process might be different. There is a reason why something must be done, and this is the reason, which is why no reason exists, because it is not true. There is no explanation available, and as it seems fit, there is some place that might determine the rest of the process, so help your soul.

Patience is a vital tool, as it might provide certain answers towards the process. You must always act patient and never rush to judgment. One month is not enough time, and that is because the process always takes years, years of labor, years of time, years of compliance, and years of researching, to the point where you have proved that your theory is valid, accurate, and believable. Time is on your side, as it always take patience to determine anything, unless the task is so easy it is meant as a joke. This is something serious, as the girls await for their next duty. At the physical amount of time it might take, there might be something that should take place, as there is nothing ready.

Waiting, waiting, and even more waiting, there is a reason to think nothing is being done, but that is only something left for the rest of society, yet it is the reason why the theory of being empty is exactly the feeling of doing nothing, so the theory is nothing less than the fact that something is going to happen. Riots might start, depending on the situation. Wars are imminent, as the enemy has shown distaste towards freedom. There is some reasons why there might be an uprising. People are dying every day and there isn't a faster process to consider. After what you might think happen, there might be an alternate sign to negotiate the outcome, but that is still unknown, so you might think .

Chaos has shown to be a disaster that will never fail to exist. It will exist until people realize that chaos is caused by propaganda and censorship. Everything is around the entire complexity of the world, as it might make sense because it does make sense. There is nothing but disdain to certain stuff, yet it might come as a surprise that something is happening, so before there might be a resistance, there could be something else, a theory or explanation that might explain everything, so that people can understand the complete details about their lives as well as their own memories. It is a time that means there will be an uprising. A government has risen so powerful that it has eliminated freedom. This government has promoted censorship, a sign that promises propaganda as well as chaos. This will not be taken lightly, as people start to rise up against the authorities. It is a reason why this type of agenda must be stopped. It must be taken as a serious threat. There is nothing that can solve it overnight, but there is a reason to think of the same reason and to apply it against the forces of evil. It is the time to defeat the Hollywood machine, the time to stand up against tyranny and evil, in order to defeat the man.

Something that was just on the news was that the Mestor extradition hear was moved backed three months, and that now, the court has asked the foreign government to take responsibility. The foreign government or also known as the Hollywood government, has shown no responsibility, as it does not comprehend any law. If the Hollywood government does take responsibility, they must understand that they have to drop the entire Mestor case, and to stop using unconstitutional and illegal shenanigans. This decision by the high court has shown merit that the Hollywood government has no case against Mestor or his website. It is a sign that is meant to promote freedom, something that might be necessary if there is a place to understand. There is no reason to answer anything, yet there is a reason to understand the basics of freedom and the rest of your opportunities. This judgment is necessary, as it supports the rest of the world, and it is a foundation to restrict censorship, the very same kind that has been noticed since the beginning of time.

At the recreation of anything, there is something that must be understood, as it does have something in common, that it is necessary to help people. Yet, it is still a surprise that something will never help people, as it might seem unnecessary, so to the rest of people, something might not be right. It has been a theory since the beginning of time, a place that existed in order to determine life and the pursuit of happiness. As you could explore this place, it could surprise you, as it might seem attractive, yet it will seduce you, and this seduction will oppose everything about you. It is meant as a defense mechanism, and is a tool to defeat everything in sight. There is a reason that it might haunt you, as it will cause everything to be determined by the rest of the world.

Thinking of nothing, there is better stuff that you can understand, as it might make sense that there is a reason to determine the reason of nothing. There is the very possibility that the end is near, but that is what people have been saying for centuries. Misguidance is a tool for propaganda, as it can help people be brainwashed, to the extent that there is a reason to cope with everything else. There is the reason to think of the exact reason why it must be necessary, and in that sense it might make the pressure or stress disappear, to the extent that it was never actually present. There is the reason why there is the possibility to determine nothing through peace and strength, and by this creativity, there exists a sense of happiness, a thing of the past, and a reason for the understanding of how life works in the dimensions.

So, there is the case, the case for freedom, the end of tyranny, and the reason to survive, all of a nature to restore order and help freedom. As it might take place, there is the place for the end of the days, a sign that might make sense, yet it has been concluded to be determined at the cost of a very high nature. The reasons can never be explained, as they are unreasonable and have no reliance. Upon the nature of everything else, well, there is a theory to cope with the non-existence of foreign creatures, yet this sign can be determined to hinder nature, and as a result, it must be altered in a way to stop pollution and to promote growth.

There seems to be an opportunity to end world hunger, but most people are unable to contribute, so governments and organizations handle the matter. World hunger has always been a problem, as poverty is everywhere, and no one can ever escape it, unless you constantly make money. But soon, poverty could attack everything and everyone. Poverty is nothing new, as it relates to a very high living standard, and since that is what causes poverty, people might never have a chance. There are some people who try to help, but poverty will always be around, and as a result, there might be something to prevent poverty, but that must be decided by people. World hunger won't disappear overnight, as people will still be starving. When people think of world hunger, they automatically think of Africa or some poor Asian country, yet, it is common in those places, there also needs to be focus on domestic world hunger. The thing about domestic world hunger is that it is more common than people think.

There, the reason of anything, yet, everything about catastrophes is defined as harmful, but there is a good side, which might refocus on creating stronger buildings. Without nature, there will never be any evolution, and nothing will ever change over time. There needs to be change, as it is the way of life, and while this might sound strange, there is a reason why it might help society come together and rebuild their cities, in order to prevent other catastrophes.

No one might ever understand, but there is always a reason to help people. As this might also sound weird, but nothing is wrong with helping, due to the fact that something bad might happen. So, the girls are just about finishing their skinny-dipping adventure, and then they decide to go take a shower, but this time, separately. Wait, what about the clothes you say, well, the computer put them in an automated laundry drop, as it was deemed necessary, and because they would wear a new uniform or outfit after swimming. Anyway, the girls shower in their separate stalls, but with no dividers. They laugh, smile, and giggle at each other. Water is dripping below their bodies, making it seem orgasmic. It is a matter of time until nothing happens. A splash of body wash, a dash of soap, and a pile of water, they all wait under the water. As soap is dripping off of their bodies, a sensation is felt, and it is the reason why something is going to happen, and it will happen shortly, but it must happen to be concise.

About time, the girls finish their showers and they head to the dryers, where they will be dried off, and then to the locker room closet. The voice speaks, and tells them to gear up with sheer undergarments, a sheer bra, specialized trousers, a sheer tank top, a specialized vest, a specialized jacket, specialized boots, and a specialized utility belt. The trousers, vest, jacket, and utility belt have built in titanium, which means they contain titanium, as well as another metal known as platinum to protect against injuries. This might add some weight but it is a necessary step in order to prevent injuries. As a result, there were never any injuries. The utility belt also contains metal, the same type of titanium and platinum found in the other protective gear. As for the undergarments and everything else, well, they are just meant for better breathing purposes. So, the girls obey the computer, and they get dressed, in order to get ready for their next assignment, weapons and defense training.

The girls are finally dressed, and they head to the training center, which is on the same floor but in another location, as the fitness center. The girls arrive at the training center, and the voice tells them to enter a room. There, the voice tells them to watch and listen to a screen. The voice then plays a video about the center. After that, the voice shows the weapons and other equipment that will be utilized in this portion of training. "Each new form of equipment will have a video to display the proper usage," proclaimed the voice. After each video, the girls were instructed by the voice that they will practice shooting with it at a specialized gun range. With that, the first video plays, the one about the center itself. There is a price to pay, but the video must be watched in order to operate the machine properly.

So, as they are watching the video about the center, and it is only about the technology. It is over within minutes. The voice starts to play the second video, which will start with the most basic weapon, the Cobalt-Henry Pacific 950. Now, the Cobalt-Henry Pacific 950 is a standard gun, but it is one of the most powerful weapons in existence. The Pacific 950 for short is the size of a water pistol, about four inches in length, and produces a straight plasma laser beam. It has a small cartridge for ammo, which are plasma pellets. Now, this gun will have a very powerful force that might take you aback, so you might want to hold onto something. A larger magazine can be outfitted, but additional pellets must be added. These pellets are radioactive when shot, so you must take extra precaution. Now, it is time to shoot.

The first weapons video ended, and the voice instructed the girls to each put on a biohazard suit. From there, the table in front of them turned over, revealing the gun. After that, the girls were instructed to pick up a gun then follow the lighted hallway to the shooting range. So the girls arrived at the shooting range, and were instructed to shoot one at a time, not at the same time. Each shot followed a loud blast that could break glass. It was so powerful, that each time it was fired that they would fall down. The girls shot one at a time, following the orders of the voice. The voice finally instructed them to drop their weapons and to proceed back to the training center. So, the girls went back to the training center, to watch another training video, something about maybe another weapon. The girls finally arrived and they were instructed to take off their biohazard suits. Whatever is used next will probably be more important, as the girls wait for the next video to be displayed, a sort of limbo exists. The voice starts the video, indicating that it is time to learn again. It is new to them that this could happen, but this is just the beginning.

The display screen shows some strange sub-machine gun, with strange features. It is introduced as the F-Mark 650, a fully-automatic sub-machine gun. The F-Mark 650 is built on plasma power, has two separate chambers, and a led monitor scope. To power the gun, it must be charged by a battery generator, which can provide a three day charge, or it can be charged by a specialized wire cable. To load and unload the gun, you must press the gray button on the side control panel, which will then release a mechanism to unlock the chambers. Now that the chambers are unlocked, gently pull their handle bars back, to open them. Once open, you have two choices of loading options, insert the ammunition directly inside the chamber, or to insert a magazine into the chamber. To unload, just empty the chamber. To close the chamber, pull the handle bars back to their previous positions. To close the chamber with a magazine, carefully make sure that the magazine has been locked in or snapped into its proper position, then slowly pull the handle bars back to their original positions. Now that the loading and unloading functions have been explained, we shall now move onto the type of ammunition. The type of ammunition used is gel pellets. These gel pellets are super concentrated with plasma. Now, this type of ammunition produces a very bright beam of energy when fired. It can cause severe burns and blindness, if not careful. Since we have covered the ammunition, now it is time to proceed to the led monitor. The led monitor is used as a scope. Once opened, a camera will activate on the back side, or the cover. Make sure the screen faces you, because if it doesn't, you won't see anything. To open the monitor, just push the white button on the side control panel, which will immediately activate the camera. To actually shoot, you must first press the yellow button, then the red button for confirmation, and then the blue button to fire. To shoot additional rounds at a time, press the green button, each time you want to fire a round. This is a safety measure built in to the gun to prevent unwanted consequences. The triggers that you might see are actually dummies, which do nothing.

Now that we have covered everything, go followed the lighted pathway to enter the specialized shooting range. The girls went to the shooting range. A wall opened beside them, revealing the weapon. Each of the girls grabbed a F-Mark 650, carefully following the instructions from the video. The voice told them to activate the camera, then to shoot and fire. Now that the camera has been activated, the girls are ready to shoot. Carefully following the instructions from the video the girls shoot and fire in a straight line. The girls keep shooting until the guns run out of ammunition. The voice then tells them to recharge the guns by returning them to their storage areas. Now that the guns have been returned to their charging stations, the voice now tells the girls to go to the cafeteria in order to eat lunch. Weapons training is now over for the day, as the voice stated, and it is important to eat so you can gain energy, as put by the voice. But before that, the voice indicates that the girls have to take a shower to remove any possible radiation that escaped from the weapons.

Arriving at the showers, the voice instructs the girls to undress completely. After complying, they undress and head to individual shower units, with no dividers intact. The shower heads automatically turn on to a special setting, in order to remove any radiation or foreign contaminants. Since this is a special shower, the water pressure is extremely high and special detergents are connected to the water supply system when necessary. High pressurized water first rinses off the entire body, from head to toe. After that, the shower head then cleans the entire body with specialized dish detergent. Then, the shower head uses a combination of soap, water, and perfumes to soak the entire body. After all of that is complete, the shower head then uses high pressurized water again. With all of that over, the entire shower stall moves away in order to turn into a dryer facility, where the girls will be completely dried. So there you have it, the girls are now completely decontaminated, and they can go eat now. With the shower being over the voice instructs the girls to put on regular clothes from the locker room. And so, they go get dressed, but decided not to put on any bra or panties, as they feel more comfortable without those items. Lunch is here.

With that, the girls head to the cafeteria in order to eat lunch. After lunch, there is another session of free time, something that is important to defeat the Hollywood machine. So, the girls go to the cafeteria. Weapons training will pick up again tomorrow, but until then, it is time to eat.

Arriving at the cafeteria is nothing new, as they have all ate in a cafeteria before, but this is built on a massive scale. So, what is for lunch, well, there is sushi, caviar, fresh seafood, shellfish, Chinese food, French, Italian, and everything else you could imagine. They grab a few of each. Not to fat shame them, but they are not fat, nor are they skinny. They are the perfect weight and body type, physically fit with perfectly toned physiques. They are also muscular, strong, pretty, beautiful, hot and seductive. You could say that they are way of your league, and they might ignore you, as you are not important enough. So, to put it in simplistic terms, the girls are better at you because they maintain themselves, and they also have a balanced diet of everything. It is interesting to note that everything is different in your world, but if you shall know, there is something else more important, and this too shall pass. So, whatever you think, something will happen, because something is currently happening.

Thinking about something, well, what else is important, as there are many reasons to construct a motive. There is a reason to indicate something, but it still has to be motivated, yet there is something more important than the rest of the world. There is something happening now, eating, as it might seem, so there is a perfectly good reason to ignore you know. There is the reason to believe that you will still be until the world will end. By the way, the world is under attack by the Hollywood government, if you haven't heard yet, so please, try to remain calm and don't panic.

Reflecting upon the dining options here, well, there is only one restaurant, which is the cafeteria, an all-you-care-to-eat buffet, with unlimited meals anytime you want to dine. Not even must restaurants will allow that, but this is in a specialized facility. If there was no curfew, then, the girls could eat here at a late night snack, but they are in training, so what else is new, nothing, I guess, or so you think otherwise. You must think that something or someone will help you, but you are mistaken, as you are neither the problem nor the solution. You are just the nuisance object that produces nonsense.

Eating, eating, and even more eating, that is what is presently happening. The girls sit down at a table. A breeze could be felt going up their thighs and they feel it, but that is nothing new. They eat until they are full. After they are finished they throw their garbage away. They are finished eating their lunch, and they decide to take a break.

Heading to the pool, they decide they want to skinny dip, yet again. So, they arrive at the pool to enjoy their free time, and strip off their remaining clothes. They jump in and start swimming, then they just decide to sit and relax on the side, where they might remain. It is sort of a sensual experience, but that is nothing new, as it could be common, because it is common, yet people are idiots. With the girls relaxing, there could be something else going on, or so you think. Nothing is as you might expect it, and it will soon diminish. As you might think, there could be a case, or there might never be a case. Boundaries are endless, but could they exist, or are they imaginary. This is something that you must be critical about, as you might determine something might happen, so you will choose to do something. As you could later dictate, there is a reason to personify everything you realize. There is a reason to sing, a reason to know, and reasons of everything else. There is the possibility that everything is happening at the same time while you realize something is non-existent. There is also the reason of the poltergeist.

Thinking back, you could say that the poltergeist is everywhere, as it is after you for no reason at all. This could be true, as it might be common, but there is nothing else, so there is something that might be true but it actually never happens. As the rest of the world knows, there could be something that is of the opposite of the world, and there is nothing that will care, so there is the reason that might attach to the rest of the world, when really, that is an alternate dimension. The alternate dimension is everywhere, and you will never escape it, and if you did, well, you were either lucky, or it was a trick created by the alternate dimension. Reasons are endless, and they might seem useless, but they help determine everything else, so they could be beneficial.

While sitting in the pool, the girls realize nothing. They are not stupid. They are extremely smart and are probably smarter than all of you combined. They can't think of anything because they must train. Taking a year off of school for training is not easy, as the school might not even be there, so they are probably fortunate. Everybody in the real dimension in 2006 is probably dead, hiding, or fighting. No one will know. The portal could be blocked or it was probably merged with nothing other than disaster.

Everything that you know is wrong. It is almost the end of free time, and so the girls take a shower with each other so that they can exercise again. Water dripping down. Soap slides down their hot and sweaty bodies. Their breasts are wonderful, and plump, filled with everything you can imagine. A muscle won't help you here. It is a sight for an epic fantasy. There is nothing wrong, as they are helping each other to feel a sensual experience. In the confines of something of a shower stall, it is not uncommon, yet some people are unbelievable, so there might be a problem with other people. The experience is pure and experimental. It can be temporary or even permanent. It is a way of evolution, a way that can influence your beliefs. This is something vital to the rest of the world. Without change, well, there will be a lack of cooperation, a lack of civility, and everything will be boring. No one wants to act the same, as some people are meant to be crazy, so there is the reason to contemplate, in order to decide.

Their shower ends, and they just put on panties, a sports bra, and a skirt, after they are dried off. They don't get any shoes, as it feels unnecessary. Besides, something could happen, but there is surely something that will happen, so there might be an excellent explanation for anything and everything. Anything can always change, as it is a part of evolution and the rest of the society, so enjoy something that is nothing but temporary. After a while, there might be something awkward, so, in the rest of meantime, you will have to entertain yourself, to a point where it might be painful to do something.

Walking or whatever you would like to call it, the girls arrive at the fitness center. There, the voice tells them to each grab the pair of specialized running shoes in front of them. The voice then tells them to put on the shoes because they will be jogging and running to build endurance. What the voice didn't indicate is that these shoes are specially designed to travel at lightning fast speeds. The girls might learn this when they start running.

For the first task, the voice indicates that they must run for one-hundred miles. This is when they all shake their heads and start to think, how they can finished this in less than five hours. It has never been heard of, and so, the girls start to run when the voice indicates. From there, the running begins. Where will they run, well, they will run in circles around the entire fitness center. It could be dangerous, but that is something that might be necessary. The girls start to realize that when they are running, they are starting to pick up speed, to the point that it is too fast.

Circles and circles, yet even more running in circles, it is a never-ending experience, so there is a possibility that people might grow tired after this activity. Boobs, bouncing up and down, as it is so fast that nothing can be stopped. The sheer force of this could kill all insects, yet, it could be possible that something will never happen. It is the risk that must be taken, in order to reduce the harm of everything else. There is nothing else that can be done, so it is only a matter of time until something is complete.

After a while, the voice finally instructs the girls to stop by telling them to brake. Braking is possible when the shoes are pointed down, so, the girls must point their feet downwards, in order to stop. It has only been thirty minutes, and the girls ran one-hundred miles. The voice gives them a fifteen minute break in order to rest. The break is over and the voice indicates that regular exercise will be the rest of the focus. The voice tells the girls to enter the gym, in order to exercise on the machines, whichever they choose. This will be for the rest of the four hours, and so, the girls start to exercise.

Time flies when you are having fun, and the voice indicates it is time to shower to that they can eat. The girls head to the showers where they will undress and take another shower. After that, they got dressed and went to the cafeteria to go eat dinner. Dinner finally arrived, but it is a late dinner, and so, it is an important part of life. Dinner is over, and free time is here again. The end of the first day of training is almost over. It will repeat itself again tomorrow until a year has passed. After a year, the girls will be ready.

Since free time has arrived, the girls decided to use this final allotment as resting time. The girls head back to their own rooms where they will each rest until the next day, which is tomorrow. By then, they will probably know the routine, and it will be possible to remember everything. And so, the girls jump into each of their beds, crashing, instantly falling asleep. As you might think, whatever happened to their room keys, well nothing, because they put them on the lobby desk, as instructed by the voice. Tomorrow is near.

Meanwhile, in another area of the facility, Rafael is currently fucking Carlie, in a passionate love affair, while Jack and Jonathan are watching. It could be an orgy, but it is just sex, or chill out. There is nothing wrong with the situation currently happening, so you might want to calm down. The banging is extremely noisy, and Carlie is moaning and panting, to the point it is pleasing her. They are on the other side of the dormitory units, and besides, everything is soundproof. So, there is something happening, but you are nonsense. Who knows what Carlie and Rafael are up to. Maybe they want a baby together, or maybe they feel sex is a fun encounter to participate in, which would also mean extra benefits.

As this fucking situation continues, Rafael impregnates Carlie, and then she cleans herself off by taking a shower, along with Rafael. Carlie has extremely perky and large breasts, and her pelvic area is completely shaven. It is a perfect vagina and clitoris, to the point where it is very tight. There seems to be something awkward, something unrelated, and something that might cause harm, but that has yet to be proven. There is a reason why stuff happens. While this is all happening, the girls are sleeping in their comfortable beds, located on the other side of the dormitories. In the point that nothing makes sense, well, nothing might ever make sense. As to the rest of the people, there seems to be something that might cripple the rest of the society.

Society, as we know it, is on the verge of extinction. There is a case to fight. There is something that can help. The thing to remember is to outnumber the enemy. The enemy has clearly shown a distaste for freedom, as if it was causing trouble. There is the absolute theory that something will always happen, and since there is a price to pay, well, there is something that must be undertaken, as it might take some time. The thing regarding life is simple. Life is a gift for most people, yet, there remains something that might determine the goals of something that might hinder the decision of something promising. There is something that might make sense, as it needs to make sense, and as it makes sense, it is complete hogwash, something that has been known to be false and a bunch of crap. This is the reason why history should never repeat itself. The reason that history actually repeats itself was clearly stated, yet, to make it simple for people to understand, history repeats itself because of the policies of certain people. These policies make no sense at all, and have no compassion for anybody. They simply believe that everything is the same as always. In the meaning of the ability to comprehend something, well, something might be acknowledged, but then, there are the times when people fail to comprehend anything, forcing the status quo to be dumb founded. Thereby, everything will change, just because of some technicality, or whatever you think about it, so, you must be determined, and yet, there is something distracting your ability to learn something.

As the next day approaches, it could mean many things, but there is something that could make that day. Meanwhile, Alison is having some type of dream, something that probably makes no sense at all, to the point that describes a fantasy. So, what is happening, well, apparently, Alison is having a fantasy of some unnamed person. Screaming in her sleep, she is not frightened, but it is more of a moaning, or something that related to the opposite effect. Who could Alison be talking to, or she is just talking to herself. Alison is in fact talking to herself. She is having some type of dream. She then screams out someone by the name of Candace. "Candace, fuck me," she exclaimed, indicated, as it seems she is having an affair with another woman. This certainly makes sense, as it is supposed to make sense. Meanwhile, Alison dreams of scissoring or fucking this Candace person, and it lasts for nearly twenty minutes, as she dreams of having an orgasm.

The next day arrives, which is Tuesday. Something that could be confusing, because the girls left on Monday, but the thing is, when they left to travel to the future, the first day when they arrived in 2015 was actually a Sunday, so they lost or even gained a day. With the second day being here, the girls are still startled by the alarm clock. They hear the alarm clock and they jump out of their beds. After waking up they put on some clothes in order to go to the fitness center, where, from there, they might train. At the fitness center they are instructed to do cardiovascular exercise routines. Their boobs are bouncing up and down, ignoring the entire thing. After that, they are instructed to swim and then do Pilates. For some time, they complete their workout. Time has gone fast and it is already time to head to the showers, so, the girls head to the showers, where they will get ready for the rest of the day. The showers are complete, and so the girls put on some outfits in order to get dressed to take a nap in their rooms.

The girls arrive in their rooms, flipping through channels on their televisions, and come across some sort of incident happening. In the middle of the ocean of Mediterranean, a luxury cruise liner is seen on fire. So, there must be a reason for this fire.

The luxury cruise liner, the Pegasus Queen, has been set ablaze by what seems to be a terrorist attack by the Hollywood government. The Pegasus Queen is renowned for its luxurious appeal towards high society. High society members are well-known for their support of freedom. This has been an attack by a terror state in order to eliminate and silence global freedom. It was a planned attack.

Tropical paradise, well, what is a tropical paradise, as if you knew. It is supposed to have everything you dreamed about, with extra luxury. Sadly, you are not part of this story, as you are currently reading it, so you must decide on your opinion or your professional opinion, if you even have one. There is something that will forever haunt you, from early to late, in the time it takes to notice the gates of hell. Something is notorious, as it might make sense, so you must make critical sense, without the entire story, or else, something bad might happen. You need to understand that everything is in chaos. This destruction of the cruise ship is a tragedy to freedom, and a win for chaos. You need to understand every detail, and it is set in stone, there is something to think of, like, think about the rest of your life. You could be lucky, yet there is something hurting the attempt to declare a win. Something has gone terribly wrong, and it is about to get worst, so decide and make your decision, because it will only get more dangerous.

Freedom is your friend, and you must understand that it is part of life, so you must consider everything while you might seem something that is vital to your interests, and in order to determine something that is global, it must make sense, or you might think something is missing. It is the way people understand the physical traits of life, and is important to your daily routine. You can help promote freedom, but it must be done in a way that will never harm society, so you must think about the rest of society.

Almost time for weapons training, the girls get dressed in their combat uniforms. Then, they head down to the training center to figure out what they are doing today. More videos might be watched, as they learned how to use two weapons the previous day. How many weapons will be used today, well, probably the rest, which is about three. These three new weapons are important, as they are very powerful, so patience and safety is of the most importance.

Arriving at the training center, the voice tells the girls to enter the room. The girls enter the room. The voice then plays a video on the screen. This next weapon that is shown is known as the M-Stat 2000, a high-energy powered magma gun that shoots super-concentrated electric pellets. The pellets are encased in gel, and only produce a high voltage of electrocution once it hits its target. So, in sense, the weapon electrocutes the target in order to subdue the enemy. It is the size of a regular grenade launcher. There are three compartments or chambers that ammunition is inserted. All shoot at the same time, or three rounds per shot. To operate the M-Stat 2000, it must be fully-charged, but it has a solar panel that will keep it going until the battery dies. There is no scope, as it is not a long-range gun. It is meant to be used within no more than two thousand feet, but the recommended distance is no more than one-thousand feet, as it can't shoot far. To load and unload ammo, push the brown button, then insert the ammo or the magazines with ammo. To close the compartments, pull back the handle bars until you hear a click. To shoot and fire, press the blue button, then push the red button for confirmation. Finally, to fire at the target, push the green button. To shoot additional times, push the yellow button. It is simple to use, and is probably the least complicated weapons.

Now, since the video is over, it is now time for the girls to try it out, so the voice tells them to head to the shooting range and grab a gun. Each of the girls grab a gun, and the voice tells them to practice with it. One by one, they each start shooting, and it reacts severely against the targets. The gun first electrocutes the target, then it sets the target on fire, causing the target to be engulfed in flames, turning it into ash, something that is amazing and scary.

Now that training for this weapon has been completed, the voice tells the girls to head back to the video center again, in order to watch another video. The picture comes on a screen, showing a machine gun-like weapon. It is in fact a machine gun, but shoots concentrated gel pellets of xenon, neon, and krypton at the same time. As like the M-Stat 2000, the G-Net 5000 also has three compartments or chambers. There is a scope for this gun, as it is capable of shooting at far distances, up to fifteen miles. The G-Net 5000 has solar panels to charge, in case of a lack of battery power. Now, the G-Net 5000 consists of a highly radioactive nature, since it is possible for radiation. To actually use it will mean something very powerful. First, in order to use the gun, the scope camera must be activated. To open the led scope, you must press the olive-colored button on the control panel, causing the scope to rise up automatically, thus activating the camera. The screen faces your face, and the camera is on the opposite side.

Now, this LED scope is also a touch screen. The touch screen feature allows you to set a target by zooming and locating. The touch screen feature also allows for adjustment of necessary operation features, such as battery life, chamber capacity, and target rate. Now, to load and unload, this is something different, as it is completely voice activated.

You must tell the gun the word "chamber," in order to load and unload the ammunition. Once you have all the necessary ammunition you need, you will have to say "shut" to the gun. The gun will automatically close and will re-calibrate, based on the information it receives. There is also a flashlight, which is completely voice activated. To shoot and fire, just indicate a distance and a target, then say "launch," then "fire," which will activate the radon energy core. The gun will then shoot and fire a blast of energy in three straight lines, forming into a single blast, after the ammunition has left the chambers. Now that everything has been covered, the voice indicates again to go to the shooting range.

Again, the girls follow the directions indicated by the voice and start shooting one by one, in a steady pace. Shortly and slowly, a high beam of energy is released onto the target. The only thing remaining of the target is a cloud of dust and a trace of light, as the properties of these gases caused an immediate reaction to destroy the intended object immediately. The light is left behind because it is the aftermath of a glowing radiation, indicating that something was shot at. It could also mean that it wants to know that it was successful. Now that this practice has been successfully completed, the voice indicates to the girls to head back to the video center, where they will learn how to use the last gun, the Hellfire 8000, a combination of a rocket launcher, a bazooka, a machine gun, and a grenade launcher. It is one of the most advanced weapons of its type, and it was invented for the sole-purpose of eliminating everything in its path at the same time. This gun is highly dangerous, as it produces super-concentrated plasma-energy along with fire, gas, and radiation.

Now, this gun, like the previous weapon, has a fully-automated led scope that slides up. The screen of the scopes faces you and the camera faces the opposite side. Once the led scope is positioned to its correct spot, then the camera will be activated. To open the led scope you must press the violet button, which will then activate the camera. To load and unload, you must recite "chamber," as this gun is also fully voice activated. To close the chamber, you must say "shut," which will then close the chamber. This gun also has a voice activated krypton flashlight and a laser.

When the gun is ready to shoot and fire at target at objects, you must say "confirm," then "shoot," and "launch," all at the same time without any hesitation. This will make it easier for the gun to understand your speaking habits. When fired, the ammunition produces a bright beam of blueish-red light, which slight colors of yellow, green, and orange. Blue is the main color indicated, as it is the most powerful in the chemical compounds of the ammunition. The ammunition consists of powdered magma, powdered sodium, powdered calcium, powdered magnesium, xenon, and plasma. The force of these compounds create a liquefied agent of what was stated before. This agent then turns the intended target into a massive pile of dust, just like some of the other weapons. Since its objectives is to destroy, it has a very high success rate, indicating that nothing can escape its wrath. Now that the video has been finished, the voice indicates for the last time to go to the shooting range to test the weapon.

One by one, the girls arrive at the shooting range, where they practice using the weapon. The practice is a success, and the voice tells them to keep shooting until no more ammunition exists. For a while, the girls keep shooting. The girls run out of ammunition when the gun indicates to replace the magazines. The voice indicates that the training is complete for defense today, and tells them to go to the showers to get ready to eat lunch. The shower is also required in order to remove any radioactive material contracted during the training process, so it is a way to access precaution. The girls head to the shower room, in order to take a shower. All at once, they remove their clothes and the shower automatically turns on to a special setting, a setting that eliminates any radioactive material, in order to prevent contamination.

Yet, as the never ending training continues, it is a

sign of progress. The girls are done showering and put on some regular clothes, and head to the cafeteria in order to eat lunch. It is a time for jubilation, a time to celebrate, and a time to understand the difficulties of how to interact with the enemy. The enemy must be destroyed, as it is represented as a hate group that promotes censorship and propaganda. It must be stopped, or it will get out of hand. There seems to be a clear message, and this message needs to be destroyed, in order to prevent the destruction of the universe. There is a reason why bad stuff always happens, and it is because of the radical element of certain people. It is not on the basis of one movement, but it is the beliefs that are a part of hatred, and this hatred is left untouched, until one day, it boils and is released into the wild. It can be triggered by anything, and this feeling only needs to make sense to that one individual, so it is in fact a byproduct for certain people.

There seems to be something else relevant, and then there is the cafeteria, which is where the girls are located now, so they must be hungry. Well, they are following a very tight schedule filled with different activities each day. It is important to know that lunch time is nothing new, but it might make sense if something actually happened, and in this sense, there seems to be something irrelevant, or so you think. Nothing is of importance to anything else, as that is not how life works, but people believe the opposite of everything.

There is no cause for anything. You might be doubtful, but this could only be the world telling you that something is indifferent. At least one thing is always indifferent, so there is a cause to celebrate something, yet that thing is still unknown in reality, and as it makes sense, there is a feeling that something will never happen because it is happening now.

Just about done eating, and the girls head to their rooms, hoping to do something, while there might be a better reason to understand sanity. There is certain evidence that might exist, but as you might already know, there are always contradictions that can occur. So, in any situation, there is always a reason to understand something that is irrelevant and relevant at the same time.

There is something that can object to the status quo, as you should already know, and it is the theory that can make or break your entire case. There are always reasons that may never conform to sanity, as it is a way to antagonize the people who support freedom. Freedom is constantly being threatened, and this has always been known, so remember something very important. Remember there is a way to object to everything about censorship and propaganda, and something that requires the knowledge of life. Life is about living to fulfill your dreams of becoming successful. You do not want to work a menial job when you are very well qualified, and this is some reason why people still don't understand anything about life.

Many people believe that life should always be about peace, but that is not the case. People who constantly preach peace usually identify as a hippie, so they might be heavily involved in sex and drugs, but nothing is wrong with that, however, that is not always the solution to everything. People need to comprehend the entire situation by using critical analysis to conduct extensive research and investigations. This is a result that will help reveal the truth, and as a matter of fact, it could be biased, but each person has a different personality, as it is supposed to make sense.

The vast majority will have issues with certain results and it only occurs because of their beliefs, so as you might further understand, something will always be meaningless to certain people. You can't always please anyone, but you might be able to please the majority, so, in order to conduct something relevant, it must be useful, and this will help the entirety of the focus.

Sanity can drive people insane, as it was proven before, but people always make mistakes. As there could be something wrong with every picture, there is surely something wrong with the opposite of everything else. Sanity is the result of thinking. Insanity is also the result of thinking, but everything is related to a mental illness. The brain is affected by some sort of defect, which can be the result of anything, but you get the picture, since you understand anything. Nothing makes more sense than the rest of the world. As you already know, the world is currently in chaos, thanks to the Hollywood machine, and their beliefs against freedom. It was a result of insanity and hatred that promoted censorship, and this was already known, even if it was never mentioned before.

Just as you leave, you might find yourself answering several questions, which might seem hypocritical, but just try to think for a few moments. You might find courage in order to see them in real life. There is nothing stopping you from achieving your dreams, and since you made it this far, it is easy to think that there will always be a dream. So, you might want to relax and think for a moment.

Half of the day is nearly over, and the girls are in

their rooms resting. Thinking about anything, well, that could be a stretch, but it is almost time to go to fitness training, and everything is coming along perfect, so there might be a time to think, for the purpose of anything.

It is now time to get ready for physical training, so the girls head to the fitness center, where everything is completed in a breeze. It was the usual, same thing, running, exercise, swimming, and today, something new, basic exercise, such as pull-ups, push-ups, and everything else. Since it is completed already, yet it went by extremely fast because of fun, it is nothing new, and the girls go eat dinner. After dinner, the girls go to the gym to exercise. There, they use the gym equipment, then they hit the showers. They feel tired, and head to their rooms. Now, in bed, they fall asleep, ready to repeat everything that happened.

One week has passed since they started training, and so, it might be a breeze. Soon, a month came and went, then another, and another, and finally, nine months passed. With three months left of training, it became surreal. These next three months would be the most crucial, as the previous nine months were. So, to put something in retrospect, there was a reason to actually consider a thing of the past, and how to organize the rest of the ideology.

In the time that passed, there have been many reasons to consider that there has been a lot of situations where everything was the result of mishaps. From the very mishaps, there were reasons to consider to abandon this entire program of defeating Hollywood. However, after further consideration, it would have been something fatal, thus, more fatalities would occur if Hollywood was never defeated. The reason why there was an immediate consideration to not drop the program was because of a certain incident, which sparked outrage against propaganda and censorship. This situation would later help the freedom cause.

Three months ago, it was discovered that the Hollywood government wanted to destroy the new country of Florida. But that is only the initial cause. The real cause that created outrage was the possible destruction and desecration of Pensacola and Saint Augustine. These two cities were the first of a kind, and are possibly the oldest colonies in what was used to be the former United States of America. America as we know it ceased to exist when the Hollywood machine decided to take over the country and government.

Here lies the possible reason why the Hollywood government wants to destroy Pensacola and Saint Augustine, which is nothing short of a coup. Since these are the two first and oldest cities in Florida, the Hollywood government would believe they have leverage over them, and in this leverage, they think that Florida would be subdued to turn back to the former land mass of North America. This scenario, however, devised by the Hollywood government would never work, because Florida has been known to fight back.

If the Hollywood government actually goes through with this plan, then Florida would start to attack the Hollywood government, and then there would be war and chaos. Luckily, there could be something better that will eliminate the threat before anything ever happened, yet, Florida has not yet learned about the possible attack by the Hollywood government. Since Florida moved away from the landmass of North America, they have erected an entire concrete border around their entire landmass, similar to a sea wall, but higher, in order to prevent outside attacks. This border also has state of the art technology, which can eliminate any threat within seconds.

After all, security is the main reason when protecting any territory, well, that is always the reason presented. The reason is to protect and maintain life, in order to prevent chaos, but chaos has been shown to outsmart everyone. As the defense system protects the national borders, it shall to be used to prevent anything bad from happening. This defense system will launch a missile or any aerial explosive object to destroy the threat. There are infrared cameras around the entire border that can detect anything, as well as heat sensors that will know the difference between good and bad. There is something that has been proven, as nothing bad can ever escape this system, as it is one of the most expensive systems in the world. Yet, each and every day, there is still a threat.

Every day, crazy people, who have nothing better to do, decide to blow up the border. These people are either insane or are with the enemy, the Hollywood government, but all the defense system does is to read the biometrics of the skin. The defense system will then determine if the object is a threat. Most of the time, the people who attack the border are just crazy, but there are those very rare and special circumstances when those people are representatives of the crazy Hollywood government. In this instance, when the person is proven to be a representative of the Hollywood government, the defense system just imprisons them, instead of killing or destroying the object. The person is than deported via ocean on the way towards drowning.

This might be harsh, but the representative of the enemy deserves to be taught a lesson. For the reason why Pensacola and Saint Augustine were targeted, this remains a very serious matter, as they provide money for the government of Florida and Spain. These two cities are the most important to survive anything, as they were the first colonies to exist in the former North American landmass. This might explain why they are very valuable. Famous people from around the centuries have lived in these two cities, even though they might have their own problems.

There are other serious problems, but these remain the most important. Value represents meaning. Without value, well, there would never be any meaning, and this might be present to demonstrate everything. There are the reasons why problems exist, as they promote change, but never-ending problems are a serious threat to society, as nothing can ever be completed in a timely manner. So, with that, there are serious precautions into the entire situation of this possible coup.

For many reasons that are still unknown, Pensacola was abandoned when it was first settled by Tristan de Luna, which was not entirely true, because a hurricane ruined everything. Now, Pensacola was discovered in 1516, but it was not settled until 1559. Nevertheless, there was a major catastrophe that killed people, forcing the rest of the Europeans to sail to new land. This would leave Pensacola without any European settlers, but everything that was built would remain, as later, it would come back, but over a century later. Saint Augustine would later be settled in 1565.

First, let's make this clear, the Hollywood

government wants to destroy Saint Augustine more than Pensacola, as it is still not known. Yet, the reason might be because of several historic sites.

Saint Augustine has been the home to the fountain of youth ever since Ponce de Leon discovered certain parts of Florida. The fountain of youth is said to prevent any aging and will make you feel young. This claim has yet to be proven, but some people have alleged the water from the springs actually made them immortal. Well, immortality is some sort of curse, as most people don't want to live forever. It is a curse that will haunt you for the rest of your life.

Today, the fountain of youth is an archaeological park, holding self-guided tours for people to experience the living conditions of the past. The park itself has a gift shop and a planetarium, along with multiple museums, and early forms of housing. It is an environment that holds something important to the creativity in everyone. People who visit will imagine something closer to themselves, as an experience to the best possible outcome.

As with any park, there are also birds, particularly the peacock, which act like crazy people. There is nothing else that will determine anything, just as there is a theory of how everything recognizes something is relevant. There is nothing but relevant information to the rest of the sacred knowledge of truth, knowing that there is a reason to live, no matter what. People will determine themselves that there is something to think about. There is nothing to think about. The entire historic downtown of Saint Augustine is filled with history as well as something useful. Everything is useful, as it is necessary to understand the craziness of life back then.

Ponce de Leon did not build the city of Saint Augustine, as later settlers from Spain did that, and then from Britain. Someone by the name of Pedro Menendez founded the city of Saint Augustine, trying to make it efficient to colonize the place. A few centuries later, a fellow by the name of Henry Flagler decided to vacation in the city of Saint Augustine. Flagler loved the city so much that he wanted to turn it into a tourist attraction for the wealthy. He bought land, built hotels, as well as a church. Yet, Flagler also built a jail after learning the current jail was located right across from his new hotel. Flagler decided to give money to the county government, and in return, the government granted his wish of a new jail.

This jail, commonly referred to the old jail, is now a museum, but in its heyday, it could hold up to seventy-two prisoners, including women, a death row unit, the chain gang, and a sick ward. It seems controversial but it was common for its time, as it was sponsored by an industrialist. So says everyone, and everyone else, yet there was surely a more odd occurrence, in which the sheriff of Saint Augustine, CJ Perry, decided to live on the premises, but it was a separate building. The house was attached to the prison but the fact that the sheriff wanted to live there was still insane. Yet, there remain something more important, in that the sheriff was mad with power, as he wanted more power. He wasn't happy with problems, so, even if you fell into cardiac arrest, well, he still wanted you to be hanged, if you killed someone, even if you already died. This was the result of power.

Everything related to the occupation of something, well, that was nothing new, as it was current to think that something might happen, as well as something that might endanger the wellbeing of the rest of society. People fail to understand anything, and as they think, something is missing. It is the result that something must be done in order to think about something irrelevant, and for the time, it is unnecessary to think about anything that is unrelated to the opposite of anything else.

There is nothing else worth appealing to, and yet there are still many problems facing the world. With the people starting to realize something is happening, there would be a riot and chaos. For the fear of anything, there is the reason to think about the reason of the beliefs.

Nothing makes any sense. The former sheriff decided that he wanted to have all the power in the county, and yet, he decided to live on the premises of the prison. Other sheriffs will not even do that, but him living next to the prison would make him the warden, or at least give him more access to the prisoners. He was surely crazy, as it was something else.

Something even crazier was the trusted prisoner program, where good prisoners were allowed to have some type of freedom. This might sound crazy, but it was in more than one state, but depended on the sheriff. So, the reason behind this was to institute reform and allow the good prisoners to work and have some freedom, which did not sound crazy. If you were a murderer or part of the chain gang, well, you were limited to certain stuff. But murderers locked away had no freedom at all, since they actually killed someone. It was something sort of crazy, yet there remains something unimportant, something that has nothing to do with people.

Everything is related, but the old jail is a thing of the past, and it must be known that something is more important. To put it into perspective, everything happens for a reason, and there is something to think about, so as it might sound, there is nothing to think that will be short of anything because that is already happening, and it will be here to stay.

CHAPTER SEVEN

Nine months came and went, yet it seems like it was yesterday that the girls just arrived, but there are still three months of training left, as well as a new baby being born within days. There is still some time to learn, yet this experience has been worthwhile, as everything that had happen is about to help them after three months. There is nothing else to think about, except how and when the portal will open.

Some say the portal is magical. Others say it is the work of the devil. The portal is mysterious, but it will lead you to strange places. The portal clearly has a mind of its own. Although programmable, most of the time it is set to a random date, either in the past or the future. There is a setting indicating whether to go to the past or the future, and then there is another setting of the date and time, as well as the location, but this setting can be overridden by the random setting. The portal is very advanced and it can cause severe alterations, leading to catastrophic events, but that only happens if it is used for evil, and not good purposes. People do have a mind of their own, and they need to realize that some things are different than others.

Where will the portal lead, well, it won't take you to your intended place you seek. It most definitely won't take you anywhere near your intended destination. It won't take you anywhere close to the continent you seek, as it might divert you somewhere else. This all will happen if it is on the random setting. The random setting overrides the entire system, and takes you to an alternate destination, depending on your choice of future or past. There is a way to avoid something like this, as you can turn off the random setting and enter in an actual date, time, and location, and it will make you feel better. If you don't, well, the random setting will override the entire system. After you arrive to your destination, the system will announce the destination. You might be surprised to find out that you are actually lost, but you must survive, so you must deal with everything that you encounter in life. One place that the portal likes to send you is to a luxury island resort in Mexico. Now, this resort is probably the most beautiful thing you have ever seen. It has the most luxurious amenities that you have ever seen. There is an infinity pool so large and classy that you thought you would be dreaming.

Besides the fact, let's talk about everything else, as it might be different. Everything is different, as it demonstrates the possibility of living in another new dimension. There are always new, yet distance dimensions out there, but the possibility of finding one is something rare. You could be living in another dimension, but that might already be true. The girls are in another dimension, currently training to defeat the Hollywood machine in 1986. There is something more possible that could strike a difference in the accord. There is a possibility that it could fail, but this is the reason that it might succeed. In any case, there is something that will always happen, and it too shall continue the rest of the world. The world is a very small place, but it is characterized as a very large environment, well, when referring to the world, people often replace it or use it in the place of the planet known as Earth. The planet Earth is also known as the world, but the meaning is just about the same, and it sounds better. The thing that people forget is that everything can be confusing because it is supposed to be that way. Everything has to have a meaning, and if it doesn't, well, there will be something misaligned with the rest of the universe, as with previous occurrences.

Since everything has a meaning, the universe also has a meaning. The universe is a combination of the rest of the planets in our solar system, as well as the different stars. The universe is the same as a galaxy, even though they might sound different. As to the meaning, well, it sounds confusing because of the name. The universe always changes, as the planets and stars, as well as the other mysterious objects in its jurisdiction have an objective of trying to keep in unison. Of course, there is the occasional black hole, which might try to consume you if you don't watch out. The black hole is this mysterious object that could be a former star or another galaxy. Either way, you won't ever escape it if you ever get sucked into it.

You might die or you could be taken to an alternate dimension, or even to a different galaxy. The possibilities are endless, and it does have something to do with the space and time continuum, so it would be recommended that you listen to your science instructor, and that might increase your knowledge. In case something does happen, there will always be a reason to demonstrate something that is worth remembering, as it might make a lasting impression upon your brain. There is always something to think about, and it will behoove you to think in a well-respected manner. There are reasons why mysterious events happens, and there could be poltergeists.

Beware, there is something that you must consider when you decide to alter the dimensions of reality, as you should already know. You should already know about the possible consequences, and if you don't, well, you will face a backlash of opposition of the most critical assessment of your life. You will find it hard to live, and your celebrations will die off in a fire. The entire purpose of your life will dwindle in a matter of seconds. There will be no hope for the rest of your life, and as you might think, there is always a reason to consider, as there is many times when something can happen. There are things to consider, and of all ideas, there are the reasons to identify with something that is known to your mind, as everything else might be a stranger. To put it into perspective, there is a reason why stuff happens in a certain way. Everything happens in a certain way because of a precise reaction connected to an even larger element. That larger element is able to produce offspring that will later grow, and in the times of a crisis, there is a reason to doubt anything, but anything can happen, or so help the other person. There is nothing to worry about, as everything that occurs is about life, and it is life itself that tries to prevent death. The focus of death is to kill everything in relation, which is connected to a specific trait and object. Once death has started there is no time to escape. Death is a powerful device, as something is surely a part of the rest of the world. There is nothing else that can help you. Cheating death never actually occurs because no one can cheat death. Any movie or film that revolves around cheating death is clearly fictitious, as that can never actually happen. You can either live or die. Dying always happens, every day, but then you might argue for miracles. Well, miracles are what people call cheating death, but that rarely happens, but they are not the same.

Depending on your knowledge, a miracle is an occurrence enacted to save a person via a spirit. The spirit helps you, but you actually died. Nothing is impossible, but there is a better way to achieve the long term goal. The short term goal just helps you until you can make it on your own. Once you have devised a plan to make it on your own you might be ready to start a new goal in life, something that will allow you to achieve your actual dreams. You know that you will be grateful once you have identified as achievable and excellent, all at the same time. Miracles on the other hand, well, they are rare, as you should already know. You should already know that when a miracle actually happens that you already died, but again, a spirit decided to revive you, because that spirit believes it is not your time to die. After a while, your heart starts to beat again, and you begin breathing, making it seem like a miracle, but it in fact the way of life.

Everything that lives a life has a reason why they

exist. Everything with a life is part of a bigger picture. The immortal beings are watching everyone and everything, as it is part of life. While immortal beings are rare, they do exist, but as humans. Even though immortals are humans they can live forever and as long as they want. But immortals have to make a sacrifice, a sacrifice that amounts to eternity. Each immortal lives for eternity, or until they decide they want to die. Immortality is a gift, but in order to be granted immortality, you must be an original creature from the creation of the universe, and you must be able to adapt to change, or immortality could be granted by another immortal after proving oneself to that immortal. It is not an easy thing to live with. Those who choose to be granted immortality know that it is a huge responsibility, but those who were the original immortals know that everything has a reason to live and that responsibility is everything.

Therefore, since immortality is considered sacred, you must use it wisely, as there are reasons why you should know. Since immortality is a gift, it is to be used only for good purposes. Evil purposes do not exist for immortality. Immortality being a gift represents the reason why the universe is controlled. Everything related to life is controlled by the immortals. Immortals understand everything about you as well as the world, so it is of importance that some things must be controlled. Without the immortals there would be no reason to live. Immortals are the guardians of the universe, and there are currently only a few that exist.

Again, immortals now take the form of humans, so they can blend in, and this is the reason immortals can access anything they want. Being human also has its limits, as being immortal might seem tedious and boring, but that is just the plan. Surely, immortals do grow tired of living, but they have to live for eternity, in order to watch the universal. If an immortal wants to die, well, they must choose a time, a date, and the reason. The most common reason an immortal chooses to die is the life expectancy clause. The life expectancy clause is something only applied to creatures, such as the majority of living animals, including mammals, amphibians, reptiles, and all other creatures. Everything has a life expectancy. Immortals choose this clause to die because they are tired of living forever, meaning that they believe they had helped to achieve their long term goal of a guardianship. The actual way that immortals die is different, as many immortals might want to commit an accidental death, but this accidental death is actually an intended suicide. It is regarded as an accident because that is what medicine indicates.

Surely, you did thought that something might happen, but there is no reason for anything to happen, as it might just be a fluke. Something rare always happens, and before, you might know that there is the reason to always underestimate the reason to think responsibly, as there is never any reason to think otherwise. People might tend to harbor conditions against each other, but there is simply an idea that might prevent stuff from happening. Nothing can be perfect, as everything has strived to be perfect. It is a special case of circumstance for something to be involved in the life process. There is the ability to think freely, as there is always the reason to consider about everything. There is something worth knowing, and each time that is current is supposed to understand the basics about life. As people might tend to agree, there is always something that is sort of overlaps in certain areas. While these areas are common, it is wise to know that these overlaps are interdependent, and they rely on each other to balance the field. There are fears that one field could outtake the other, but if that ever happens, well, something bad might occur. It very might well develop something that is so evil that no one would want to live. There is something to think about as it is recommended to learn about everything, and as a result, it would be wise to consider anything else. There is clearly something else in existence and it is here to stay, as it is an evil spirit.

Immortality is no joke, and if you think it is, well, you are mistaken, as it takes a lot of energy to guard against the forces of evil. It is the sure way to guarantee that nothing bad ever happens to the universe, and if something did, well, there would be catastrophic events, and these events would start to cause chaos. This chaos will then lead to something that will attempt to destroy the rest of civilization.

Imagine something so awful that you thought it was your friend. Your friend always behaved but it decided it wanted to experience everything. This made your friend a crazy person. Nothing can stop your friend now, and it will only be a matter of time until your friend decides to destroy everything. This should never happen, as it will indicate something that will bring censorship. Nothing will ever be the same, and there will be the reason to admire something that is not real. Of course, there will be the opposition, whose goals are to promote propaganda and such, and that is nothing new, as some things never change. To prove something wrong is not an easy task, but they believe the opposite. At the same time, there is an abundance of hope. Hope is everywhere, and if you want to know something, there is a reason to believe, something that is not common for the rest of the world, when something happens.

There is hope for anything. As you might already know, hope is everywhere, and nothing can ever change that. For everything that exists, there is always a reason to believe, and this reason changes with time. Everything can also be unfortunate, but that is something else to consider, and if you do, well, there is a chance that any type of misfortune is extremely rare. There are those who experience misfortune because they are in the wrong place at the wrong time. These people who believe that they are always unlucky feel like that they have no reason to live. They believe that they are being targeted for no reason at all. In reality, they are only experiencing this type of misfortune because of other underlying events that are supposed to happen. Even if they weren't there the misfortune would still occur, but they would never get to experience that feeling.

Every time that misfortune is granted, it makes the person feel ashamed, something that is common if you are trying to hide something but someone finds out, and then the person who finds out decides to tell it to the world. This friend has no trust at all and should be ignored. Of all the things that occurred, it should be noted that no one deserves a public shaming, unless, of course, you are in some sort of medieval era. This punishment of public shaming would then make sense, as it was common in the middle ages. It was also common in the seventeenth century, during those damn witch trials, which were clearly political, nonsense, and fabricated by certain people. There is nothing else to believe, as some things are always meant to end in some sort of ritual.

It is the rite of passage to determine the meaning of everything, and it shall help you to determine the data of everything, which might find something important. The theories behind everything are part of life, and they help motivate the rest of the world. It is common to think that nothing will happen, but this notion needs to understand that nothing is always going to be the same. In every circumstance, the entire process changes, which causes the whole theory to become obsolete. This new founded result will have a severe impact on life, as well as the rest of the world. The theory needs to evolve in order to become relevant to the rest of the world. At the one time it might seem important, there is another piece of information that might change forever, and this thing will develop into something that should never happen in any form of life. It is the result of a mutation, something that is meant to be deformed. This new object will be different from the rest, and people will stare, looking for something that is not part of life. Everything will be determined by something, but it must be a coincidence, since something is present.

Clearly, time is changing. With three months left, there is still the theory of where the portal will take you. The portal should take the girls to 1986, but it might take them to a luxury Mexican resort, where they would have to travel to another dimension. The reason to stay on the opposite of the meaning is something that has to happen immediately, as there is a sign that will change the status of everything. There shall be a reason that might not want change, as it might determine that there is a physical bond, which might result in attraction. As far as something else, there is nothing to worry about, and it is the fact that something is important no matter what is true.

Everything has something to do with nature, and it is because of that there exists a bond between forces. These bonds enable people to understand everything about the reason to understand life. Life is something that is meant to attract anything it sees, as a way of hope, a way to live, and a way to promote. There is the reason of how to promote, and this reason might determine the fact that something is changing, always, as a way of life that maintains something important to the rest of the environment. The environment is something that you should already know about, as it was mentioned before, so you should know the facts. The environment is part of nature and it helps promote growth and stabilization in the food chain. The food chain is a part of life and it helps organisms live and survive. There is nothing wrong with nature, as it is part of the ecosystem, which is part of the bigger picture.

Ecosystems are very important to the rest of life, as they are what takes part in a natural environment. The entire ecosystem is the environment in which organisms live. Very likely, it is a part of the overall food chain system, a part of life that promotes growth, as well as stabilization. Being that something always happens in the ecosystem, it is important to understand how it works, as they help each other to survive the conditions. There is something known as survival of the fittest. Now, this theory proposes that only the strongest of the species lives and the weakest dies off. This could explain why the strongest of the species always attack everything else, as it also implies how the food chain works. The food chain is complex and confusing, yet there is a reason to its insanity and mentality.

For the food chain to work, there must be a balance in everything. If a predator kills all of its particular prey in the habitat then there will be a lack of food. This lack of food would then mean that the predator will starve to death and later would become extinct. This lack of food could also mean that the predator would have to find another type of food to eat, in order to evolve its species.

For instance, everyone regards the human as the top of the food chain. Well, the human might be top of the food chain, but the humans also have many predators such as the snake, the shark, the poisonous spiders, and the venomous insects that cause diseases. There are some humans who are not afraid of anything, as they are fearless, meaning that nothing frightens them. The human is also a predator in some kind of way. There are many predators who target the human, only because those species are afraid of the human. The snake is afraid of the human, as they believe they are the enemy, so the snake decides to defend itself. The shark could be afraid of the human but they hardly attack humans because they eat fish.

Predators are species who target other species for food or other conditions. Humans target everything, so that makes humans the top of the food chain, but humans may still be targeted by other species. Even though a lion or tiger might seem like a predator, those two species regard the human as an enemy, and if the human acts in a certain way, the human might become food, thanks to the interactions between the animal kingdom. Then, there is the meaning of prey, which is different. Humans are both predators and prey in the food chain, as there are always species who want to eliminate other species.

When thinking of prey, it is important to note that they are the ones who are being hunted and killed. Anything can be a prey. Plants can be a prey, but then, there are some plants who can kill the predator, just because of evolution. It remains a fact that there is something in the midst of something new. It is a part of life and there is everything to live about life. There are the important factors that demonstrate the reasons of insanity as well as the rest of sanity. The system is built upon the conditions of restrictions, as it maintains an important balance on society. There is nothing more important than the way of life. Since everything affects life, it is important to differentiate between the factors of how the world operates. There is something for everyone, and it will take some time to develop a personal relationship between species. As well as the thing known as the circle of life, it is important to learn about the increasing change about the entire ecosystem, since there are reports of never-ending pollution, which might cause mutations. Mutations, as you already know, are genes or traits that alters the rest of the body. These mutations change the entire function of how and when species develops. Mutations can cause disease, but in some species, they can actually be good. One example of good mutations are the plants that are immune to insects. When the insect attacks the plant it is impossible to penetrate, causing the insect to either day or to fly away. Yet, insects can later evolve to be immune to pesticide and other poisons, meaning that the plants will die if the formula is not updated.

For the reason of mutations in plants, it is not that important to alter their genes, since, in the end, the insects might attack because of evolution. Evolution is the reason behind everything, as it is the main point why stuff happens in life. There is nothing more important than the circle of life, as it is the way of the future, and the way of living.

There comes a time when life itself is questioned. Many people have been questioned about the meaning of life and their role in society. Each person is different, and some have refused to answer the question, as there is no meaning to life. Life might have a meaning, but it is complex, and to that point, there is a time when it is unavailable to understand. There is a theory to everything, as described in a complex environment, and each time mentioned, everything has a relationship with each other, to the point that everything is the same or developed from the same master race. No, this isn't about racism. Racism is a form of discrimination, and people always think that racism is not related to discrimination. Well, for many years in the United States of America, racism was actually illegal, because of idiotic politicians who believed white people were the master race. Now, this is the same ideology developed by Hitler and his plan to remove the Jews from Germany and Europe.

When Hitler and has cronies developed his master plan to expel the Jews from Germany and Europe, he did so that he wanted to eliminate them from society. Therefore, he also devised a plan to send them to a distant country in Asia or somewhere else. Present day Palestine was an option, yet, there was also the option of Madagascar. Both plans never actually went into effect, as there were many obstacles. There was something that could not escape the grasp of other people. One issue was the failure to defeat the German enemy, yet it was a conscious decision made by the national socialist party that Jews were bad, and that Jews caused the destruction of everything. There were some Jews that Hitler actually protected, a doctor, and maybe some other people. It was the cause of a national agenda created by a failed student, who later became a failed artist, yet, this same person was also a vagabond at some point in his life, to think he could succeed. Also being a former convict, he only went to jail because of a failed coup, but the judge sympathized with him because the basis of the coup was to ignore the reparations from the first world war. And so, while in jail, Hitler had many fans, who gave him food, which caused him to gain weight, but later lost it all after finishing his short sentence. While in jail, Hitler didn't want anyone to succeed him, and he didn't care if people ignored his cause.

Hitler knew the reparations were unjust, and that they only represented the outcome sought by the allied governments. Germany never caused the first world war, as you should already know this, as the cause of the war was the killing of Franz Ferdinand. Austria did not like it when their royal heir was killed. The attack by Serbia was an automatic declaration of war against the Austro-Hungarian Empire. This declaration of war caused the central powers to attack each other, as there could have been confusion. In the end, Germany was blamed for everything, as they had to be blamed, since they needed a scape goat. There is the feeling of how this could have happened, and it only occurred because of the simplistic ideology of constant war.

Then came the idiotic fourteen points by Woodrow Wilson, who held a doctorate in History as well as Political science. History is a good discipline, but Political Science is just nonsense. Everything that Wilson believed in was a lie and a fallacy, as all his plans failed. Wilson believed that government was the solution and could fix everything, and the same applied to Truman, who was another idiot president. Both of them believed war was good, and that being the world police was a good idea.

Today, the world police is viewed as a bad idea, as no one needs to be the world police. Government should be responsible for their actions and to their people, but the governments failed to understand this ideology back then. It is still important to note that not everything can happen overnight. There are reasons why things happens, and it will result in the people of the world determining the outcome of the future. For the rest of your life you might think something is bad, but there are some opportunities were you can escape certain elements, so you must think otherwise. In the end of civilization there is a reason to understand anything, and as a result, there could always be a problem, so, to alienate the problem, there is something that could be ignored in the attempt of creating a plan to develop the past and future.

This now brings the attention back to racism and discrimination in North America. Since racism was legal in the United States of America in southern states, and maybe some northern states, there were huge problems. Blacks and colored people could not sit together, as segregation was everywhere. Segregation was the rule of law in the south, and people who ignored it could be arrested. There were riots and protests, along with the occasional death threats.

People started to meet in churches. People created special organizations to deal with the threat of racism and other forms of discrimination. One fellow was named Martin Luther King Jr, and he held a doctorate, and there were some questions concerning his dissertation. The dissertation probably contained a fair amount of plagiarism, but he was later acquitted, some say because of his success to change the world and to prevent segregations.

During this time of radical ideology, there were these rules known as blue sky laws or blue laws, also known as Jim Crow Laws. Now, nobody by the name of Jim Crow ever existed, as it was a fictitious name invented by a white actor about a black slave or servant figure. Convenient, huh, well, it was typical for the time, as the whites believed that blacks were inferior to the rest of the society. Whites feared that blacks would take their jobs, changing society, and taking over everything. It is the same thing today, but today, this scenario applies to computers and technology. Technology could be dangerous, said too many people, but in the beginning nothing ever happened, as it was probably controlled in a manner that limited its capacity for world domination, something that is present in society. It is the feeling of certain activities that there is a cause for this racial matter, as it was probably already explained. But to reiterate it, the cause was because of hatred and white supremacy. As explained before, the whites believed they were the master race, and to put it into that perspective, if you were not white you were a defect to the rest of society. This has always been the case in American society, but not all people liked the idea of mistreating the people in society, no matter what color they were. It was a fact that the northern states had a much better humanitarian policy than the south. It wasn't really part of southern policy to institute equal freedom. There were really a backwards country. Everything about the former United States was backwards. Public policy was outdated and promoted censorship and propaganda. There was a serious threat to society. Public officials accused people of being the enemy, which promoted propaganda, as they wanted everyone to support the mission of nationalism. There is nothing wrong with nationalism, but too much nationalism will eventually lead to something known as fascism. This ideology known as fascism is actually ultra nationalist. This means that the people and the rest of society think they are better than the rest and that they know more than anyone else. It is a case of jealousy and power. Corruption is widespread, and nothing can stop them except for the opposition or the resistance.

For the resistance to exist, there must be a reason to fight. There must be a serious threat that will harm society. There must be something that will promote censorship and propaganda. If any or all of these things happens, well, a resistance will form, and it might be in secret. The resistance might hide in order to escape any brutality. People have a sense of not knowing anything, because their ability to learn is basic. Not all humans are like this, but most humans know nothing about life and society. The fact that humans thrive is the fact that they are even living. Humans could be described as the master species, something that is relevant to everything else in the world. The theory behind anything is that it must relate to the physical attractiveness of the meaning of something related to the resistance of the night, or something hideous might occur. There is no proof of anything, and as it is stated, there is the reason to think otherwise.

Many times have passed where there is a reason to believe in anything. It could be a force of nature or it could be something else. There is nothing else that can help, unless it is a miracle, so there is little chance of something happening, and the end might even have a surprise for you to watch. Even the beginning could have you wondering how it could happen. There is the ability to teach the effectiveness of the reason to anticipate the quality of life. As some things develop, there is a plan created from the beginning of life. It is a plan of why there might be the reason to instill the creativity of the society. There have always been some objections, but just as they arise, there are other reasons why they are not even worthy, as the reasons don't even make any sense. It is the wording itself, along with the intended meaning, that the explanation is hogwash, because it targets certain people in society. This kind of wording promotes hate speech, something that exists today, but it will never disappear, as society is still too ignorant to ever learn about freedom.

Other people did exist, besides Martin Luther King Jr., people such as Rosa Parks. Yeah, that Rosa Parks, the person who refused to move. Rosa was in the correct seat, but she was told to move to a different location. Rosa obeyed the segregation laws, but it was the bus driver who didn't care. The cause of the incident was a white person boarding the bus, and there were possibly no more seats on the white side of the bus, so Rosa was told by the bus driver to go somewhere else, a place that seemed unknown. Well, Rosa was arrested, and that arrest sparked outrage. It is common to protest against these laws, but it was discrimination, a form of policy that abolishes equality.

Now, Rosa Parks did not want to promote chaos, she just wanted to sit in her seat with no commotion, something that obviously did not happen, hence, the arrest. Well, again with King, as he had to attend college in the north, as they were more aligned with the rest of society. King did not want to end racism, because he wanted to end discrimination. King probably knew that racism would still be around you years, and it would probably never disappear, but the feeling was just mutual. King also wanted to end police brutality, something that is widespread in the present Hollywood government. But, it was not to last, as King was shot by someone who probably hated him. Today, King's role of a freedom fighter still lives, but there is still hatred, and this hatred is not going to disappear, as he also knew it would never disappear.

For years, everything sparked about racism and segregation, and it was something about government involvement in society. Then, there is the goal of world domination, a controversial topic worth discussing. World domination, the Roman Empire, a history of everything you thought was wrong, well, as you might already know, it did exist, and for a very long time. When you think about world domination, you might think about the Roman Empire, or even the failed League of Nations, and the current United Nations, something that still exists but has shrunken dramatically in the last few decades.

Something that is current, as well as misleading, is a place
of weirdness, and a place to abandon society, to a point
that is worth to understand by research. As many might
think, the idea of world government or world domination
is a bad idea, but that is not the case when done correctly.
The reasons are known that it could be overbearing and
evil, but with the right leadership, these two ideologies can
promote freedom, much to the liking of skeptics.
Depending on the focus, there might seem something
controversial, and it could be because of all the
misinformation and propaganda that people try to
promote.

World government is not easy to accomplish, but
the Romans were able to dominate several countries for a
very long time, only because there were very few
governments that existed. What this means is that
governments existed but they were not even big enough to
control an entire country. Still, there was Egypt, but that
was controlled by a pharaoh, but it was not really a world
government. The Egyptian government only took care of
their people and no one else, but it did work. The
governments that did not work were the local
governments, because they invented crazy laws that often
change every other day. These laws were also contradicting
the rest of the laws in society. Local governance were
inefficient and had no actual meaning. Sure, there was a
world government, but it died when something happen.
The cause of such a catastrophe divided the Roman
Empire into two separate kingdoms, an east and a west.
Now, the governments that were not big enough to
control the country were the small local governments
because each local government wanted to control the

country, but they only had authority in their municipality. This made everything uneasy, as it probably infuriated local government leaders. Nothing much changed, as today, local leaders still get infuriated at state, provincial, and central governments. It is a thing of the past, as well as part of the process. There has been nothing wrong in society to them, but they want power in order to prove a point, many of them who believe they can make government more efficient for the people, but in fact, they made it more bureaucratic, something that confused them. It is part of compartmentalization, also known as dividing departments into several units that only is allowed to complete and know a certain task. People are infuriated at the idea of compartmentalization, as it shows nothing but real and absolute reluctance to the rest of society. It is part of the problem, something that central government supporters believe is part of the solution. Well, those supporters only know hogwash, as they were brainwashed into believing something that supports censorship. Something that was believed to help had the opposite effect, leading to something that should not exist.

As the will of the people develops, it is part of the plan to understand that some governments hate each other, while other governments want to help the people. Well, nothing ever stays the same, and it will only be a matter of time until something bad happens. It is the point that strives to promote freedom. Everything has been contradicting the entire system of free movement. Restrictions have plagued society forever, and that might not end in the entire lifetime of your existence. It could be a miracle that something needs to happen, and there is a way that might promote the freedom to the rest of society.

It is the courage that will be demonstrated to the rest of society and culture. Culture is everything about your heritage and lifestyle. Culture makes you unique, as nobody is the same, unless you are a clone, but even clones deviate from their master plan. The master plan is simple, to obey the rules, and nothing else. There is room for negotiations and other formalities, but just as you think, there is something else that is present. The world is not simplistic, as it has always been complex. Much to the understanding of periodic research, not all of this research has been right. People who research might want a special target, or something that is to their liking. It is most relevant that sometimes the data will be skewed to a specific point of interest or something else.

There is nothing that will determine something otherwise, as depicted in something other than the fact of life. It is of the satisfaction that counts, and that might sound good, but there is no meaning to this theory of new founded glory. There is still some indications that it is currently in development and the process won't end until there is a reason to believe it is correct. In all likeliness, this theory will never see the light of day, as there is no room for it in the entire universe. Everything will have to be modified in order to make sure it is aligned.

So, how is world government accomplished, or how does it fit into this world, well it is easy and complex. There must be a constitution established. Any type of declaration of independence is optional, but it is recommended, because it might be necessary in order to explain the reasoning behind the creation. As for the establishment of the world government, well, the constitution will explain the majority of everything. There are many ways of how to create a form of world government, but different ways are never the same. No one has to follow the global manifesto of how to create a world government, as not everyone likes a predetermined document. The government itself is the executive branch. The legislative branch should be some type of international parliament where people are elected by their constituents. The executive branch will determine the distribution of seats along with everything else. The executive branch can block anything by the parliament. In essence, there is also the judicial branch, which just interprets the law. So, for any sake, the parliament can pass legislation, but so can the executive branch, in any case.

In all likeliness, the executive branch has a cabinet within the realm of the government. The members of the cabinet are hand-picked by the chancellor or the Prime Minister. The chancellor and prime minister are also considered royalty, and are part of the royal family for the world government. The members of the cabinet can sponsor legislation and can bypass the parliament. If members of the cabinet sponsor legislation within the executive branch, well, it still needs to be approved by the chancellor and or the prime minister. If legislation is introduced by parliament then the legislation will proceed to the cabinet. From there, any cabinet can strike it down or remove wording and sections, along with amendments. If parliamentary legislation is struck down by the cabinet, it won't move on to be signed. If it does not get struck down, well, one member of the cabinet will sign it, and that person who signs it supports that legislation, and from there, it will move to the chancellor and or the prime minister, who has the final say on the entire piece of legislation. If it ever reaches the chancellor and or the prime minister, either can reject the legislation, by refusing to sign it, and they even can take certain sections out or even have the power just to sign and agree to certain sections and not the rest.

So, you might say, well why this type of process, well, the thing is, this type of process, with the executive branch and the cabinet acts in a form of double checks and balances. It is made sure that the law is not unjust and that it never violates any freedom or human rights. The process to approve or deny legislation might seem tedious, but it is beneficial in the end. The members of the cabinet are actually members of the parliament, but they are not located in the parliament. They are called members of parliament because they are nobility, they decide the fate of future laws. The people elected to parliament are either members of an assembly or members of a council. This type of world government uses the cabinet as a stepping stone to make sure nothing is abused. It creates a balance of power. Now, you might say this is confusing, and it is, because while the cabinet is not elected officials, they still can create laws, and they are nobility, so they really have some sort of leverage in government. This can cause something to be prevented. It is known that people exist as critics, yet there are people who might support anything, for the reason of not understanding the complete process.

Furthermore, why is there royalty in the possible world government, well, royalty makes sense, as the members of the royal family could prove to be a fundamental asset. Each member of the royal family is either a chancellor or a prime minister. Yeah, you know, and I already know what you are thinking, that there can only be one of each, well, there is, but the rest of the royal family make up the deputy chancellors and the deputy prime ministers, and finally the high chancellor. Nothing is new, as this probably could be feasible. The royal family would have a duty to act upon, and this duty might coincide with any laws and even foreign relations. There is something that can be described by the thing that is still unknown, but it must be certain. As the way that parliament works, well, that is just described as an international parliament. Parliament would have the authority to nominate the judges. It is important to note that the cabinet and or the chancellor or the prime minister can approve or deny the candidate judge. If approved, the judge will serve a term in office, and when the term expires, the judge can run for election. It sounds relevant, but that is just how it makes sense, but people might disagree, so you might think something is either wrong or right. There is an option to determine what is wrong, yet everything does seem right, so you must understand the process before it ever begins, and alas, you might understand, as it is complex. To the point that something makes sense, it could be beneficial to anything, and as it does make sense, there are reasons why there is the possibility of overlapping. So, you might think it is a miracle of some sort.

Well, now, there is also the judicial branch. As previously explained, the judges are chosen then confirmed by the executive branch. The supreme court is a different entity. Everybody on the supreme court is hand-picked by the chancellor and or the prime minister. The justices and assistant justices serve a life term. These justices are also the attorney general and assistant attorney generals. Yeah, it is a lot of red tape, but once you find out why, it is only implemented in order to balance the entire system. It is not meant to discourage, but was meant to enhance checks and balance in a broken system.

Everything else in the constitution describes the focus and the reason. The reason for a constitution is to make sure everything is balanced and to make sure nothing bad happens. The goal of a world government is to promote peace. World government would be responsible for regulating other governments. It is a goal by world government to instill equality, to help the people, and to provide free access to the necessary freedoms. This might sound like something to end world hunger or even a charity, but it is in fact not a charity. Charities are non-profits, whose goals are to make sure everything is right in the world. Charities make sure no one is ever left behind. It is a goal to institute the rest of the world with charities, and there are several ways to do this, but there are reasons yet unknown to the rest of the society. People must determine anything relevant to their circumstance, and it shall provide opportunity to the future by promoting everything in the present, to ensure happiness.

Now, you might say that world government is the same as world domination, well, that is incorrect. World domination can be a good thing, but it can also be bad, if used in the wrong context. World domination as you know means that a person or a group of people want to take over the world for certain reasons. This could be because they believe the world is going in the wrong direction or that they just want to be a dictator. If it is the former choice, then the decision might lean towards the direction of a world government to establish some rules and boundaries, and they will setup a society where they will make the rules. If it is the latter choice, then it is being used in the wrong context. The dictator choice would enable the instigator to take over the entire world from anywhere he/she is located, and this is what most people think about when learning about world domination. If world government is established with the basic liberties and freedoms that promotes equalities, then it would not be considered world domination, unless the people in charge never obey their own laws. So, to explain it in a simplistic context, if a world government is established and the people in charge do not uphold their own rule of law, such as the constitution, it would be considered world domination, thus, making the people in charge dictators, which would mean that it is being used as a shadow or puppet government. This is nothing new, as it was explained before, and the reason behind everything is exactly the same. The puppet governments are controlled by a mysterious figure, and the goal is to instill fear, or a lack of freedom, promoting censorship and propaganda. It requires an outside force to come in and create a form of controlled society. The puppet government or shadow government is governed by an external force of people who have aspirations to tell people what to do. World domination has now become restless in a society where it was supposed to be helpful. It is now a form of sudden death. This might sound like the definition of a Communist, Marxist, or even Socialist society, but even those are not as severe as the puppet government or the shadow government.

Communism is a form of government where the leaders tell you what you can and can't do, but you still have basic freedom. Communism can have several groups of political ideology, and it can form to a spin off, which it has over the years. There is something about communism that makes it useful. Usually, people only want communism to exist because of the bad people. The communists want to eradicate corruption. Corruption always exists, but too much of it is bad for society, and that is why it must be eliminated. Corruption will lead to propaganda and censorship, and it will stop innovation. Communism has tried to prevent corruption, but it is still early to tell if the plan is efficient. Communism now show early signs of eradicating corruption from society, and that is a good sign, since communism has branched off into other movements, and it is possibly leading the way to abolish a corrupt state.

On the other hand, there is socialism, which could be a branch of communism, but that is whether the leaders believe in communism. Socialism just implies government should control everything, but there should be an abundance of choice. For example, socialism promotes universal healthcare, something that could be controversial, but in this system, healthcare is available to everyone free of charge. Of course, everything is paid in taxes, but it is still a better society. Opponents will try to invent propaganda, but it can be easily disproven, to the point that it is actually funny. In a socialist economy, everything is regulated fairly, as the majority of the businesses actually listen. This could be done in fear, but there are other reasons. It is in fact a good system, as well as everything else.

Now, a Marxist society is a place where the government wants to promote protest by eradicating the bad entities. The leadership in Marxist societies believe that the businesses have disrespected the workers. The workers need to stand up, but it needs to be done in a way that government can regulate the workforce in a more efficient environment, an environment in which the workers have freedom and are treated fairly. Marxism is a form of socialism, and it might sound like communism, and it possibly is, but for any reason, they are all separate societies, forms of government that decide to create rules and standards to abide by in order to live a quality life. Neither of these societies, whether it is communism, socialism, or Marxism, ever promote terrorism, as they know it is bad. In fact, these societies condemn any act of terrorism, as it demonstrates something that promotes terror, which is the opposite of their beliefs. It is a matter of time until something changes.

For sure, there is something about change. It was the usual thing to do, and as you make sure it was part of the situation, there was something that never made sense. There was the realization that something bad was happening. It was something that could only promote propaganda, but then, it became clear that there was an agenda, an agenda that did not care about anything. The precise details about the rest of the situation could be scattered or even isolated, depending on the scenario, or what it might seem. There is clear evidence that something is happening, as it is made sure that something is in complete control. This outside force is the cause for everything, and it wants to make sure that some things are never achieved, because if they are, well, the entire plan will be ruined. As far as everything else goes, it is a fact that is certain to entertain crazy people, as there are multiple scenarios that are part of the entire scheme. As far as everything else, there are serious threats to society, being that something is endangering the environment, or so you might think, as the way to control the future is a threat to the immediate action.

As with everything else, there is nothing that can remove anything, so everything could be considered a lost cause, which might make sense, but what does that actually mean, well, nothing, as it is a result of something that has no meaning in life. The entire process is about patience, and it applies to everything, so just as you might think, there is the reason to outsmart everything else. When you experience something, it can cause something to happen. You will feel energy that may surprise you, for the simple pleasure of helping you survive. You can achieve nothing but the best, and as it is determined, there is a reason to understand the critical environment of such a nature.

Then, there is the realization of what is happening. It might all be happening all too fast, people kept saying, but what do they know, as it is considered a weakness. Something must be done or there might be something in the works that could disturb the natural flow of the ecosystem. There is a way that can help, as it might be determined from the exact same thing, so as you might say to yourself, nothing can be the same as always. It is the thing that remembers the most is a wild animal, as they have the memory of a champion, or so you might realize. It is the passion of something that is meant to strike a deal between you and the rest of the world. There is something that could make sense, as it might sound the same as the culture of the wild. Things of the past have caught up with you, and they are about to attack, so, you might think you have to fight back, but your plan fails, so it is within your heart that you decide to give up and to face the music. This plan to give up is normal, as it demonstrates people being cowards and chickens, and to face something like this, you must either fight or run away. Running away might be your best choice, that is if you are outnumbered, but even if you do decide to run away, you might be killed or turned into a zombie. It makes no sense at all, as it was never meant to make sense. There is a clear reason that current events are causing nature to run an evil course of action, something that has no ability to make sense. It is at the precise moment that there is something in the clear that is happening for the people to learn. There is a reason why this is happening, and as it does, there seems to be a nuance of epic proportions, something that is used to the ability of showing the progress of anything. It is the cause that something is not the same as anything, and there are constant ramifications of the theories that lead up to the information claimed by the rest of humanity.

There are causes for actions that never existed, and as they make sense, if they do, then there is something wrong with the rest of society. Not everything is supposed to make sense, as it demonstrates something wrong with culture. Culture is unique, and nothing is the same, but society has a unique aspect to culture. Everyone is unique, as you might already know, and it is fact that there is time to understand everything about life. There are reasons to start taking risks, and you might need to comply. Tasks are everywhere, and it is important to question the possibility of something that might never happen because it might happen. Each time something happens, there is a reason to ask for the quality of life. There is an abundance of opportunity, so everything can remain the same. As you might consider something that might happen, well, this might exist, or that might exist, well, there is evidence to support that there are reasons why certain events happens. The focus of something might make sense, but these event are the real reasons for the rest of life, as they promote something that is hidden. The reasons will always remain mysterious, and as they made sense, well, nothing is of present value. Everything is stuck in the realization of a collapsed society.

Boom, and so you think something is in imminent danger, well, it happened in the past. In 2003, the Hollywood government, in their alternate dimension, decided to invade Iraq, because they felt threatened. Iraq did not provoke anyone, except for the Hollywood government because of domestic and foreign policy. The Hollywood government felt Iraq was a threat because of the current leader of the time, Saddam Hussain. The justification for the invasion, weapons of mass destruction, well, that intelligence was flawed, as no such evidence existed supporting that claim. Moreover, no sovereign nation has the justification and jurisdiction to take out another sovereign nation. Saddam Hussein did not do anything to the Hollywood government. The Hollywood government felt threatened because of jealousy, which is not a good thing to seek revenge. It was also a case of revenge, but what did Iraq do to the United States of America, as it might seem worthwhile, well, absolutely nothing. The entire evidence was flawed. Everything about the attack was flawed as it was determined someone just invented the evidence, or they might had a reason to seek revenge. It was simply a case that was proven wrong in the media, but not all media likes to admit defeat. There are some politicians who still support the invasion even though the evidence showed no signs of weapons of mass destruction. Well, all of the politicians supported the invasion today, because these politicians live in the alternate dimension created by the Hollywood machine, something that you should check.

Precautionary measures were never taken for the invasion. No research was ever conducted. Everything was flawed, and the evidence never existed. All biological weapons that ever existed in Iraq were destroyed years in advanced, but the politicians still did not care. It was something that they would not admit. No one wanted to admit defeat. The case was flawed. You have foot soldiers marching one by one to the beat of nothing more than a dirt ground. There is no grass, no cement, just dirt. Dirt is everywhere. It will make it impossible to navigate, as the dirt might turn into mud. You will now have a tough time walking. Everything will be dirty. It is something that is nothing more than a slippery road. It in fact makes it a slippery road, since everything is now wet. The dampness of the rain causes people to slip and fall, causing injuries, which might lead to bacterial infections. There is nothing that will help anything. It is the reason why there might be something wrong with society. Everything is flawed in a way that nothing ever makes sense. The theory behind everything is that the cause is a bunch of garbage. The whole thing about the basis of the attack lacks justification. You have people saying that the invasion by the Hollywood government was necessary in order to prevent biological warfare. Those people are paid shills who want to promote propaganda and censorship. They never want to admit defeat, even though they know no evidence exists.

It is a way to show that they want to have a very powerful influence in society. The shills want to promote a bunch of lies, something that is located in a fantasyland. They are in a fantasyland, as everything they say can never be trusted. The cause is not justified. It is a weak failure by everything that was ever created. There remains something that has no meaning in life, as it is a way to demonstrate dominance. Yes, those shills want to have power over your ability to seek freedom. They want to end freedom, but they believe freedom is a threat to everything. They are the people who promote censorship. Remember, censorship is bad, as it promotes propaganda, which is also a factor of terrorism and the risk of isolation. It is a task which they want to succeed. Nothing is more important to them, as it demonstrates a lack of understanding. People can no longer trust the government in an alternate dimension. It might be an exact replica, but the alternate dimension is evil and filled with censorship, causing misinformation.

Censorship causes propaganda.

Propaganda causes censorship.

It is a byproduct of an overzealous authority.

These things contribute to the demise of authority and society. It is a weakness. There is no other solution for them. Everything has no meaning.

It is the cause of the event.

The theory behind deceit is part of destiny.

As everything is nearing, there is a place that can determine the physical asset of the world. There is an eerie problem with their solution.

People will believe anything.

The shills are everything.

The news is supposed to tell the truth, believed by most people.

People believe the news is not propaganda.

Some news channels just report propaganda, and others report the facts.

Propaganda news agencies are funded by the Hollywood government. There is no sign of stopping, no sign of retribution. Everything is happening for a reason. There is a case by case basis. Nothing will ever be the same. The idea of something being haunted is the same of going nowhere in life.

It happens for a reason.

Shills know where you are hiding.

They want to make sure you don't do anything controversial, something that might ruin their plans. It is a thing for the shills to consider fraud and deceit as a means of power. Without those two objectives, they can never succeed in their ultimate plan of censorship and reducing freedom for the entire society. It is something that is controlled, in a manner that might seem illegal. They don't care who you are, as it might seem illogical for you to even think. There are reasons for this logic.

Everything leads to intelligence.

The Hollywood government hates smart people. They hate people questioning them. They believe everything they do is correct and just, because they see questions as being the enemy. It is something that is common in life. It is a reason that keeps on happening. It is illogical. They are afraid that questions will eventually lead to more freedom. They hate revolutions but they started one and eventually had a huge success. But, since they gained their power by deceit and fraud, they have also mistreated their own people. With their authority, they have contributed to several events that still plague the world.

Even though they created an alternate dimension to rule the United States of America, they are still stuck in that dimension, but it will eventually merge with the real dimension, if nothing is stopped. It is a way to take power from the legitimate authority.

Power is everything to them.

The whole story will never work, if deceit does not exist.

It is a plan that currently works in the alternate dimension. The plan would cause questions in the actual dimension. People will be questioned and put on trial in the real dimension. Hollywood would be in trouble. The rest of the governments would shun the Hollywood machine in the real dimension. It is correct to say that people will not live to see the Hollywood machine in the real dimension because people will protest their ideology. It is the plan itself that will upset the people of the real dimension. People in the real dimension are not idiots, and they will demand answers. In the alternate dimension, the Hollywood machine now known as the Hollywood government, refuses to answer any questions. All questions, they believe, are said to be a form be freedom and blasphemy.

The Hollywood government has yet to answer anything relevant and useful. Everything is deceit. Their invasion of Iraq was deceit. The war was deceit everywhere else. It is a form of manipulation that is favorable to the initiators. Everything is built on a lie.

Everything is a lie. It is a form that relates to propaganda. It is unreasonable to span the globe with deceit.

Here comes the world as we know it. There are huge changes in store for the rest of the people. Nothing will be the same. It is now part of life. There is no evidence if it ever spread to the real dimension.

Precautions must be addressed.

Precautions must be understood.

There must be a plan to decide the best fate of the future.

The future looks dismal.

It is a failure by the rest of the world. No one saw this coming. Everything was supposed to change for better. Now, everything is worse off than ever before. People still don't care in the alternate dimension. Everything they try to do ends up thwarted by the Hollywood government. The perpetrators who try to remove the Hollywood machine find themselves humiliated in front of people. They are humiliated, dressed as clowns, sometimes with no clothes on. It is a sad case for the rest of society. No one will ever take it upon themselves to do anything.

People must realize that something needs to happen. It is the reason that must make sense. It is the reason that must demonstrate the best opportunity to help the reasons of preventing destruction. It is the opportunity to seek a reform in the justice system. There are reasons why this stuff must happen now, and it is in fact the correct time to figure out a solution. The time is near.

Everything is near.

The world is round, not flat.

Idiocracy must come to an end.

As everything starts to begin, it is the dawn of a new day. The world is constantly changing.

What's that?

There is nothing there.

This is the example of hearing stuff.

You start to develop problems.

You might think you are going crazy.

People might send you to the crazy hospital.

There is a plan to humiliate you, starve you, and to do stuff you never want to do in life. It is a price that some people have already paid for. Everything that promotes freedom is against the Hollywood government. You thought you saw everything. It is a clueless idea to think about nothing, as nothing remains the same. It is the choice that you must make.

Decisions are ready.

Decisions decide fate.

It is the opportunity to seek reform, to end the constant chaos.

Wars are everywhere.

This government promotes terrorism.

Terrorism must be stopped.

Everything relies on a fallacy, a belief that is against tradition.

It is the goal to decide the fate.

At the time of fate, you must understand, that there is a seeker. The seeker is everywhere. You must not hide. It is the seeker who solves the problems. It is the seeker who decides the fate of everything. The seeker is constantly watching, but the seeker can be anything and anyone. It is a form of invisible governance.

It is the reason of insanity.

Evil is everywhere.

The timing of certain events will determine your fate. It is the goal to appreciate nothing. There is nothing there. There is nothing relevant. It is a clue to solve. The precise moment in history will determine the fate of something that yet has to be determined. As persistent as it is, there is no way to stop this kind of evil in the future. There must be a plan where you travel back to the past. Only there will you find the way to defeat the enemy. The future is filled with an impossible task. Anything that happens in the future is impossible to prevent in the future. It is designed that way to ensure protection.

Determination, a goal in mind, a way to read the theory of the focus of the event.

Everything is related. It is the form that counts. It is the precise measure of the current condition. It is the reason why it exists. The plan for anything is the reason to solve the problem. It is a puzzle. Nothing will happen overnight, and if it does, well, it is just by chance.

Clearly, something is happening.

Nation building, well, maybe.

Saddam was framed. He did nothing wrong.

Framed for what, nothing but propaganda and false evidence.

It was a sad day.

The Hollywood government convicted Saddam on false intelligence.

There was no proof of anything.

The trial was orchestrated to promote and sponsor terrorism. It was a reason that backfired. The Hollywood government didn't care.

Everybody seemed happy.

People shouting, "Saddam is dead," joyfully, as if something was going to change.

Well, nothing changed, everything just got worse, and it was now time to create the possibility of something being irrelevant.

People fled.

The Islamic terrorists retreated.

The Islamic terrorists started to denounced terrorism.

Terrorism was now pursued by the Hollywood government.

Islamic terrorists feared for their lives.

Islamic terrorists gave up their radical ideological movement.

The Hollywood government became the lone instigator and initiator in terrorist attacks. People started demanding answers.

Nothing could be supported.

It was a plan by something other than the creation of a false idea.

Globalization is everywhere. It could help. It is hurting. The alternate dimension is an evil destination, it is a place for deceit and fallacies. It promotes censorship and propaganda. It is clearly insane.

Saddam was hanged.

People thought it was for a good cause.

It was later found out to be misinformation.

Everybody who supported the trial and execution demanded answers, as they were misled. Everyone retracted their statements supporting the trial and execution of Saddam. It was a time for new justice. It was a time to support the end of terrorism. It was now time to end unnecessary occupations of other sovereign nations by the Hollywood government.

Everything was a mistake.

Information was a mistake.

Decisions were mistakes.

Nothing proved to be correct.

It was a shame. It was a sham. It was a scam. Nothing felt correct.

It is the thought that counts.

That is bullshit.

Nothing ever counts.

Everything is a systematic failure. It is meant to fail. It is a part of life. Nothing needs to be perfect. Being perfect means nothing in life. It is not about perfection. It is about how you complete the goal. No one ever needs to be perfect. The entire situation is part of the bigger picture. It is part of life, something that is meant to strive for opportunity. The formation of a new front. There is a victory parade. There is something that is current in nature. Everything is part of the situation. It is a requirement that something must be done. The situation is specific in each account. There is the reason that acclaims to be the rest of the world. There is something that must determine society.

As people want to be involved in something, it is something that must count. The entire story is not relevant to the rest of history. History is constantly changing and it is a part of life. Something needs to be understood, and it is the result of something unrelated in nature. There is a physical attraction to the rest of the portion of sanity. As it grows, there is a side that is mentioned that will depend on the rest of the relevance. Everything that you might imagine is the same as the entire result. It is a small organism that exists only in nature, or something that is meant to derive something other than life.

Alas, creativity has been the detriment to the loss of words. The Hollywood government never cared about creativity, as they only care about greed. The Hollywood government hi-jacked your creativity, saying it belongs to them now. They don't care because they think they created it, but that is only the beginning. It is a shame that interests want to change the system. Interests have changed the system, and some of those interests need to say out of politics, but that isn't possible when the Hollywood machine created the politicians. The Hollywood machine is now the Hollywood government, and they created some type of artificial human, that resembles a real human, but it is actually an android. It is fully capable of being a human, and it can act like a human, but it is clearly a robot.

Something that hasn't been realized is everything. It is the result of something that is mentioned to create the reason behind the insanity. It is not always a just cause, it is a complete sham that makes no sense whatsoever. The complete chaos is part of life. It has always been part of society, or something different. The same thing applies to everything, and as it takes place, there is a goal in mind, something that is irresistible, to the taste of attraction. It is the reason that something is at the proper sense that there must be a current situation, yet, nothing has proven itself to the world. It is a shame, but it is utterly confusing, to the people and to the rest of the world. Nothing has worked, and something is unreliable.

Focusing on something that might make sense

sounds plausible, but as it might be determined from sanity, there is a reason why there has been the physical altercation of the natural universe. Somewhere and somehow, the Hollywood machine was able to make a carbon copy of the universe, but formed it in such a way that promotes nothing but chaos. It is such a sad world. It is not knowing what will happen next. There is no hope for society in this alternate dimension. It is a case that is confusing, everywhere, for the utter nonsense of chaos.

Propaganda everywhere, as it is deemed necessary to end freedom. It is an assault on society. It has become reckless with nowhere else to go. There are very few reasons to justify this alternate dimension. Everyone is hiding. There is no reason to escape, but people are scared. No one from the Hollywood government knows where the HEPTAGON is located, and they do not even know of the existence. It is a reason to be hope that the enemy never finds out anything about the resistance.

Lost causes are always there, and then there is the result of never-ending nation building. The Hollywood government, and its predecessor, the Hollywood machine, have constantly propped up dictators in this alternate dimension, but soon, the dictators learned about the true meaning of their power.

Dictators decided to ignore the Hollywood government, and decided to open up their countries to the rest of the world, something that wasn't recommended by the Hollywood government. Dictators opened up trade routes and started to hold democratic elections. The Hollywood government didn't like that, but they couldn't do anything. Everybody started to realize the goal of the Hollywood government, and it was the goal to promote a unilateral agreement just for the United States of America. The Hollywood government didn't care about the rest of the world, just themselves.

Riots happened.

Chaos was everywhere.

Insanity is king of the world. There is nothing else available. It is at the height of its goal. It already changed society. It is the reason that something must be done, or it might not help.

It was the reason to understand.

There were the qualities of life.

It seemed accidental.

Was it a mistake?

Nothing would ever be the same. Something must be done to prevent this from happening. There is a crisis at hand. There is nothing else that can happen. It is nothing that exists. It is a part of life. There is a reason for the thing to be able to understand why the people start a rebellion. There must be a reason, as it was never clear. People start to resist. There is nothing available.

Democracy!

Autocracy!

Capitalism!

Government is everywhere. Big brother might find you. Not all governments are evil. Only evil governments target their own people. It is a waste of time and money, and yet everything is used to make baseless claims.

Damn the place.

It is a thing of the evil generation.

There is nothing that can help anything. It is against the future. Freedom is at risk. There is nothing that you can do. Everything will die. There is nothing that will lead to more educated decisions. It is a way to control the future and the quality of life.

Everything is shrinking.

There is something that must restore freedom.

It is the measurement of anything important than the basis of movements. Everything must change. There is nothing else that can happen. It is a case that can show the rest of the world the sanctity of harmony. It is the reason that nothing will ever be the same.

Opportunity is diminishing, day-by-day, and as a way to escape it, there is no room for error. There is nothing else that will remove anything. It is a risk that will continue to be debated. People are constantly unable to determine the facts of something useful. There is nothing but acid. There is the creation of everything evil. It is the price that has been paid. It is the reason that must be determined by the future of the universe. It is nothing that can escape. It is everything that is wrong with the attitude. It is the utter nonsense created by misleading people.

False information.

Misleading information.

Censorship.

Propaganda.

It is all the same. It is meant to destroy the real truth. It is happening now, in the alternate dimension, built by the Hollywood machine. It is happening in real time. It is at the central of attention. It is meant to qualify as something other than the real value of life.

Life is vital. It is part of why people must live. People must accomplish something. Other people are just living because they are balancing the universe. At every stance, or anything that happens, these people might die, because they were just meant to be born, and then to die. It might seem tragic, but that was the original intention of their birth. Immortals are not born, and this never applies to immortals. Immortals choose to die, and they do not die fast or easy. These people who were meant to die in an accident or in another type of incident were put here to die. It is the truth, but it might not make any sense. These people might die too easily, as it might demonstrate the need for people to die. It is part of a quota system. There is nothing that will prevent their death. Eventually, they will die. It is some form of regeneration process. It sounds scary, but it is a part of the cycle, a cycle of life and evolution.

The tree of life.

The eternity of life.

Life itself is plagued with sins.

Immortals hardly commit sin.

Jesus was not an immortal. He tried to commit few sins as possible. Sin is everywhere, but it was just invented by organized religion.

Organized religion is everywhere. It is not supposed to be scary. Organized religion might seem radical, as some members of churches have shown distaste to anything. To them, the churches, religion must be everywhere. It is a sign from God, a sign that is promoting propaganda. It is a way to brainwash people. There is something wrong with this crazy picture. There is a reason why this is constantly happening, and it might lead to destruction.

Besides the facts, there are very few facts. There is nothing that can help. It is part of the system that needs an overhaul. It might seem impossible, but there is a reason to destroy that notion. It is the reason that everything happens for a reason. It is the opportunity that might cry wolf. For the purpose of sanity, there is a way to determine nothing from the outcome. It is a precise measure. It is something that must be achieved. It is simply part of life.

Something that can be remembered is something that can make sense. There is a reason that something makes sense. It is complete nonsense. There is nothing that is able to understand the ability to take place. There is the ability to understand anything. The belief of something in a futuristic environment like this is unbelievable. How could there be something worth evaluating. There is a reason to understand anything as it might make sense. There is the thing of the past, a reason to understand the misfortune of events, in the same time it takes to read the present.

There is the absolute reaction to teach something to the future of something that is other than the resistance of the critical patience of the rest of the world. There is nothing that can help. It is of nothing important to the theory of how to dedicate something to the world. There is nothing that will help the future. Everything is set in the tracks. There is something that will eventually turn people into human centipedes. It is the result of science. It is the result of something that might never make sense. It is the result that something is looming in the environment. It is the present value of everything related at face value. It is the time that might count, for the theory of just appearing, to counter the consequences of the rest of the world. There is a theory of how to engage in solitude.

Inattention to everything is always happening. It is

the cause of everything. It is the reason that something might happen to the rest of people. There is nothing that can actually take place, as there might be something that takes place. The utopian society might seem irrelevant, but it is here to stay. There is a reason to acquire the attention of the reason behind the quality of the data. There is something that might hinder the relation between everything else. There is the reason why it might happen now. It is the reason for the theory and the notion to have something never in common, as they are always in common.

Bright lights.

The sign of alien invasions.

It might be inevitable.

There seems to be something wrong.

Nothing will lead you to the cause.

It is the reason that everything is behind the reason, to the cause of the meaning of something that is meant to analyze the attempts of gratitude. It does not make any sense to anyone. It is supposed to be that way. There is nothing that will ever get you to change anything. There is nothing related to the theory of something that is the reason to stand still. There is the possibility that something is working. It has to be working, right, well, there is something for everyone and it can be caused by anything. It is the result that there is something of the importance that there is the reason to think that there is nothing to investigate. There is something that is happening in the current fight for the reason to help. It is the thing that might save the future. There are events that can cause the real problem to hijack the rest of reality. There is the option of nothing.

At last, there is no ending, because this will never happen, but you might think there is a reason to this madness. There is nothing that can help you. There is the reason that you might face critics. You will have to face critics as there is the reason to understand the real issue behind everything. There is the reason that you will insist that something must be relevant when there is nothing that so important to the value, since it has already been achieved long ago, and yet, it is the exact opposite of the things you have learned about life.

Nothing is important to your life. There is nothing important to anything. It is of no value.

Trains are not moving.

There is nothing in your mind.

You are a complete mess.

You must be crazy.

You are being brainwashed.

Nothing will be determined by the reason of your sanity. You are sane, but you are also insane. You are a mental patient. You have lost everything. You need to find out what's wrong. You are scared. You are hiding in fear. You must examine some history in order to completely learn about your situation. You are afraid that this is only happening to you, but you must realize that there are other people in life who exist. You must be willing to accept your fate. It is of utter importance that you complete everything that is important in life. You think this might happen to you, but it is only happening in your mind. You just realized that you were having a dream, a very bad and weird dream that made no sense in your life. You must be confused and you should be, as it relates to something important in your life. It could mean anything. There could be a lack of fun in your life. You might be even suffering from depression, as this will indicate emptiness. You must be empty, as this is the reason that makes the most sense.

Everything completes nothing.

The rise of anything is related to the rest of everything else. It is not really supposed to happen. There is nothing that can be prevented. It is the true value that makes sense at all.

Nothing makes sense.

Everything is confusing.

You eventually thought Hitler won, well, then there is a surprise.

Hitler escaped.

Hitler fled.

Hitler didn't face any trial.

Well, that is a complete surprise. You were hoping Hitler would have taken over all of Europe, well, it didn't happen like that.

There was never any war crimes trial.

The Hollywood machine didn't win.

Hitler didn't win.

It was a waste of time of money.

But, Hitler defeated the Hollywood machine.

However, the Hollywood machine rebuilt itself a few years later. The war was over. There was nothing Hitler or the Hollywood machine could do. You could say that Hitler won, but that would be false. Hitler gave up, as he realized that fighting was a waste of time. This strategy confused the Hollywood machine. It was a genius policy. It was part of a goal to stop brutal attacks.

Hitler returned government and policy in

Germany to a better place. All hate and propaganda was later abolished. Hitler wanted to do this all along, but he found a way to finally succeed.

Hitler, well, he retired from government.

Hitler moved with his wife to New Zealand, where he later died. It was a match that was complete in paradise. It was a tropical paradise.

Nothing could be better. It is something sort of happy. Everything went as planned, and so you thought, but the rest of Hitler's organizations were abolished, but were transformed into a modern military and police, along with other social programs.

Something that is crazy might sound crazy. If it does sound crazy than it must. Hitler transformed Germany into a utopian society before he retired to New Zealand, after the end of the war.

There has never been anything good about a utopian society, as people try to say it will lead to chaos. People believe utopian living is propaganda, but they fail to understand that a utopian society is possible. What makes it significant is the quality of life and freedom. You would have thought a utopian society is possible, but people believe that communism is a utopian society. Communism could be a utopian society, but there are certain laws that make it seem less likely. A utopian society is possible but no one has ever proven to succeed in creating one. A society might be utopian for one person but might be different for the other, as it is an ideology of what is needed. Utopian qualities are different for each person. Not everyone will live in a utopian society since it is unique to their life. The utopian society is a place where everything could be perfect, it is a place where people never have any troubles. If you never have any problems you might be living in a utopian society, but other people will dismiss this as nonsense. It is a part of life that might be absence. There could always be a problem with the way people perceive the goal to experience new things. There is a reason why there is opportunity, and as the world starts to identify with everything else, there could be a feeling that might happen.

Utopian societies once existed everywhere, and it would seem that people faced problems, as there were always problems present. No society is ever perfect, and there is a reason for that. Instead of imagining something that you think is impossible, think of something that is relevant to the rest of the world, something that can be easily achieved. You might come to a conclusion that is more likely, as it might be possible to demonstrate in real life. When you think of a utopian society, you might always think about flying cars, sky scrapers, beautiful jungles and forests. The wilderness is everywhere, and it is such a beautiful sight to imagine and to stare for days. Well, this thing, as you imagined, is not a real utopian society, as it is just your imagination of dreaming about a fantasy. Like I said before, the real utopian society rests in your capability, but real places do exist, but they are limited in size. Anything could be a utopian society. A small Mediterranean village might be a utopian society. Part of Greece might be a utopian society. Today though, utopian societies are hard to find, as they are very rare. The utopian society might be in your mind, but you must be willing to avoid problems. You can make it a utopian for yourself, while others might feel it is the most despicable place they have ever resided. It is just a case of preferences, and as it might seem, there are still utopian societies that actually exist. It depends on the quality of life, as well as the way that people want to live.

New Zealand was transformed into a utopian society, as it was later to be possible to achieve such a dream. Besides that, Hitler went into retirement, as he realized it was a lost cause, and he wanted to end something that should have never taken place. It was a time for wounds to heal, and a way to demonstrate a renewal in activities. It was a reason to decide the real fate of everything, something that has nothing else but new and improved standards. It was a cause for Hitler to refocus on his failed passion. It would be time that he try to accomplish something old to achieve new fame. It was something that might sound crazy but there was little time. There was nothing important about anything, as there was a reason to solve with time. The time riddle is everywhere, and as it is achieved, there is a case to celebrate for the rest of society. It is a case that mentions the equality amongst the rest of the people. There must be something that is current with time. There are reasons why this must happen, as there is always time to learn, yet there is a failure to accomplish the reason to relearn. It is part of society. It must be used in order to help the rest of people. There are reasons why society is bad. Utopian societies are not perfect, as they are often hidden in very dark places. There is nothing about life that can be determined to control the rest of the reason behind the reasons. It is a place of chaos, a place where nothing is impossible, but there are insane laws, as that might determine certain actions.

Utopian societies are located in Greece, but in

general, utopian societies are known for their insane laws, which are never relaxed. Their laws are generally very troublesome.

If everything was the same as normal, there could be something that is happening, as there is a true meaning to something other than the correct state of mind. In the notion that something is other than utopian, it is regarded as a police state, but that is not the vase. There are several proponents of a police state, only because those supporters want to have a vast amount of power. It is at the current situation that there might be something wrong with the rest of the people or there could be something that might be imagines as the way people think. It is never the right theory to decide what will determine the quality of life. There is nothing that will be determined to suit the rendition of something that is the quality of time. It is why there might be the reason why the system is fixed, which might make sense to people when you explain it to them. From there, they will evidently say that they knew it all along and that this evidence proves their point of something that is against society. It might make sense as there is a reason to believe everything, and for that purpose they might think that something is happening, for the safety of the rest of the world. There is something that will happen, as it already has.

Several things might happen in this utopian society, as it was already indicated. You would think that I am in a utopian society, but you don't know my identity. You will probably never learn my identity, as I have never introduced myself, but I might, but I probably won't. You only know me as someone who knows everything. It is something that is mysterious to you. I could be anyone, but what about the rest of the people. There could be something going on in your life that is detrimental to your family. It should be of the utmost importance to you that something will happen. There is always something that might occur along the line, as there is always a problem in life. There is something that is adamant about the physical abilities to comprehend, as it might tend to demonstrate the ability to learn in the workforce. There is something that might never happen. It is the reason why you must clearly identify the resources to everything with the possibility that might be determined, as there could be something that is happening. It is nothing short of the tale of something that might happen. There is the reason why there might be something that is happening, as it might make sense, to the rest of the people, but there is a short end of the deal that was never mentioned. It is of the possibility that the utopian society never even existed. As for the cause, well, there might never be any cause, as it could have been just imaginary, something that is all too common, and a way to distinguish the possibility of a false conviction. It is a feeling that is based on nothing, and the reason behind false testimony is just to seek attention, whereby the alleged victim can get money or out of their current conditions. These alleged victims are either delusional, mentally ill, scammers, or even intellectuals, but the first three are the most common, because the intellectuals are smarter than the rest of those people, because they know how to never get caught, but they choose not to get caught. There is some sort of conspiracy, but this is not really happening, as it is just a figment of your imagination. It is a reason why they think something might happen, but there is no reason what is happening.

As people start to live with society in the realms of culture, to the point where civilization has started, there was always a reason to determine the cause of everything. It was the reason to determine the precise measure of something that could be obsolete, and it was the precise movement that is the reason to encounter the mysterious creature. A force of nature is at the very cause of the intended plan, as there is nothing wrong with anything else. There is nothing that will conclude the simple plan of the reasoning behind the veil of the current situation. It is nothing but trouble, as it has always been this way. Society has been something important to people of the world. It is a fact that must be proven, and it has been the fact that there is a reason to consider all options, as there could always be an outlier, or there could be something related to the emotion of the exterior. There is nothing that will happen to the rest of the world, unless there is something that is nothing. There is nothing that will fix society, as there is no reason for fixing. If there is something wrong then there would be an interaction amongst the peers of the people for the cultural rendition of why there must be a civilization. It is a reason why there must be something wrong with nothing.

Utopian society could be everywhere, as it has been clearly been demonstrated by countless numbers of people, as it could have existed. There is also a false feeling that you might get, and as for the true intentions, well, there is something that should happen, as it might indicate the reasoning behind everything. There could be a closed door, as it could indicate anything, or there could be something that resonates to the opposite effect. There is nothing that might happen. It could happen tomorrow, or it could never occur, as there must be a mysterious event, to the extent that no one will know what has happened.

Eventually, there will be an uprising. Maybe it shall happen because of everything in the world, but the exact cause might mean nothing. It is the cause that might appear to be the most brutal. It is something that might tackle the bigger picture of everything else. It is the reason why there might be the temptation of everything, for the reason to target something that is not worth reading. It is the rendition of everything else that counts. It is the theory that mentions the slightest moment of courage, to the extent that there is the complete reason of insanity. The reason that something is happening is the reason why there is a happening. At the reason why there is a reason, there might as well be an opposite reason, to dictate the indication of something other than the theory of being an asshole. There is nothing better than being an asshole you say, but there is something that is located in the theory of a field of dimensions, a sign that something might be in the horizon. Everything has a theory to describe the notion, but it is in its current form, a sign that might appear unusual. It is the reason why there is the option to stand out in front of others. There is time to settle within the opinion of the sign that must encourage the time to set sail. It is the prophecy that must reign in the thoughts, a reason to determine everything behind the enemy. There is something worth to acknowledge, as there is a reason to demonstrate the need to prevent disaster. It is at the moment that nothing happens. It is the moment that something is the result of nothing. The signs show something is about to happen, a way to understand the community, in a new form that must able to concentrate on the periodic episodes of the theory that binds time. The results would be nothing about your life, but as a record, there would be something related to your meaning of quality. It is something that is not supposed to measure anything, but as a tool for the utopian society, and in that manner, there is something that might be able to consider the rest of the pack, a new motion to sign the type of cast that will promote nothing. There is nothing other than the reason to promote nothing. There is the reason to determine nothing.

After everything has been achieved, it could be determined that nothing ever happened. It is the result that manufactures everything. It is part of this utopian society you decide is necessary for civilization. It is the fact that the world demands civilization, for the real reason that might surprise anyone. To the account that might always be the same, there is a price that people must pay. It is the fact that there must be a real reason to interact the policies to enforce nature, but there is something that must never be determined. It is the reason that intellect must be encouraged. No one wants to be named the village idiot, and yet there is always that person who becomes that local idiot. It is nothing common to a precise measurement of insanity, as it might have been nice to ascertain certain information. There is nothing that can hide, for the reason that is known might discourage some people from doing something. Everything is important in life, and it is a reason that must be the real notion to fight the sign of something other than nothing. People will be people, and this will always be the case, as there is a complete mess with everything else.

People have better things to do, as there is nothing more important than life. As it might determine, there is a constant reason that people always fight. There is the reality that something might happen. It is the place we live in. It is the precise moment that is never happening. It is the reason that must happen. It is why everything happens in a very strange occurrence.

Civilization, zombies, and utopian societies, they are entirely the basis of something that could make sense if there was a reason to understand. There is constant emptiness, which differs between life and death. It is time for the people to realize that something is happening. It is the time to build the new civilization, the time for control, and the time to tell people that there is a reason to live. It is time to announce the dawn of the new civilization. There is time to prepare but it must be fast.

Everything else is a mystery to you. It is exactly why there must be a reason to survive. It is the reason that must live. It is supposed to happen, as there is nothing more that could help life. Importance is patience. Importance must be dedicated. Life is always about mistakes. It is a part of life that must be determined by something that is being acknowledged. It is the reason that must be capable of handling the situation. There is a utopian society on the very outskirts of your imagination. There is reality. It is the fact that something is happening. It is reality that must have a choice in creating life.

Death is part of everything. Immortals only die when they choose to, and this should make sense to your brain. You must be able to learn and keep information. There is a reason why you shall always study. You must memorize, and as you do, there is always a surprise, as this might be the end of your reality. You might have to fight soon, as you might face extinction. There is a life that is fighting to continue to erase your habits. You must cope with everything. It is the true reason why you must be able to understand the quality of life. There is a reason why everything might apply so quickly, in a fast paced environment. It is the fact that something is in the current universe of how to learn the goal of society. Society is a part of life, and it relates to the importance of everything else. There are several reasons why it must be completed, to the point where nothing shall ever be determined.

Life is life, and as life is determined, there is always something that might prevent it. Life is a miracle, and if you never take advantage of it, there would be nothing to live for, as it would be an empty chair.

You must be able to comply with the meaning of life, as it might help to guide your future someday, for eternity.

CHAPTER EIGHT

L̲ife is important to the rest of society. As it
is reflected amongst everything, there is a reason to live.
There might be something to live for. As with all
lifeforms, it must start from something, as there is a birth
in the HEPTAGON. Present are the instructors of the
girls and no one else. It is the baby of Rafael and Carlie. It
is a baby girl, who is named Hannah. The celebration is
short lived, as it dies a minute later for no known reason.
With that, it is on to something else, a funeral perhaps, but
there was never any baby, and this incident between Rafael
and Carlie about impregnation was something that was
never true. No one was ever impregnated by anything, as it
would be something short of nothing but nothing. It is
surely something to think about, but now there is time to
learning.

Learning is fundamental, they always say in school,

well, it is, but this is a different type of learning. With only three months left, it is time to heat things up, and there is always something that could happen. It is the result that matters. As training is currently in the process of gaining every day, it is about time to focus on something. It is a new day, and there is just a short while until something must or might happen. There is something that is going to happen. It might happen now.

So, with training almost to an end, it is time to begin more active training, focusing on more defense and offensive measures. This will make sure that nothing escapes from the rest of reality. It will be part of something that will happen to end the political strife. It is part of the complete ideology of time. Remember, a utopian society can be cruel, but if you ever encounter a dystopian society, well, you would be trying to leave once you arrive. It is simply the fact, and there is nothing good about either society, unless you always obey the rules, in which, the utopian society would be a better fit, so it is the time to begin something new. The dawn of a new day has arrived.

It is now dawn, and the girls are beginning to commence their first round of fitness exercises. Time by time again, there is a complete schedule, filled with the same exact things. It is exactly the same as before. History will always repeat itself, and there should be something changed. For history to repeat itself, this would mean that the forces of the Hollywood machine will just keep getting stronger. It is the focus not to get any stronger, and there shall be the reason to gather the same meaning of what has yet to happen. There is the case that nothing ever happens. It is the reason behind anything that consists of the reason to answer the reason in order to notify information.

Nothing is better. Swimming is swimming. It is nothing but the same, and it shall never be equal. It is the reason that this exercise fitness program is to promote a strong cardio-vascular regiment. It is something that is meant to signify the reason to show strength amongst the real reason behind muscles. You must learn how to exercise in order to become stronger.

Walking and walking, well, they are running, and that is something that is important. Special shoes are utilized, as they will help to prevent any cramps or illnesses. This was probably mentioned before, but if you never knew, well it might be a case for amnesia. It is something that is meant to deter the complex form of everything else. Something that is always relevant might be the issue of everything else, as they might equal the presence of nothing. It is the sign to show that there is nothing but disaster, and this might happen in the case of anything.

Every occurrence might have an opinion or a reason to live, but there could be the reason to imagine the single most opiated opinion of something such as nothing but the best, so there is the reason of something but the quality of civilization. It is time to answer the truth about what is currently going to happen. The real question is the type to exist in a complex community. It cannot exist in the most simplest forms, but there is nothing with the reason to question anything. People will remember the reasons to gather everything in the reason to have the functionality of reasoning behind anything. There is something that there is simple, but this is a disguise. It is a disguise that seems simple because it was always meant to be complex. In reality, it is actually very complex, so there is always a reason to answer the question to solve the single most outrageous thing you have ever heard.

Afternoon has arrived, but why would you care about that, as that has nothing to do with anything. It is the answer to solve the actual reason of something that must take the real truth. It is everything that must be the real goal of the true meaning of life. There must be a reason to solve the time of destiny. It is the quality of life that must be with the others in order to lay with the most possible reason to exist without the quality of life in order to live with the functions of the complete environment. It is complex and that is the way it has always been.

Passing has never been the most gracious thing, but another day had passed, and it is the reason to answer the true meaning of why it is time to tell the real answer about everything. It is the time to notify everything, and by this notion, it is almost time to defeat the enemy. It is the time to answer the global question. It is the time to answer why there must be a reason to destroy everything else. It is the reason why something is always happening. There is something that must be conclusive, so there is a reason to live. There is a reason to understand to study the conclusion of how to gather the true information. It is the exact result that must be the reason to hamper anything. It is the time to tell the entire quality of information. There is nothing that will be able to determine the true notification of everything that must be the true story of theories.

Another month pass, and soon, there are two months left, and it went extremely fast. Time flies when you are having fun, and that is what people always tend to say, but could that ever be true. Well, that could be true because you are ignoring time in order to achieve a goal. It might not be fun for your body, but you are determined to complete a goal. It is the reason why there must be the reason to answer the precise measure of something and there is always the reason to see the type of questions answered. Days end and end, and as they happen, it is the focus of something that might just happen without any reaction. This feeling can always be mutual, as it might happen every single time, and for that purpose, there is a reason to live. There is a reason to determine the possibility that something is in the beginning of the reason behind the true match of the possibility of the reason of nothing.

Feeling something is nothing but a thing of emotion, and it is the reason why there is always a problem with this, as nothing will ever qualify. People will always use their emotions as a way to justify something, and it is the true reason why justice is blind. It is the reason why there is the opportunity to succeed.

Morning and day, as people might determine that something is wrong, it is a sign that denotes why there must be an obstacle. It is the reason that must be qualified. It is the reason that must be ascertained, in order to make for a new room. There is something that is objective about the world. There is something about each season. There is a reason that it must happen, and everything must happen today. There is the reason that it is actually something with nothing but the other signs of hope. Everything goes second-by-second, day-by-day, and to that extent, there is always a reason to question the reason behind the personality of the problem. It is of the focus that must be determined in order to figure the correct measurement.

It is everything that there is the true quality of life, to the extent that nothing will ever be the same. There is the new opportunity to determine everything and this will be the reason to question opportunity. People must answer their own questions, as there is simply a mysterious anecdote to the reason behind nothing. There is the quality of life. The physical interactions between how everything how there is the personality of how to determine something correct. It is the reason that is correct. It is the reason that day and night are the opposite. The opposite of something that might make sense is the real reason of why there is the true possibility of how it might make sense. It is nothing that everything is the reason to determine the thing that must be the never-ending reality of nothing. There is nothing that there must be the real reason that is ever correct.

Correctness is nothing but propaganda promoted by the shills. As you might know, there is a simple interaction of how there must be several reasons. Shills are very widely used, and you should already know this, as it is a sign of corruption. It is a sign that must make sense to certain people, and there is always a reason. There are the reasons to take time to determine everything, as it is related to nothing. It is the reason why there must be the new opportunities to question the true face value of why there must be freedom. It is nothing new, there is something wrong with society, as there is nothing wrong with people, just the people who control the government.

Complete nonsense. Nothing is normal, and it will always be determined to ask something that is wrong with the entire scenario. It is the time to take action. It is now the real reason to answer nothing but there is something or there is now the patience to question everything else. There is nothing else foolish than anything else, and this has always made sense. It is the opportunity to take time. Time by time is the real reason to undertake the passion of something that must make sense. It is the reason to question nothing but the true value of insanity. It is the sensation of something that is now that must be determined to recite the correct passage in order to make sense. There is nothing more suitable, but there is the reason to ascertain nothing other than nonsense, but there is nothing other than the real reason to take action, for the opportunity is happening. It is now the correct time to start a revolution.

Well, there might be something happening, as there is always something happening. It is a part of life. It will never end, as it is a part of life. Two months flew by fast, and there is only one day left of training, but what would happen now. What would happen tomorrow, as there is a reason to demand the answer. It is the eve of the new revolution, the time where there will happen in the past. People will travel to the year 1986. With one day left, there is something still to gain, but will there be a note to find how to prepare. Well, there could be, as this might be needed to plan the attack. It is the time that must succeed.

As it might sound certain, there is nothing wrong with how society is living, but there is a reason to think that it is ending. It is a place to understand the facility of the way it can interact with people, but there is trouble with the rest of the world. There is something that resists the urge to take the time of inconsistencies.

People please, as there is nothing wrong. It is a simple pleasure, and it might show some distaste, but that has to be with the audacity to determine anything. There is the type of person that must adhere to nothing, and as the reason to think, there is nothing wrong with anything. It is the result of something such as the reasoning behind nothing. It is the reason that nothing will ever get done, or so you think, but there is still hope. It exists in the form of something but there is nothing to the creation of something. Hope means that there is the reason for something other than the meaning of life, as it takes time.

Behind everything is always a sign of progress, well, today is the day. It is about time, and the girls walk to the lobby of the HEPTAGON to find a note on the front desk. The note seems surprising, as it might mean something or it could indicate what will happen next.

Hello Girls,

Today marks your last day of training, so be proud of it. As a result, you have come so far. Remember, there is a reason for the fight, there is a reason for everything. This fight matters, as if the people of the Hollywood machine are not defeated, then there will be an immediate backlash, something that might have dire consequences. Everything happens for a reason. It is for that reason why there have always been rules and laws. It is for that reason that some things were always meant to be. To handle any situation, there is always a goal in mind, you must be prepared for anything. Preparation is key to solve anything. It is part of the reason why there is sanity. To highlight the major points of your journey tomorrow, this note shall be divided into four different sections, with this part not counting. First and foremost, everything will be about what you will encounter. So, now, the sections are the introduction, the what to expect, how to survive, and the conclusion. There are also subsections in certain

*sections. You might find some of this material very useful. Not only
will your journey to defeat the Hollywood machine be vital to history,
but it shall also be a very large stepping stone to fight censorship,
propaganda, and terrorism. By doing this for humanity, you have
shown courage, bravery, and strength, by demonstrating specific skills.
So, you must consider everything before you leave town tomorrow.*

Introduction

  *Your journey begins tomorrow at 0800 hours, where, at
that time, you shall report to this lobby, fully dressed in your complete
gear. Your complete tactical gear consists of colored sheer-laced
brassiere, colored sheer-laced panties, a tank top, a bullet-proof vest, a
jacket with built in protection, pants with built in protection, combat
boots with built in protection, and a utility belt with built in
protection. Built in protection simply means that that item of clothing
has metal inside of it to protect you from any harm. The metal is part
of a specialized system that attempts to repel any objects that
threatens to subdue the person. You might get hit by something, but,
if the system works, the enemy object would be repelled.*

  *As per everything else, there is a reason why you must be
ready to fight. Today is your last day to train. While it might not be
a busy day today, this note is just a briefing to tell you about
everything that you might encounter, but that is a separate section.
Now, everything that you do tomorrow might affect the future. It is
part of life to understand the reality of something that will be the
forces of nature. Your goal is to instill a plan of harmony.*

  *With everything in chaos, you might not have enough time.
There could be several occurrences in which you might face something
with a lack of understanding. This is normal, but everything should
be related to something. Right after you arrive in the lobby fully
dressed, a portal will open. The portal has a mind of its own, and it
shall take you to a target location, however, if something happens*

with the settings, you might sent to a random place. This is due to the random setting. To help you get out of an era you shall also be given each a time watch. Wear this time watch, each of you, and set it to the year 1986, the month of March, and the fifth day, which should be a Wednesday, if the portal takes you to a random location.

About half of the time, the setting is set to random, only because of a computer glitch. Now, each of the random locations might lead you somewhere, but they are all a distraction. Everything that you will learn today will help you better integrate into the past. It is part of society, so, be careful. The current time is 0700 hours, so, you will have some time to learn about anything today.

What to Expect

When you first arrive to the lobby tomorrow morning at 0800 hours, you should already be wearing your complete tactical gear. On the lobby desk there will be five time watches, and each of you will put one on. After you put on the watches, you will have to wait for a few minutes, until the time portal opens. Once it opens, you will each enter it one at a time, but before that, you must get your weapons and other gear. Your weapons have been stored into a large but compact backpack.

Before you leave your rooms tomorrow morning, you will find a backpack in the closet. This backpack must be carried on your backs at all time, and it is vital that you never lose anything. The weapons and their components have been specially modified just to fit. In order to use one, there will be a new tactic used. Each weapon has been modified into a small capsule. In order to turn that capsule into the appropriate weapon you must throw it on the ground. Upon throwing it on the ground, you will see the weapon in front of you. It is recommended that each of you deploy a different weapon, in order to reduce the amount of chaos that might happen.

Now, it is time to talk about the time portal and everything else related to time travel. As indicated, you must wait for a few minutes for the portal to appear. The portal has been set to appear after you grab your watches and put them on, but lately, there have been some issues. As of last night, the portal has been displaying signs of malfunctions, and this has cause several things that might happen in your world, but they could be a sign of progress by the Hollywood government. There is a good chance that the portal system has been hacked by enemy forces. It could be due to pranks by kids or a plot by the Hollywood government. At any rate, you could be sent to a random location that could take you to a distant location.

Right now, the system seems pretty stable, but it could malfunction at any moment. You must be prepared for anything, as it will demonstrate priorities. There are three random locations where the portal might send you, which are Mexico, China, or New Zealand. These are the most known destinations that the portal likes to send people when the random setting is initiated. For all purposes, you will attempt to use your time watches to escape.

As with all random things that might happen, there is also a possibility that your time watches could take all of you to each of the random locations before taking you to your intended destination. If this happens, just remember to be patient, as there is a possibility that your time watches could have been hacked. Each location is part of the world, but some are not even in the alternate dimension. Right now, all of you are in the alternate dimension created by the Hollywood machine. You will go back in time to the year 1986 to prevent the Hollywood machine and their androids from taking over the United States of America. For all purposes, all of the destinations you might end up going to won't be in the alternate dimension, as they will be in the real world. If you do end up in your intended destination, remember, your will expect some stuff to happen.

Intended Destination

New York City is your intended destination. When you arrive here, everything should be normal. Your arrival will be March 5, 1986, the day when the Faberx Corporation bought the United States of America and its government. While it might be normal, be warned, as everything could be a trap. Expect a parade a few hours later, but nothing else, as this deal of a purchase has been in the works for months, and it was known that the Faberx Corporation would complete the entire purchase. The Hollywood machine is watching everything, but they don't care who you are. To them, you might be members of the national guard or part of the police. The Hollywood machine already knows that members of the police and military have been deployed to oversee the entire parade. Don't expect too much chaos here, as there is something to fear.

Upon arriving at your destination, you will want to know what to expect. Your mission is to find the Hollywood machine and to kill them, but they are not that easy to find. They might be everywhere, so you must be certain to find them. If you see any chaos it could be from the Hollywood machine. The Hollywood machine has attacked this parade when it first happened, but they have also caused massive amounts of deaths. For months the Hollywood machine had been working on creating a time portal, and they achieved that goal, so now, the Hollywood machine activated that portal and created some type of alternate dimension, which is where you are now. The alternate dimension created by the Hollywood machine, as you know, has chaos and everything else that is bad for society. It is a dystopian society that you must realize.

Everything else about New York City should be obvious. While you are in Canada, you are still in a safe location, as the enemy does not know about this place. It is something that no one even knows about.

Mexico

If you arrive in Mexico, it would be somewhere in Cancun or the Yucatan Peninsula. You would arrive at an all-inclusive, luxury, tropical resort. Keep in mind, you must find a way out fast, as this might cause a distraction. Everything that you see here us real, but there is a chance that certain stuff might disappear, so, when you look back, you might be surprised.

China

This is something that will be the most challenging random location where you might end up. If the portal sends you to China, there is no knowing of where it will take you. You might end up in the middle of nowhere such as the Gobi Desert or you could end up in some sort of tourist trap. The most important thing you should know is about the location you end up. China is filled with hard terrain to navigate, and as a result, you might have difficulty with the entire destination. It is a place with extremely high elevations, and you might get lost, so, remember, anything is crucial. In order to escape, you must use your time watches. Be careful here.

New Zealand

There is only one place that you will end up, the beach. You will be standing in sand. There will be buildings around you, but you must understand about everything. This place won't be as dangerous as the rest. It is probably the safest destinations you might get sent to, but you still must be careful.

How to Survive

Surviving is an integral part of this operation. You won't know how long you will be at these destinations. You could be at these places for a while. Your time watches have a built in GPS and can instruct you to find the nearest shelter. You will notice whenever *you arrive at any of these destinations that they are all different. It is a manner of instinct.*

Survival skills are an important factor of this journey to defeat this Hollywood machine. For one, you do not want to create a riot. You do not want to get caught in anything that can harm you. When you first start out, you must be ready. You must always be ready. Patience is to be used at every obstacle. It is important that you keep a close distance between yourselves. If anything happens, then, there would be a reason to worry, but basic survival skills are necessary. For your purpose, your backpacks also have the necessary survival tools packed into a very convenient located, and are in a different compartment than the weapons. As you already know, your backpack is the basic military issue, and if that wasn't made aware to you then I apologize. Your backpack has two large compartments, both are divided with their own zippers. The first compartment, or the rear compartment, contains your weapons in a capsule form. The second compartment, or the front compartment, contains food and beverages in pouches. Then, there are two side compartments on each side and three other compartments that are in the front.

For your purpose, the two side compartments on each side holds a knife, a whistle, a fire starter, matches, a flash light, and a small compass. The three compartments in front consist of maps, mirrors, a compact satellite phone, a drinking flask, and a state of the art survival kit. Keep all of these items as they might be necessary, as you might encounter something.

As per obstacles and unintended objects that might target you, there is a few things to know. When you first encounter something, you must realize that it could either be friendly or evil. If the object or thing is small, it is probably some evil creature. Sure, it might look cute, but it is in fact deceptive. Large creatures are actually friendly. You must remember that none of these creatures are good, because they are all evil. One thing that might seem hypocritical is that of the niceness or meanness, but even though they show different emotions, trust nothing. Everything that you encounter might be the enemy. You are facing some very dangerous situations. You could encounter IEDs or other things that explode. Be careful of everything. Terrorism can be anywhere you encounter. It is something to remember that you must determine what will happen.

Lastly, as you prepare to survive on this journey, remember, everything can cause chaos. You should know that there is a reason why you have gotten so far. You must realize that civilization is everything to the rest of the world. Everything is meant to have a life, and it is important to try.

Conclusion

Let's review some basics, you are on this mission to defeat the Hollywood machine, you are going to 1986 to prevent an alternate dimension from being created, and you are to ensure the longevity of a peaceful transition for a government that supports freedom. You might not know what you are looking for, but you must wait. When you arrive, you should wait for a parade. Now, you might arrive in some of those random locations, and there is a chance that the parade already concluded. If this ever happens, you can reset your time watches, and you will be back on course. When you finally arrive in New York City, remember the parade. There will be members of the Hollywood machine waiting to cause chaos.

After the parade begins, there is a good chance that people will start shooting or burning down buildings. These people who are causing these things are members of the Hollywood machine, and they must be stopped. You should shoot back. You should treat everything as suspicious activity, as you will not know who is the enemy. There might be people who are against you and there are people who think you might be crazy.

Now that we have covered the basics, it is important to

know that some people might put a target on your head. In order to prevent the Hollywood machine from becoming too powerful, you must destroy their building in New York City. You must burn everything that is connected to them. It is important to know that they might think something is happening, but they will try to escape. Remember, there are things that the Hollywood machine can do that will amaze you, but you are to ignore everything. You might end up in a trap, or you could end up dying. Whatever happens, know one thing, if you succeed, you will automatically return to the year 2006, but if you fail, you will end up at the HEPTAGON. There is also the possibility that if you succeed you will end up in the year 2006, but there could be chaos, in which you might be automatically transported back to the HEPTAGON. As everything can be classified as chaos, you might be surprised. There could also be the possibility that even though you succeed you might end up back at the HEPTAGON.

Remember this, everyone is counting on you. You could be the last hope for civilization. Always stay focused, as there will always be constant distractions.

Good luck,
Your Instructors

After a while, the note seemed too explanatory and possibly repetitive, but that could be for a possible reason to determine quality control. Everything became normal, as it was supposed to be normal. Today is the last day of training and it should be a breeze. Without a doubt, there is nothing that can stop anything.

Fast forward later in the afternoon today, where each of the girls are walking out of the showers naked with water dripping down their bodies, heading to the dryers, and after that they will do something. Time has flown by so quickly in these last twelve months, as it only seemed like it was just yesterday that something happened. It could be a matter of fun or it could just be a coincidence. Whatever the issue, there seems to be an overwhelming support for anything that might happen tomorrow.

Everything happens quickly, and like that, it the last day of training is over. Tomorrow the girls are headed off to the year 1986, and whatever they find, they are sure to find something relevant, or at least there will be something in the fields of relevance. Just like that, it is almost curfew, and to that point, the girls are not that tired, but they head up to their rooms to get ready for tomorrow. It is going to be a new day, and nothing might ever be the same, so there is a reason for anything.

The next morning arrives. The automatic alarm clock wakes up the girls at 0645 hours and will not turn off until they wake up. It is now time to get prepared, where they must get suited. But first, they have to take care of their personal hygiene, where it is a must that nothing is dirty. One be one, they each take a shower in their own bathrooms, all at the same time. After that, they all take care of their other needs. It is something that is relevant to the mission. Now, it is time to get suited.

One by one, all at the same time, each of the girls prepare to get suited. First the bra and panties, then the tank top. Then comes the vest, the jacket, and the pants. Now that all the basic garments are on, the utility belt is attached and finally the boots. This took about one hour to complete, and just like that, it is now time to grab the back pack in the closet. Now, each girl, for the last time, locks the door behind them, and they head to the lobby to get their individual time watch.

Five minutes remain until the reporting deadline, and it just happens like that. All girls are suited up with all of the essential equipment they need. It is now time to wait. This could be a while, but there is a possibility that it could just happen instantly. There is the case of being sent to a random location, but nothing is sure yet. It is a matter of life or death, and as people make decisions, something must happen, for the reason that might make sense might lead to an epic disaster for no reason at all. It is a reason that there could be something related to the destruction of humanity, but there could be something wrong with the rest of civilization. For all hope, there is a reason to succeed, and there is a reason to decide. There is something else that could explain the reason to demonstrate nothing.

Everything depends on the essential need to survive, and if something happens, it is the reason to demonstrate the willingness to defend the world, as there could be something wrong with civilization. There is something that must wait, for the time is now.

Three minutes later, and the portal starts to appear, and all of them enter at once. It is now the time of no return, but each can return with the time watch, if anything happens. There could be a cause to alarm, as something terrible could be happening right now. No one will know what is happening but there is a theory of deceit. The girls are now time traveling to the past, but something just doesn't feel right. It could seem that something bad has happened, but that might be something else. Alas, the girls finally arrive, only to notice they are in a tropical paradise. The girls have arrived at a random location, the one in Mexico, and they must figure a way to get out of here fast. There is a possibility that it will lead to defeat, but something drastic happens, as they now see some sort of android, and it is firing lasers, so now, they must escape, so the girls try to activate their time watches, only to find out that it takes time. The time watch takes them to China, then spits them out in the middle of the Gobi Desert. It is hot, and then there is a time shift, which takes them to the northern part of China, where everything is freezing. The girls try again to activate the portal by their time watches, and it takes them to New Zealand, in the middle of an island.

Immediately, the girls knows that something is wrong, and they try one more time, and finally, it takes them to their intended destination, New York City. The parade is only a few hours away. It is almost time to defeat the Hollywood machine. While it might not be definite to handle the situation until there is something happening, it is a sign of competence to show that there is a reason behind something. At the most, there is a time to think of the past. There is a reason to know the fate of everything else. It is part of your destiny to understand life.

Minutes start to pass, and nothing will be left, until there is something to think about. Now, hours later, the parade starts. It is very noisy, and what seems to be a normal occurrence. There is something sort of nothing, but this is usual, even for parades. Parades usually cause a lot of attention, leading to certain riots and causing chaos, but only if people start it. Nothing seems unusual yet, as it is still early. The parade has only started about a minute ago, and it is still early for any commotion to start. It is with the most distinct opinion that the members of the Hollywood machine are still waiting for a particular event to occur. It is a sign that it must be well orchestrated, something that might have meaning to the rest of the world. There is nothing that will cause the demise of something unless it has been initiated. There is reason to believe that something is currently being initiated in order to start chaos.

After it was apparent, something still believes it will never happen, but you should never rule out anything, as it could always be misinformation, a relevant task to believe when something must be hidden from the public. It is a sign that must show disregard to freedom as well as the pure and simple act of censorship. It is promoted by censorship, as a reason to stop freedom and to promote propaganda, in a way that seems outrageous to everyone, while the very few that still support it. There is a reason for this puppet master theory, as it does make sense to the belief that something will strike at once. There is nothing sort of short that will lead to something other than a disarray of hope. It is something that must be curtailed, with the hope that it must be prevented, in a way that must support freedom, in order to end this type of process that constantly supports propaganda and censorship. It is nothing new, as it was used before, so there is something that is the reason to support the theory of the ending of something that must be relevant to something, but it must be the opposite of everything else. It is the process that this entire theory is in the hopes of nothing other than the belief of a bunch of nonsense. It is the sign that must be heard, as it is the reason that something is always happening. There is always the theory of an inevitable event, and this might occur because of anything.

Inevitability has been awkward in recent years, as

it could have been prevented, but certain people refused to compromise the entire situation. It is part of life, but that is nothing new. To the effect of something might happen, well, that is always the case, as something is always going to happen, and to put it that way, there is a reason why there must be chaos always happening. It is in fact because chaos thrives on unexpected events in history, which demonstrates the meaning to everything. It is nothing short of crazy, but that is nothing new.

As a way to deter anything from happening, there is a reason why the parade is happening, to celebrate the new life of the United States of America. It is part of life that might change something. It is part of the never-ending conflict between freedom and censorship. It will help everything in order to promote freedom. This is not the end of the world like most people think. It is part of the process to structure the focus of policy, to seek new leadership, under an era of new time, and it is by that account, that it is the reason to celebrate the period of the pursuit of happiness, as it relates to a better environment to live in. It is simply part of life, and it needs to start.

Within the last few hours, many things have occurred, but this parade is almost over. There is some sort of hesitation on the part of the Hollywood machine. It might not even happen at all. Something could happen soon, but it is still calm, with no riots taking place. Everything is calm as well as peaceful, so there is nothing else to expect, or you could think otherwise. It might be a coincident, but they must be waiting for something. With only five minutes left, the parade is almost over, but the last float ends with a breeze, so, there is the case that the enemy forgot about the whole situation, but that would not be the case at all, if you know about life.

Instead, after the parade ended, there was chaos. People started firing guns. The gun fire was loud, and many people started to scream and shout. It sounded like it was from a movie, but it actually did happen. The Hollywood machine wanted to make sure that the parade finished in order to launch their attack. They did that in order to let people watch something, so that their experienced would not be ruined. It was a mastered plan, well-orchestrated, in order to demonstrate a high rate of competence. It was the reason why it was excellent.

Well, people started to scream and panic. No one knew who was doing what. The girls tried to find the people who fired the guns. It is something that was apparent, but there could be something wrong. The perpetrators could have escaped, but they were hiding in plain sight. It is a sign to understand, to take a chance that something might never happen. It could happen to anyone, in any point in time, and it must be the reason why something is always random to cause chaos and riots.

Soon, yet enough, Erica spots a person with a gun, and she shoots him, but he escapes. The suspect later falls over, but gets up, only to fall down and die later, within minutes. When the parade goers see this person die, they start to panic more, as they believe something is after all of them. It is a sign of weakness.

Whatever happens might show signs of radical new improvement, but nothing happens yet. Nothing is in the mood for anything. As people start to run in fear, there is more chaos. There are hordes of people running away, causing people to be trampled on, leading to injuries. It is mass chaos. More shots are fired, and there is more chaos.

People are afraid of what is happening, but there is a good chance that it will not end. It is a cause for an alarm, a meaning for something that makes sense but actually lacks the authority of something. When something happens, it could seriously impact the weight of the program, yet, there is proof it does absolutely nothing, so there is a reason why there is never any help.

Focusing on something like this parade is simple yet complex, to the point that something does not even make sense to the highest power. As the girls try to figure out what is happening, something happens, but everything is the same. The girls shoot more at suspected members of the Hollywood machine. More fear is present, like it is new to everyone. It is nothing new, but people are acting like idiots, where everything is irrelevant. The situation is seen as a complete disaster to everyone. It is seen like there is nothing wrong. Another person suddenly dies, and it is a member of the Hollywood machine. People are outraged, but they are the true cause of the riots. The people are starting to burn down buildings, start fires, and cause damage to every structure they see. It is seen as a cause to show some demonstration, but this is not a demonstration, this is a riot, filled with chaos and everything else that promotes the destruction of civilization. It is part of something that needs to end. It is dangerous.

Most people are still running scared. No one can stop the people causing damage. It is impossible to stop. People will always be afraid of anything, especially if they do not face any danger. It is something that never makes any sense. Even when people see a building being burned down, they act as if they are in imminent danger, even though they know they are nowhere near the proximity of the location. So it makes sense to those people, but in life, it makes no sense to anything.

As chaos starts to close the streets of the city, it looks like it will never end, but there could be a reason to end this situation. There should be something that will happen, and it should be part of everyday life. It is a part of life that needs to make sense. It is something that has always been present, but there is nothing new that will demonstrate anything, so it is old news. Chaos and riots are nothing new, but as they rage on in New York City, there is a sign that keeps a distance between everything. If something bad happens, there is no one responsible, yet the real thing is the basis for culture, and as it appears, it has been attacked to support propaganda.

Regarding about anything, there is a solution to solve anything, but the existence is mired in deep trouble, along with crazy people who have no hope for anything. As many people still die, there is still a way to admire the situation as a matter of life or death, but the near solution is nothing new, so it must be taken seriously. It is a time when there must be some action. There is a reason to take a stand, as it might be necessary. It is important to state the fact rather than the opinions, as opinions lead to propaganda, but that is not always the case.

Everything is in danger, danger of the populace, danger of chaos, and anything that relates to a crisis in hand. There is something that must be done, and it is important to realize that it must be realize, for the reason is to support the true hero of something that leads to overall freedom. There is something that will make sense, as it might take time to realize the entire situation. It is a crisis to take action, the time when it is needed the most.

There is a reason to admire the true appreciation of freedom. It is a sign of respect. It is something that constantly makes sense. It needs to happen now, as it relates to the rest of the world. It is part of the whole society, as it makes sense towards the meaning of life. There is something that always make sense. Something seems right about this, as it should make sense. There is nothing wrong with freedom.

Chaos and riots continue on the streets of New York City. Suddenly, something happens. There is a time shift that takes the girls to Mexico. So now, something is wrong, as they are trapped in Mexico and are attempting to head back to the United States of America. Something could be wrong with the time watches as they are not working. It could be a sign of sabotage, but no one ever touched them, except for the girls. It is a sign that must mean something. They are not in 1986 anymore, they are in the present day of a tropical island paradise.

It was clear that something went wrong. When something goes wrong it usually means something is in danger, and this danger has effects on the entire global impact of people. It is the sign that mentions nothing but the radicalization of idiots. People need to realize nothing as it is in the midst of something new, and there is the way to solve the idea of something that has nothing but considerable attacks upon the nation of the state. It is the reason that happens to be nothing short of the reason behind the real issues of the day.

There are two paths that are spotted by the girls, and they must decide which one to take. These are basically a fork in the road, but no one knows what it is actually for. There are claims by the natives that it is meant for witchcraft, in which the devil is responsible for everything. Other people have claim that these two paths lead to happiness and fun. And then, there are those who say it leads to nowhere, that you are just going to walk in circles, but you think you are walking in a straight line. Looks can be very deceiving, as they are always confusing. You never know what is going to happen to your life. You are stranded in the middle of nowhere in a tropical paradise of the beach in Mexico. One thing you might ask is how is it possible there is a road in the middle in the beach, and well, the answer might surprise you, as it is a sign of mystery.

Amelia, Alison, and Elizabeth take the northern path, while Melissa and Erica take the southern path, both hoping to find something to escape. What leads to something strange must come from somewhere. It is a sign that is very apparent in nature. So, on the northern path, it seems usually normal, and there are trees, animals, and other fauna, along with other foliage. It is a sign of growth, something that was meant to indicate that there is a reason to indicate that there is something right with the system. On the southern path though, you thought it would be different, however, it is exactly the same, a carbon copy of sorts. While this might sound strange, it might be exactly the same thing. Both paths could lead to the same location. It could happen, as it has previously did occur. What happens next might surprise you, as both paths lead to a dead end. The girls are reunited at the end of the paths, even though they were going in different directions. This entire situation could have been a crazy distraction that was supposed to do nothing. Well, there is a sort of strange activity, something that is not supposed to occur in the midst of a journey. It is a sign that has yet to be the center of attention. As long as something is happening, it might occur.

So, there is now a chance to figure something out. There is a strong chance that the girls will walk past the dead end, and so, as they were curious, they all decided to walk past the dead end, all while they had to cross high weeds and other nuisance plants that seemed agitated. Something very mysterious is happening, and it is leading to something that might sound strange, but it is not on the course of what might be expected. What happens next will surprise you, as it should be a surprise.

After crossing these wild plants, the girls come across some sort of old Mayan pyramid. It seems old and rundown, with no one in sight. It might as well be haunted or could display something that is not common in nature. It is part of something larger, maybe some sort of conspiracy. It should be worthwhile to identify the meaning of this object, as it could be beneficial to the entire investigation. There is a chance that this is nothing sort of new. It was hidden in a secret, yet mysterious location. There is some type of thrill behind this object. It is something that you should never venture alone.

Theories, results, and everything else, well that is the reason behind everything, as it relates to a complication in society, but this pyramid is not a complication, rather it is a sign that they must enter. So, without hesitation, the girls enter the pyramid, and they see torches on the sides of the walls, and so, they each grab one, but they still need fire, so they get out a fire starter from their backpack. The fire starter lights up each torch into a thin yet strong flame. It will help guide them to the mysterious path, and it could lead to the destruction of the Hollywood machine. There is no knowing where this pyramid will lead the girls, and as it might be expected, there is a cause for action. There is a reason to determine mystery.

Long winding tunnels, leading to dead ends and alternate paths, as well as crazy and strange objects. There are mysterious objects within this old, unstable building. There are writings on the walls, telling about families who faced misfortunes as well as opportunities. It is a sign that must lead to something, as this pyramid is starting to have a funny feeling to it.

Complete darkness, nothing but shadows appearing on the floors. It is completely dark. The only light emitting is that of the torches. No one can escape it, as it is located everywhere. There is nothing that you can do to stop this from spreading. Everywhere they go, it is a hidden turn. It is a very long passage. No one knows where they are going, as this is the first time they had ventured out to this mysterious place. It is surely filled with mystery, but there is something to this interesting journey. There is something that is new to this escapade, as there seems to be a familiarity to this entire situation. It seems that people might have traveled here before.

Paths have been crossed and it has been clearly displayed in order to determine the precise determination of the century. Sure, it is simply a debate of the past, but there is an increasing sign to promote nothing. Amelia sees the end of darkness. Light is in sight, as the journey is almost over. It looks like it is very close to the end of a tunnel. Something seems a bit tedious, as there is sense to discover something that made sense before. The theory of the sign is, is that if it is light, then it might be light, because the end of the tunnel should be near. It should never be taken seriously because it is not meant to justify anything. It is simply something that was meant to decide some fun.

Without a doubt, there seems to be something that has always been courageous, as traveling through a damp, yet dark tunnel in a pyramid sounds insane. It probably is insane, let alone everything you might end up finding. There is no risk of joining something, other than to neglect the very clear tactic of handling a situation.

Clearly, or whatever you believe, there seems to be something wrong with the picture, but nothing is ever in the spotlight because it previously controlled the spotlight. To the point of something that was meant to destroy something there is nothing that was meant to determine the precise goal of the theory. There is never any just theory as it clearly just promotes censorship and propaganda, but by the reason of insanity it could be the reason to destroy the end of the civilization. It must be the reality that must take place. It is the reason why stuff exists. For the same exact reason that is the theory of evolution, there is nothing wrong with how life evolved. There is the theory that there is the complex civilization that promotes everything else. It is nothing but the reason except the fact to control life. This event must be prevented in order to restore the faith in humanity. It is a sign that is best suited for the notion of developing nations, and by this act, there is time to mention nothing other than pseudo tactics of why there is nothing other than the sheer place of confusion.

At last, the girls finally see the end of the tunnel,

or whatever it was in the pyramid, after nearly ten minutes of noticing. It took some time, but it might not be the end, as the end is nigh. The end of this tunnel in this pyramid is not something new, as it was used before, but no one ever found out the reason to establish such a cave like building. It is now the end of darkness, as the girls start to approach something new. Now, it is time that they finally exist this long journey of not knowing where it could take them.

Exiting the tunnel was finally a success, but it seemed daunting, as after they all arrived in the presence of the new light, something happened. There was a collapse, and it sounded like the pyramid. Looking behind, Alison realized that the door disappeared behind them. This was a strange situation, as it seemed familiar, but the ending might not be over. It could be that the reason to exit caused some structural deficiencies, but who would ever agree to that, as people have always objected to that type of sentiment. It is a sign that was meant to promote. The real story is where are the girls and are they safe. Well, the girls are safe, but now it looks like they are in some type of glass house with foliage in every direction. Of course, the building is enclosed, so, they are safe, but something else might happen. Their time watches tells them that they are located in Canadian wilderness.

So now it even gets more stranger, as how could you travel from Mexico to Canada in a very short distance, well it could be explained by these shoes that they are wearing, which can travel at fast speeds, but they are specially modified to prevent you from finding out. It makes perfect sense but they still have no clue about what happened, and they must try to find a way back to New York City. One more time, the girls try to activate the time portal again by using the time watches, but nothing happens. It would probably mean that they are stuck here, or it could lead to a complete disaster. There is nothing that could happen, so there is a reason to be afraid. There is a way to escape but there is also a way out of this building. There is some type of crazy event that is happening. It is surely perfect timing for everything to happen. It is a result of mysterious, yet strange events of history.

Noticing a door, maybe a way out to exit this glass building, the girls use it, only to find nothing but a weapons room. It seems like the outside is near, but that is just an illusion, in order to fool people. People think it is a glass house, and it is, but on the inside, as well as the outside of the building, there is a cloak that makes it seems the entire place is see through. It is built as a protective system to fool them, in order to prevent intrusion. So now, there is the question of how something finally exits this building, and it must be known now.

Now, there is a way out, and Erica found it. Right in front of Elizabeth was a door, and Erica saw it and then opened it. There is now a sigh of relief, as there is now a reason to think something is going in the right direction. After exiting the door, the girls finally are outside in the deep forests of Canadian wilderness, but the door then disappears behind them, like magic. It shocks no one now, and they must find a way out, or so they think. The Canadian wilderness can be a strange place, as it was reported that zombies could live here. There were reports of zombie attacks in recent years, but no one ever found that to be true, and if they did, they probably never escaped. It was a sign that could mean nothing.

Outside, in the open wilderness, the girls start to hear strange noises, as it could be anything. It could also be a zombie attack or even a wild animal. There was sound, and this was the result of different noises. It sounded like many different creatures, but no one even knows what it was to begin with. As the girls continue to explore this wilderness, something starts to appear, but is moving within the bushes. The girls split up, hoping to find what is going on around them, and as a result, this could have some consequences, it could mean that something is watching them, or something is the result of the overall meaning of life. Something might attack, or it seems that something is making an attempt to scare them.

After three fours of roaming the wilderness, there is something that happens. Someone is in need of help, and there is a loud scream. Alison is near, and is the first one to help, but something happens to her. Instead of what might make sense, there is something else that might be the result of something. It is a crazy and strange experience. The person screaming for help does not need any help, and instead, he tricks Alison or anyone could help him, as a way to mislead people. The alleged person in distress was hoping it was a female who helped him, so he could actually do something. When Alison is not looking, the person gets up and headlocks Alison, forcing her on the ground, and then ripping her clothes off with his hands. Now since that happens, he attempts to sexually assault her, and he does, but Alison enjoys it, and in doing so, she actually kills him by playing along. Alison decides to kill him when his eyes starts to close, and in doing so, it is nothing short of crazy yet exhilarating. Alison rips off the head of the person and it is revealed to be an android invented by the Hollywood machine. It could be just be a coincidence, but the thing behind the motivation to try to forcefully have sex with someone is nothing new. This android was just a creep looking for attention, but there was something wrong, the victim actually enjoyed it, but then decided to take matters in her own hands. There is a possibility that something else could happen, and as it makes more sense, there is something that makes sense.

Without anything contributing to the entire factor of existence, all things can be the result of a death. It is the result that makes people the statistics of life. It is the theory that motivate haters of all types. Reforming civilization is always happening, and it is by the distance of the future that something must happen. It is the result that must be changed in order to control the situation. There must be something that controls the situation, in order to stand up to the rest of the statistics.

Now that the person or android is dead, Alison gets up. She is completely naked and exposed to the wilderness, since her clothes had been ripped, yet some portions are still on her body. It is her back and front that are exposed. Her ass, boobs, and pelvic area can be seen. It is something different because it is different. Now that she is standing, Alison needs to clean herself off, and so, she is in need of finding a shelter, and the time watch tells her it is five minutes away, so, for five minutes, Alison walks barefoot and partially naked, and completed exposed to the entire Canadian wilderness. Her body is exposed to the extreme winds. There is a slight breeze, and it is feeling like it wants to start a war, but that is nothing new, as it is normal when the wind wants to do that. For five minutes, it is nothing but a cool and breezy environment, even though it is still part of the summer cycles. There is something important to this case, as it must be careful, otherwise the people involved must decide to do something. There are cases for an easy way out.

Anyway, Alison finds the shelter, and it looks eerie familiar. Actually, it is just a small log cabin, but it has a complete shower facilities and everything else that is part of a house. It might look small on the outside, but it is actually extremely large, since everything important is entirely underground, just for security purposes. Alison decides to enter, hoping to find something. The door shuts behind her and makes a loud bang as she enters the log cabin. She looks for a place to shower, and possibly new clothes to war, and maybe similar or the same as that were torn off of her body. A draft is felt, but that is just the air. It seems like a view of the past, or something irrelevant. It is a sign that there could be a poltergeist here, but there is no proof of anything, as there is no reason to believe anything. Alison finds a bathroom, after taking stairs down to one level, and she sees that it is open. She removes the remains of her torn clothes and places them on the floor. From there, Alison takes off all of her accessories so they don't get damaged, and then she cleans herself off from all the dirt and other substances that were on her body.

It literally takes half an hour to complete the shower, as some of the dirt is extremely sticky because of water and tree sap. The water pressure is also very low, and that could be the result of terrible maintenance or age. At any rate, now Alison now has to find some clothes, which she has to walk completely naked, probably dripping wet, because there are no towels in sight. It takes about ten minutes to find some sort of closet, and she opens the doors, revealing that the clothes she was wearing was similar in nature. So, Alison puts on some panties, a bra, a tank top, a vest, a jacket, pants, a belt, and boots. In fact, it is exactly the same clothes that it makes this place feel strange and weird. There is also a backpack in the closet, and so, Alison grabs it and leaves the other one behind.

Soon after that, Alison grabs her time watch in order to find a way out. Now that Alison is better suited to handle something after this strange incident, she goes back outside. All of the girls are split up, but there could be a reason for this. As Alison is leaving this log cabin, Erica enters, and somehow her clothes had been ripped by something. Well, the clothes of Erica were ripped and torn because she went under some bush that a piece of thread got caught in. That thread later resulted in a rip, and revealing her pristine body. Don't be fooled, because these bushes in the Canadian wilderness are extremely powerful. Some have claimed that they are alive and are constantly assaulting people. So, now that Erica is exposed. As Erica wanders around the cabin, she hears a noise, but that is only Alison. Erica does not know that another person has been here, and so, Erica must now get some new clothes, after she realized that the bush ripped up her current clothes. Erica finds a bathroom and she takes a shower, then finds a closet. Erica puts on new clothes after taking a shower. It is the same closet that Alison was in a few minutes ago. So, Erica is now fully geared up, she now heads to the kitchen, but finds nothing. Erica only came to this log cabin looking for something to eat. Failing to find some food, Erica leaves, shutting the door loudly. Erica goes back to find a way out of this wilderness, and by chance, she looks for clues.

After Erica leaves, Amelia finds this same log cabin, five minutes after, but out of nowhere, she is zapped from the sky. Her clothes are now missing, so she sees this cabin ahead and opens the door to find new clothes. Amelia immediately sees a bathroom, and decides to take a shower, because she feels dirty, and not just from the wind, but from this strange incident that happened. After taking a shower, Amelia walks completely naked to find a closet, and to put on the same gear as Alison and Erica previously did before leaving this cabin.

Ten minutes pass, and Elizabeth finds this cabin, only to have her clothes ripped off by some wolf. She is completely naked and sees the door to the cabin, and then finds the bathroom to take a shower. It takes about fifteen minutes to complete her shower, then she walks completely naked to a closet to find some clothes. She finds the closet, but is interrupted by a strange noise, coming from the front of the cabin. Somehow, Melissa found the cabin, but before she entered, the wind decided to strip her naked. Anyway, Elizabeth ignores the noise, but notices that she is still dirty, so she decides to go back to take a shower. With that in mind, Melissa enters the cabin, and finds the bathroom door, and it is not closed. Melissa hears water, and sees Elizabeth naked, taking a shower. Elizabeth starts to notice Melissa, and finds it strange, and Melissa takes off any remaining parts of her clothes, in order to shower with Elizabeth. It is nothing new, but it has been a very strange day, for the reason of something else.

Elizabeth and Melissa start to pleasure each other in the shower, and it is a sensual and sexual experience. It is something that is meant to be private, but the door is opened to the bathroom. The girls start to climax to each other, revealing moaning and pants. It is an excited experience, as well as a mutual friendship. They continue to climax until they have reached an orgasm, in order to feel the most sensual thing possible. After several minutes have passed, they rinse off and head to the closet, completely naked, and dripping wet, to put some clothes on. Now that they are inside the closet, they see the necessary clothing and put it on. After that, they try to find a door, hoping to find their way out of this Canadian wilderness. It is something that was strange. But, now that Melissa and Elizabeth are in their group, they still have to find Amelia, Alison, and Erica, because they are on their own. It is something that could be dangerous in the near future. It is something that is a part of everyday life.

Now that Melissa and Elizabeth are ready to leave, they get all of their other stuff, resulting them in finally exiting the log cabin. Everything is the same, and it is the exact same thing that everyone sees. There are still tall trees and other foliage present. Everybody is still in this vast Canadian wilderness, to which no one knows how they got there, but it is surely a mystery. It is a time to understand that not everything is the same. Everything about this place. It is life that must matter, and it continues to grow in a vast community of plants and creature. As anyone would have expected, there is something else to this nature event of how life is controlled but that is a different story, it is an event that is never to be mentioned, as long as there is life present, a case by case basis that demonstrates courage, to the idea of something important.

Ideologues are constantly changing, and they must

in order to keep with the times, but there are reasons why there are times when there is a constant plague. There is nothing else that can be done, but there is a course for action. There is a time to set aside and to be motivated. It is the time that must be constant in order to change. It is the reason that must be different in order to secure the benefits of the idea of something other than society. It has all the appearances of the thing that you might imagine, but just as you take sense, they will continue to motivate the simplistic plan of the way people live.

Globalization, the way of the future, is the same type of nonsense that can harm people. It is the same reason why there is the reason to kill it. It is a threat and helps the thing of the future. It is the time when there must be change, and the way that must be motivated to achieve the dream of the past, in order to achieve the future. There is something that must change, for the safety of something that needs to make sense. It is something that must make sense, to the same type of civilization that has no idea of what is happening. There must be a hearing, something that must be the reason to understand society.

Without anything, there is the possibility of something bad happening, to the point that there is the reason to maintain the period of hope. It is described as the feeling of something that has no hope. It is part of life, the part where society and civilization form the landscape of the complete economy. It is the complex form of life that must be maintained in a unique atmosphere. It is part of the new thing of the past, and it is constantly evolving, to the extent of new freedom.

Civilization is changing, but this Canadian wilderness has been here since eternity. It is a very mysterious place, as you should already know. It is a sign that something will happen, as it was meant to happen, so as the saying goes, there is always time to achieve your dreams, but there is a reason to navigate with patience. There is a reason for this, and it has to be used carefully, otherwise there will be a constant problem in the eyes of your ancestors. It is the time when deceit is powerful, and it needs to be battled. Plague will end up killing everything, and it would be the result of a lack of sanitation. Before clean water, everybody just dumped their waste on the ground below, and that caused all kinds of diseases, particularly diseases that will kill you if you don't get medical treatment. That is why you must already sanitize yourself, as you can kill the bacteria and viruses to prevent any illness. It is something that was meant to help you but people are afraid of everything these days. It is time to know that there is a time to achieve. There is a goal in mind to offset the situation.

So, what happens, well, there is something that might sound strange, but there is probably no way out of this wilderness in Canada. The only reason they know why they are in Canada is because of a time watch. Out of nowhere, there could be something that will happen soon. It could be something that makes sense, or it could be something that has issues. Either way there is a chance it could be something that is deadly. It is something that you do not want to mess with, as there could be dire consequences. There are reasons why this stuff happens, and that is why it must stop from happening in the future.

Suddenly, there is a noise. It is the noise of swaying leaves on trees. It is present that something is happening, but it might just be the wind. There is another sound, and it seems like there is movement in the bushes. There is the time to think about what is happening, as it is time to navigate the situation of the past, recalling your footsteps. It is time to signify the absolute truth about what is happening, for the future to be bright. Melissa and Elizabeth here a noise coming from the bushes, and they believe it could be a rabbit or some other furry creature. So now, the thing or object reveals itself, only to be identified as Erica. Now that Erica has found two of her friends, they can be happy together, but Melissa and Elizabeth only stopped walking because of the noise coming from the bushes. So now, Erica, Elizabeth, and Melissa all tell each other about the log cabin that they found in the wilderness, and how their clothes were torn off their bodies. Out of the bushes, Alison appears, and tells everyone how some creep perverted android sexually assaulted her, and how she killed him. Now that only one is missing in the wilderness, they walk so that they can find Amelia. It is probably that Amelia is looking to find a way out of this crazy place.

After half an hour, Alison, Melissa, Erica, and Elizabeth stop to rest. Then, a noise is heard from the leaves of the bushes. It is a surprise waiting to happen, as the thing appears. It is revealed to be Amelia. Now that the girls are all united, they ask each other questions and tell them about the log cabin they found in the wilderness. It is something that is mysterious, something that doesn't even make sense. They all concluded that they were completely naked, front and back, but with some clothes remaining on their legs and arms, when they entered the cabin. This sounds mysterious, as they now concluded that it was a requirement to be naked to enter the cabin, but they are also surprised that they found the same type of clothing that was in the HEPTAGON. It could be strange, but it could be that this log cabin is part of an elite camp to secure people from abnormal threats. It is rather by chance that they all found the same exact building, and by that, the way they imagined that something like this would ever happen. The full force is now happening, as there is a sudden realization that something isn't right in this place. It is a sign that something is expected, but no one knows what that is, because there is a chance that it could lead to something that does not even make sense. It is something that now starts to make sense, and as it relates to the past, it might be related to the future. There is the realization that a bad thing will start to happen, as it might precede something else, but to that extent, there is a need to investigate this something, as there is no knowing of what is hiding in the bushes. It could be something dangerous or something cute, but everything in this wilderness can deceive you, as not all life forms are capable of being nice. If you expected that, well, it could be a lack of realization. It is just a part of life and something that needs to make sense, as it does make sense to figure out the best tactic. What one person might believe could be the exact opposite to the person standing right next to you. Complete nonsense, as you would say, but that is how life works. Life is a very complex thing and if you don't comply with it there is a good chance that you will fail, and this might lead to certain distractions that might call your beliefs into question. It is simply a thought for discussion, a way to realize what might happen, and a way to determine the exact case of happiness. It is the time that might show the differences between good and bad, the thing that might make sense but it never does, but that exact reason is to be the true focus of anything, even when it never makes sense, as there is no reason to understand anything. There is simply no idea that is unique to everything, as it must make sense to the whole world. This idea is flawed and it must be fixed, so that it doesn't confuse people. There is a reason why this happens and it is the reason to determine anything, so there can be some peace.

The road to civilization is a confusing one, and it will probably never make any sense, to the point that must be a never-ending relationship with your neighbors. As people start to realize, there is a reason why everything happens, and it can occur because of beliefs, but there are no beliefs in this Canadian wilderness, since it is the reason why everything happens for a reason. The Canadian wilderness is a place of deceit, and you should already know this, but if you don't, then there is a reason for an excuse. With all of the things that are happening, it might sound fine to just forget why you are even here. It is the reason that surprises everyone, as there is no reason to support anything. People must be able to maintain their lives, as a way to survive, in order to gather a reason why there is time to answer the precise meaning in life. There is a shortcut, but shortcuts lead to deceit, and you must be able to navigate the entire situation. Shortcuts are only to be used by professionals, specifically, immortals, people who can't die but can choose when they want to die. It sounds confusing because that is how it is supposed to sound, so stop your complaining. It is the real meaning of what life was meant to be and it shall be the focus of anything that is part of the cycle of civilization. It is the form for which you must maintain and understand, and it is to be used sparingly, in order to maintain something that is very limited in nature. It is something that you do not want to mess with, as altercations will lead to the reason why you are presently here.

Without fear there is no life.

There is no life to understand, and it is not clear.

People must understand, and they must handle with sanity. It is a case to solve the meaning of life. It is the reason why there is no life but life. It is the reason why this place in Canada is so deceitful, and it is the reason why something must happen in order to stop the time of a global power that makes no sense.

Out of nowhere, there is a loud sound, and the girls can hear footsteps. It could be anything, and it could be that there is a possible attack. There is something that could happen. The creatures must reveal themselves, as it would be a waste of time. More footsteps can he heard from the exact opposite directions. It could be that something is trying to surround the girls, since this part of the Canadian wilderness is packed with vast bushes and other foliage. There is only a single path marked in sand, for this section of this crazy place. It is completely surrounded by nothing but mass foliage, and this is where people might die. For the rest of the purpose, nothing might happen, but it will happen, since it is the reason to think.

As the sounds and footsteps near the girls, they believe something is about to happen. Then, something comes out of the bushes, and it looks like to be a zombie, and so, the girls activate their guns, but as they kill one, the rest of them keep appearing. One by one, it appears that they are multiplying by the dozens, hundreds, and then thousands. It appears that they are increasing in size at a way that seems impossible.

The girls keep firing their guns, but nothing happens to remove them all. They now know that they must run while they are shooting their guns, with their heads turned facing the zombies in a sideward position. They can stop, but then they must continue to run. It was utter madness. Where was everybody, and where was the backup. There is no back up, as everybody who is supposed to help is currently present. There must be something wrong with this scenario, as you usually see more people coming out of nowhere, well this isn't that scenario, because that scenario is always fake. This scenario is real and it is part of life. It is what is different between everything else and it must demonstrate the aspects about life.

Carefully shooting to avoid any injuries, the girls continue to shoot at these zombies. It seems like they won't disappear as it appears that they must be modified out of something. They could be zombie androids, but they should have been killed already. It is something that makes no sense at all. It is a complete surprise and it might end in disaster. If anything happens, then there could be a collapse of the entire civilization, which could cause the entire society to eventually die off. This situation would tend to get more dangerous as it continues to grow. There is no stopping of anything, and it might not even make sense. It is what the meaning of life might stand for but it is the reason that could cause the entire blow of the century. This can only have one outcome, and a bad one at that, if nothing is done to stop these zombies from attacking. It could be that something is happening but that is the current situation.

Running in circles, that is the point of the very well-known objective, well, that could be this case, but there must be a reason why. There is a reason why this might happen, as the entire Canadian wilderness is a figure eight, also known as an infinity sign. There could be the possibility that the girls are running in circles but they don't even know it, so it could be confusing for them. It is a reason to believe that they currently do not know what they are doing, and this might even make sense. Nothing is in order to happen, as there are constant fears, which might eliminate the true meaning of why this life exists. It is a sign that makes no sense, and it is the story that helps guide the people of the world. There is still time for hope as there is always time to celebrate the consideration of a healthy debate. It is for the future that there should be the necessary qualities of life, that there shall be nothing forgot. After all, there is always a constant fear of retaliation and this fear can cause anything to occur within the entire distance of time. That is why there must be some limitations imposed, which are considered to be permanent and invisible boundaries.

As people suspected, there is time to understand the willingness of time, and as it succeeds to a fate of new and a constant rate of harmony and freedom, the movement shall grow into a utopian society, but you never want a dystopian society, as that makes no sense at all, since it is a complete nightmare. It is actually madness that causes people to start chaos, in the form of riots and anything that people can think of. It is part of the problem and it must be eliminated from the entire society, altogether.

Remember, there is time to remember, as there is a reason to remember. You do not want to forget about what happened to society at large, but then, you do not want to end up stuck in this Canadian wilderness, with all kinds of strange creatures, and possibly, rapists. You want to escape these badlands, as that is what people might tend to call this type of area. It is why there must be a way out, in order to solve the situation, as there is time to solve something, with regard to life and humanity.

Humanity is something that you must live with, and if you decide to destroy it then you might end up dying yourself. You could also face this strange wilderness situation, and you will be stranded and all alone, to the point that you will develop a phobia. You will try to escape this wilderness if you ever come into contact with it, but you will have trouble finding a way out. This will cause significant problems for your health, as you might never gain a well maintained life cycle.

For everything to end, there must be a reason to start a mild conversation. This is when the realization will come into play to determine the outcome of something big. It will be revealed that something wasn't true, but it will also reveal what has happened in real life. There is a sigh of relief, as something is discovered. It is a sign that must determine the efficiency of life. For many people, this means that there is always a constant fear or there could be a constant fear, but it is probably only lurking in society to wait until there is a weakened system. There is something that might make sense to this, as it will reveal nothing but the truth. It has to apply to the rest of the world, yet it must be maintained to help the plagues from spreading.

Helping out with anything, there is a reason to fear that something is going to fail or fall on top of you. Then you would be crushed, for some apparent reason, and this might never make sense to you. It is the epitome of life, as there are surely some strange things that are supposed to happen. It is just a part of life.

People, people, there are other things to worry about, and you should hope you are in a safe place. The girls are in a place of danger, and you could be responsible for their fate. You must decide if you want to help out, or as you might encounter something even more dangerous. There is something that you might encounter. There is the reason to think about life as well as the beliefs of other people. It is a game to you, isn't it, and you still refuse to respond. It must really be right for you to refuse to answer any questions, yet there is something wrong with society. The rest of society must be incapacitated, but there is a way to fix that, you can slow time to an indefinite halt. It is responsible for you to freeze time to save something, but you are neither helpful nor responsible. You are a complete joke and you must make amends to be happy with your life. It is part of the society that you must control your urges. You must be willing to accept your fate. It is a time to show strength, a time to determine aptitude. You must be hopeful something doesn't happen to other people.

This is a complete mess. It is something that makes no sense at all, and it might never make any sense, as there are problems all around. The girls are stuck, and they must find a way out of this situation. They aim and shoot again, only hoping to kill these zombies indefinitely.

It is a sign that is not showing any difference. The girls run again, but faster and faster, they pick up radical amounts of speed, and something starts to happen. Somehow the girls ended up in a much distant location. It could be the result of time travel or even a time shift. It proves not to be a time shift or time travel. It is just something that might make more sense than usual. Everything is different, but if it is neither, then it has to be something, well, it is probably the result of hyper speed. The shoes must have accelerated the girls to a distant part of Asia, but if they are in Canada, well, how could they walk on water, well, there is a good explanation for that. The shoes automatically freeze time, resulting in everything being still. Nothing is currently moving when the high speed shoes are activated to go at full speed. Because of this unique feature, you can walk on anything, but magma will still melt anything, so you should stay away from active volcanoes. It is the reason why it must be a part of life, for the reason that there is the possibility of safety.

So, the reason comes now, where exactly are the girls, and why in Asia. Well, it seems like they are located somewhere in the greater Tokyo area. Tokyo City is known for its populated areas with constant tourists. If there is ever an incident here, something like a zombie attack, well, there will be massive deaths, as the people will be hopeless, only because there will be massive pushing and shoving against each other. This movement pattern would cause great difficulty to escape the deadly escape. It is hopeful that some people might escape, but it could be the reason why there might be massive amounts of casualties, along with many fatalities. Many people might die, but others might only get injured, and so, there is the reason of how to handle a situation like this. With timing an important issue, it is a part of something larger, a complex mechanism that decides the fate of everyone, and no one must decry this situation. This can be the solution to anything, as it has been known to reveal useful information.

Reality kicks in, and the girls start to realize that time has stopped for them when their shoes were activated. Even though these shoes are from the log cabin, they are still the same as found in the HEPTAGON. Time is still stopped and it might start to resume in a few seconds, minutes, or hours. There is still enough time to achieve something, and it must be completed.

CHAPTER NINE

Just as something strange happened, the girls now realized that they traveled extremely fast, effectively stopping time, to the Tokyo City in Japan. Time has yet to set, yet it might be soon. There is a crowd of people, but they are not moving, they are completely frozen in time. There seems to be a railroad or some type of metro train, yet, the train is not moving. It is in suspended animation, as everything else, and there is nothing else that could happen. So, there seems that there are multiple things that the girls can do. They can either start time again by stomping their shoes on the ground, wait for suspended animation to stop, or to walk on the tracks. It is a difficult choice, but the girls choose to walk on the train tracks. There is not much information to know about, except that this place resembles the Narita Airport Train Station that is below ground. The train resembles the Narita Express or NEX for short. The Narita Express is extremely fast for its type as it resembles a modern metro train, but can travel up to eighty miles per hour. It is not built on standard track gauge, but it would be narrow. In fact, the track gauge is considered narrow. Almost all trains, except for the high speed bullet trains, use the narrow gauge track in Japan. The high speed bullet trains use the standard gauge track, as it is better for speed.

As the girls try to find a way out onto the train tracks, they see people everywhere. This train station is completely insane. There are crowds of people everywhere, and since they are frozen in time, it is still too crowded, and so the girls must find a way to squeeze past. It is extremely hard to pass these people, as they are in the way, and there must be a better solution. There is something to still think about, and it is about the same as always. It is the amount of time left until suspended animation will end. Right now, the girls still have two hours left for suspended animation, which is indicated on their time watches for some odd reason. It was simply a time to enjoy yourself, but there is a war to fight. There is a reason to find a way out of this crazy and insane place where there is no room to move. It is a situation in which there must be a move. Something must be done in order to achieve the goal, as it is simply a part of life. It is part of the overall goal to achieve the freedom of something that was meant to achieve nothing, yet there is a constant movement of people who fail to recognize anything important, as it is the reason why they always lack the efficiency of the world. Nothing will always be completely concurrent, and it shall never be the same or even the exact opposite. There should be no relation at all to the entire agreement, as it is simply a matter of life and death, as it might make sense in the end.

After finally making it past the crowds of people and the train, the girls climb down onto the tracks so that they can explore the situation, which took about ten minutes to get out of a massive crowd. Everything is completely frozen, and now there is less than two hours left until suspended animation is over. This is very valuable time on their hands, as they can find a way out of this place. It is something that could lead to more clues, which could lead to more clues, and could lead to the reason why this is happening. It is simply the result that something is happening, as statistics clearly show an anomaly of an algorithm. There is a complete mess and it can be fixed, in a way that has every right to attempt a new life.

As the girls continue to walk on the tracks, they finally find dirt next to the rails, in which they can finally walk on. This dirt, well, is partially gravel, is a much better surface than metal or wood tracks. The railing on the tracks could lead to injuries, and as a result, everything could end in a matter of seconds or minutes, all because someone tripped and fall, because they made a mistake when walking. It could also mean that the person is just plain clumsy and things like these accidents always happen.

Anyways, as the girls are continuing to walk on the ballast, yes, the gravel and or dirt mixture, that is what it is actually called in order to protect the rails, the girls find it is a long way, and they have to enter extremely dark tunnels with limited lighting. After many tunnels and half an hour later, the girls finally see signs of building, yet they also see more trains stuck at the stations because of this thing known as suspended animation. While everyone else is currently in suspended animation, the girls are the only people who are not affected by it, because they are wearing the specialized shoes that started it all.

There is only eighty minutes left, and they must find a way out of this crowded metropolis, where everything is frozen in time due to their shoes. Don't get me wrong, there is nothing wrong with Japan, but the girls where never even supposed to come here, the entire incident was a mistake caused by shoes. Tokyo and the rest of Japan is a beautiful city and country, filled with excitement and fantasy, with dreams and everything else, but there is no reason for the girls to even be here at this present moment in time. It is probably a diversion.

Twenty minutes have passed, and there is one hour left until suspended animation ends. The girls finally see a good station to climb out of, and it is Tokyo Station, one of the best train stations in Japan. The girls climb up on the edges of the wall protecting the tracks. One by one, they each attempt to climb to the platform, and each of them succeeds in doing so. Now that they are in a main train terminal there must be something else to find out. There could be more things lurking here, yet it is crowded, but not as the previous train station, which was below Tokyo Narita Airport. It is a sign that can help. There is no reason to be alarmed, as there is nothing more than help. It is a major cause of how to solve the issues of civilization, but there is a current situation that might say otherwise. There is something that might seem alarming, but that might always occur, so the position on the matter is that anything can happen because it will happen, which will result in something always happening. It is not the end of the situation, as there is still a long ways to go, and it

shall last forever as long as the people are in harmony, a
path that seems confusing.

After the fact, everything should be resolved, and
it is normal to indicate that something is in the current
situation for the purposes of nothing other than games. It
is the purpose that something is done, and it is the case
that something must be motivated, so there is a reason to
live in the time of deceit. It is the time when deceit is in
the middle of everything, and you might get distracted, but
to prevent this from happening, it must be an epiphany
that will later turn into the realization that something is
going to happen, which will result in the prevention. This
practice has always seem to be very controversial, as it
relates to something that seems crazy, but the other crazy
thing is that of this thing called suspended animation. This
type of reaction that blocks movement but still allows
creatures to live is the result of some scientific claims.
People have constantly feared that there will be something
wrong, and in order to defeat that bad spirit, something
must be done. There is always a way that must be
defended.

Since the girls have arrived on the platform of
Tokyo Station, they have wasted a total of ten minutes,
and so now, there is only fifty minutes left until suspended
animation ends, which could be in disaster. It is time that
they take action, and so they decide to exit the train
station, to find a way out. It takes half an hour to reach the
local streets, after looking at maps to decide where they
will go. Now that the girls are out of Tokyo Station, they
only have twenty minutes left until the end of suspended
animation. This might not be enough time to figure out,
but it might seem unusual, as it might have a current

situation to deal with. There is always something to battle against, as there is a reason to identify with the most plausible explanation. It is the result of what you want, and how you must think, in order to admire the true feelings of life. It is the complete nonsense that people try to promote that ends up as propaganda, and it shall be the demise of something other than freedom. It is the cause of advanced evil.

With only twenty minutes left, there is not much to do, so the girls walk past the frozen people stuck in the middle of the road, hoping to find a way out, and it is the feeling that something might happen. It is the reason that something will happen in a few short minutes. Now, far away from any buildings, the girls are in the middle of the road, and see some type of weapon. It resembles some type of grenade, but there is no reason for it to be here, as it does not make any sense. It has a lack of responsibility as well as a meaning of destruction. The complete theory of an object exploding will lead to nowhere. It must be part of a very easy distraction, but as you may expect, there is about the time that it could take time to figure out the reason why it is still present. It is constantly changing, and to that extent, there is always a reason to accept humanity for the sanctity of life, to promote freedom, and to end censorship, which will be the way of the future. This case simply takes an enormous amount of time, and you must be patient, for the reason will reveal itself in daylight. There is nothing else that could happen, and as it might sound strange, there is time to fix everything in peace.

Time is running out, since there is only one minute remaining until suspended animation ends. It is near in sight, and it might reveal something startling. As far as other people seem to notice, there is a lack of a debate, with absence as the main result. Since nothing will nothing to resolve an issue, there is only one issue to contemplate, which is to wait, and to wait for something to happen. With only a few seconds remaining, suspended animation has ended, and people are starting to move again. Everybody is minding their own business as usual, as it relates to something that is common in everyday culture, unless you are causing a disturbance, which could lead to riots and even more chaos. It is the result that simply matters, and it shall remain the result that is the real reason for the entire debate. It is the reason that there must be consideration, in order to achieve the new goal of peace. It has been awaken, and it shall be used to order the new goal of happiness.

The girls have no idea where to go, as they are confused, and so, they find a helicopter, which takes them to the tallest building in town. From there, they can see just about anything, and it might be of better help, or it could help them to provide results. There have been the main reasons to continue anything, as there is a constant fear that raises doubts within the entire community. It is that result that must maintain life, in order to achieve the most possible goal in the world, which is harmony and peace, but is almost ready to take place. With that in mind, there is something else to think about, something that must maintain the balance of time, in which it is critical to evaluate the complete overhaul of any problems.

With the girls at the top of the highest building in Tokyo City, there might be something that can be found. At around five minutes after reaching the helipad, the girls start to see what resemble zombies, and so, the girls fire at them, and they start to fire back with lasers. The girls must activate some weapons that were never activated before, and so, they each grab the most powerful weapon that they have, which is the Hellfire 8000, a modified advanced weapon that will kill instantly. One by one, each of the girls start to use the gun, remembering the instructions and their training. It is a very complex, yet simple gun, which makes everything seem so obsolete. The guns are now ready to fire and shoot, and so, they aim at their targets, a bunch of flesh-eating zombies that have no clothes on. All that exists on the zombies are falling body parts, each getting worse and worse by the second, so there is something that must be done.

Confirm.

Shoot.

Launch.

The gun is ready to fire. In a stream of multiple beams, the gun launches super-concentrated plasma-energy along with fire, gas, and radiation on the targets, who are the enemy, the zombies. Radiation only activates once it hits the targets, and with that, something new and daring happens, maybe a change of hope, a plan to start peace, or even some reason to understand life. There is smoke amongst the zombies, as the Hellfire 8000 was meant to kill and or destroy everything in sight. It might take a while, but the smoke will clear, revealing the aftermath of the situation, in a way that seems strange.

During the attempt to destroy the zombies, people started to hear loud noises, but they did not do anything yet, as they thought it was nothing, but seconds later they heard more noises. People started to run in panic, causing chaos and riots. Keep in mind, the people who started to panic only did so because they might be afraid of anything, even though if they are not in imminent danger. There is a saying to all of this commotion, and it will never end, because that is the way some people act.

With people now in constant panic, more people start to fear something, as it was transmitted in a strange way that caused chaos and riots. So far nothing has burned down and that is a good thing. Nothing has attacked the people yet, but people always get scared. Panic is everywhere, and it is about to start in a more strange way. There is nothing to fear, as life will be feared itself. People are starting to trample on each other, as it has only been five minutes since the hordes of people heard the noise. One thing it might be is the cause of fear, which is always the meaning of something. It is the reason why there is something to figure out, as it has meaning to find destiny. The destiny will occur, then there will be something else that happens, but since this thing is happening right now, the zombie attack, there must be some ground rules set into motion, which simply means everything else is irrelevant. It is a task that has been useful in the past, and as it goes, it will continue to be maintained, for the reason of something that promotes harmony, peace, and freedom, for everyone.

There is more to anything as it constantly happens, so as people might develop certain tendencies, there are reasons why they exist, and it occurs within their attitude, for the fear always remains. Fear is just a part of life, but it is part that is frowned upon. Some people are afraid of anything, and you are seeing that right now, so as you wonder why people have different moods, it is because of genetics, as a way to understand the basics about life. Everything has a reason to live, and yet, there is also a point of origin, but what happened today is crazy. People started to panic only because other people started to panic, but the point of origin was only linked to a few people. Those people fear that something dangerous will always try to happen to them, even if they don't face any danger. It is a sign that makes no sense, in which they are the crazy people, for which they cause riots and chaos, but dangerous people can do that too. It is a sign that something must happen, in order to reveal the way of transparency.

Since everything is changing in a vase new constant environment, there is something else important, and it has to relate to everything. It has to relate to life, and how the entire world revolves around the creatures of the night. It is a nice topic to discuss, but it is of the most importance that there will always be something to happen. Within the distant future, there is a reason to think about your past, as there is reason to believe you might be hiding something. It is something that might cause chaos, but you should be able to control it in such a manner that it will be impossible for anything bad to happen. The reason to the unknown is to hope and dream. There is time to accomplish anything, as it relates to movement.

It has been a while since the smoke appeared, and that means the Hellfire 8000 did its job perfectly. There is still smoke, appearing as something like smog or fog. It is something that is blinding people, only because they are going near it. People know smoke when they see it and they know it can be harmful to the body. The smoke will be here for a while as it takes time. Meanwhile, more people are starting to trample each other, because they are not looking around. It is complete hopelessness. Nothing might ever be the same, as it might make sense, but it has no known actual meaning in life. It is a thing of the plan to promote the mind and the soul, and as a way to understand biological chemistry, to a point that something is accomplished. Life is about change, as everything needs to adapt in a society of the entire ecosystem. It is life itself that has to maintain the reasoning behind something most important to the strategy of the people. There is always hope and there must be freedom, in a way that is benevolent.

Since hope is the origination of everything that wants to transpire, it is the reason that must evolve into a reason of destiny, a time to understand why life acts as it does. There is a constant change in atmosphere, as there are many reasons why stuff happens. It is the reason to understand, and as it makes sense it shall grow into the claim of evolution. Sanity is at its finest, and that makes all the sense that is possible. It is probably the reason or part of the consideration why people are acting like children. There is no reason to be afraid yet people remain fearful. This does not affect everyone, just a select few. It acts like a communicable disease, something that spreads from person to person, and through the air. It could be a reason why it might be so contagious, yet, as something makes its rounds, there is a reason to mention, that fear is everything that makes you support censorship and propaganda. All are related to the larger picture of a police and surveillance state. When this happens, there is a lack of oversight, causing select people to undermine the entire system. It is something that should never exist, and as it takes place, this is a time when people feel threatened, not by government, but by external forces that seem to exist.

Except for one reason, the external force could be imaginary or it could so far away the force does not want to take a chance. People tend to live with fear, and if they do, they a negative view of the world. People in constant fear of anything will always find a way to cause panic, riots, and chaos, because that is how their body works. It is happening because of nightmares and odd dreams. It is a time to remove fear from the face of the dictionary, a time to promote freedom, in the name of harmony, peace, and freedom, to engage the pursuit of happiness. There must be peace and war must come to an end. War causes chaos and it proves absolutely nothing. War is the reason why there is always a security and surveillance state, it causes the police state to appear. This must never happen, but it has been used before, as a way to control the enemy. It is time that war does not appear in any form of any manner, to the fullest extent, in order to make a change. There is nothing else but a change of heart. It is the way that must be achieved, in order to make the creation complete.

After what happened today in Tokyo City, there seems to be an overall consensus that something bad has happened. Certain people started to panic, thus, causing other people to panic. This whole situation caused chaos, riots, and everything else that you don't want to happen. In something that might sound strange, the police try to stop the panic, but they are ineffective, because the people are running and screaming everywhere that the police are being stepped on, falling to the ground, and bleeding. It is a bad day for the police, as all they were trying to do was to stop this chaos. Several officers have died, and so have many people. It is a result of chaos, and a feeling that this was planned well in advanced. It is the sign that some people might have been waiting for. Everything must make sense, and it sounds like this is complete nonsense. It is something that is the reason to prevent chaos. It must be prevented, as if it proceeds, then there will be anarchy, something that you never want, because that ideology promotes hate and chaos. It is something that will lead to misinformation, the way that anarchists achieve their goals.

Much is to say, but that is just normal. It should be normal but this situation in Japan is abnormal, a reason that has no meaning in reality. Something must be the result of something bad, and it can be related to the meaning of life. It is insecurity that causes the police state, but that is not what is happening here. Today, there were zombies, and they probably wanted to harm the people. It was a very strange occurrence, as this might have been the work of the known Hollywood machine. So now, after three hours, the smoke disappears, and it is revealed that the zombies turned to ash, dirt, and any other small grain of nuisance. Now that the zombies are destroyed, there is another problem, the people in the city, but then they see the leftover of the zombies, and now the people cheer.

Meanwhile, nothing happens to the girls. They use the helicopter to get off the building and fly to a secret location with no one watching. It takes a while, but the girls finally landed in a safe location, where no one can find them. The girls try to run, and it appears it works, as they return to New York City, where the parade is over. In Tokyo City, it is the next day, and there is a massive parade, after celebrating the deaths of the zombies, but now, the girls are in the city of New York.

New York City looks different than before the

girls left it. There is destruction everywhere and people are starting to loot, and the only thing to do is to drop some type of bomb. Good thing the Hellfire 8000 can be pointed downwards from a flying object, turning the ammunition into a dangerous bomb. Now, the girls must find a plane or a helicopter, and this could solve the problem once and for all. The Hollywood machine would be destroyed forever. As quick as you could, there is a need to change the entire plan. The girls have to look for some building to use as a safety area, but even better, they need to use their time watches in order to avoid any radiation, by escaping before something bad happens. It is the result of the past that might make the immediate difference. As a way to determine any field, there is always a way to define the exact replica of the environment because of the way life works. Life will change as a matter of fact without anything holding it back. There is nothing that will attempt to keep it from going, as it will always be the choice to continue something.

Everything evolves into a peaceful matter, as it was expected to. It is nothing to mention that there is a case by case bias against each claim being made, and without those claims everything might lead to chaos. It is a matter of a small amount of people to determine something because such critiques are vital to the importance of how things and object end up living. It is the choice that matters, in order to set a complete unification of how to live with the ultimate sacrifice. It is the best opinion to set that there is a reason to unite the people and the objects to the next level. There is still much complication with anything involved, and as a result, there is the feeling of something bad happening, for the feeling of lost activity. It is the plan to figure out a way to get out of such incidents.

Such incidents are why there is constant nagging and other such complaints. If you nag, you must not enable to the rest of the world, but there is a reason to determine the new idea of freedom. Incidents like this rarely happen, and as a new result, there is the reason to anticipate the entire crisis of a new enhancement. It is the reason that there must be a new case for the entire situation, but don't worry about your crazy utopian society, since they lack freedom, for some part of the law. It is simply a distraction to manipulate you, and as the way distractions occur, they try to change the subject without any prior approval. It is the cause that might change your mind about how to live your life. Everything is not candy, so you must decide how you will plan something like blowing up an entire city of people. Regardless of what happens, there is something that might lead to a new consequence, whether it is related, but it appears that things start to change with the dawn of a new era, and it is nothing new, so there will be a cold environment of what it means to handle the most serious matters. At times when it might lead to a bunch of crazy interactions, there is a reason to demonstrate that there is an institute to help the rest of the people, despite the lack of injuries. It can be a life or death situation, but there are always many reasons. There are always critics who fail to understand the importance of anything, and as such a debate, there is a reason why there must be hope, a reason to help others based on their needs. It is the reason why there must be compassion for anything, but never expect a handout or an entitlement, because those things should not exist, due to them being constantly abused by the populace of users who are always enrolled.

Entitlement or handouts, as some people call them, are an abuse of the system, as people think they always need them, just because they qualify. They think it is important to their life and how they live, when really, in actuality, half of those people don't even need entitlements. They only want it to save some money or they believe it betters the world or other situation, that everything will be more tolerant. The world will not be more tolerant of anything, as there are still people who will object to anything. There is nothing wrong with expressing your views, but there is something wrong when you try to force your views on other people. Some people believe that other people should listen to their views and to follow one universal view that supports special characteristics, well such views have been proven to be extremism, as those views lack meaning. Everybody should have their own view, and it should not be made by one single person who supports an extremist case, such as the idea of environmentalism, which wants everyone to stop driving certain vehicles, or animal activists, who support a ban of food products made from cows, chicken, and other land animals. These extreme causes and views lead to nothing but a lack of educations. Animals were created to be eaten by other animals, and humans are considered to be a part of the animal kingdom. It is part of the rest of the world that there must be acceptance towards multiple views. People who try to force their views onto another person are trying to indoctrinate that other person. That indoctrination leads to brainwashing, and it will confuse you. In order to avoid being brainwashed you must be willing to hear what people say, ask questions in your head about the subject matter, and then conduct some online research or book research if you don't have the internet.

Case by case situations will only happen very often, as people try to brainwash you, they must be crazy, or it might be the reason to attempt to do anything. There is the reason to accept something that will lead to nothing. It is part of the new life, so, go, as you might be pleased, in a sign that will promote longevity.

Without any hesitation, or you might think, there is a time when you might decide. The girls find a building tall enough to launch their attack to stop the Hollywood machine. It seems quiet but that is only the case because of destruction. This destruction by the people only happened because of chaos that caused riots. These riots got out of hand and people started to burn down buildings. You would have thought that the enemy planned to attack the buildings, but they are smarter than that. The Hollywood machine wanted the people to cause chaos and riots so that there can be a reason to establish totalitarian leadership. It is the goal of the Hollywood machine to establish a state of terror, in order to promote propaganda and fear. It is done in a way that blames the populace for starting such events. It is part of why that no one should ever be trusted. So, with everything in chaos, it might seem that everything is also in ruins, but that is not always the case, but in this particular situation, it is the case.

So, as you might have it as something else, there is nothing else to expect. Buildings are still standing, but others are in ruins, and some have been demolished by arson or demolition, by certain people. It is the case that affects the entire situation, as the reason that there is something that must make sense. For the fear of the people might eradicate something that might not make any sense. It is a part of the complete life that is granted by something that wants to control you. It is nothing wrong that will attempt to regenerate anything, but there is a cause to do anything, as there is always something.

The girls must find a way to climb the building, or to get to the top of it, and then to escape by using their time watches. Global fucks to anyone who cares or who doesn't give a shit. It is the civilization of the environment to nominate the position of a global effort. It is the most important and time consuming efforts of the century and it can take too long to understand the complexity of the very situation that stands. For all eternity, there are choices to be made, and without those choices, there will be chaos, to the tune of something that produces nothing but propaganda. In something that went wrong but had no effort, it shall be the most important thing to construct. There is the feeling to negotiate the decision to properly navigate the scenario, as it might relate to something other than hooliganism, but in any shape or form there is a way to navigate the type of situation that might harm people in the past and in the future, for the simple purpose of nothing other than patriotism. It is the fact that there is a long standing analysis of the subject in order to mention the simplicity of such a task. Not minding your own business is something that you should never do, because you do not need to know everything. You do not need to know what the person is doing. Whatever your neighbor is up to just ignore it, because if you interfere you might end up in trouble, and you will never be trusted again. So, as you decide to do something you must understand the reasons why you are under attack.

Beginning with anything that is relevant, there is some appreciation for a heroine, yet it often gets ignored, for the reason of feminism. The goal of feminism is for women to be treated like men, and there is nothing wrong with that ideology. The problem with feminism occurs when it gets political, which leads to all kinds of feminists. These extreme feminists want entitlements to everything, and they believe that laws should be changed just to reflect their ideology. These extreme feminists want to force their views onto everyone that lives in the world. It is a failed strategy, and it is often met by criticism from the pundits. Forcing your views onto other people is not a good thing, as it is considered rude behavior that shows a lack of respect for the rest of the world. Whatever you might think, it is something that is the reason to think about freedom.

Now that the girls have found a way to climb the building, they have to assemble in an orderly fashion in order to avoid from being trampled upon. The girls found a stranded helicopter, in the middle of the woods, or the place known by Central Park. The girls fly the helicopter to the building they found, then land it. By now, it is time to think of how to navigate this plan, but Central Park used to be a very busy metropolis, but now it remains as a gateway for torn down foliage, after it was attacked by the Hollywood machine. So, there remains something important, in that, there is a reason why terrorism is bad. In all accounts, the place known as Central Park was burned down by a bunch of arrogant evil people, who cared about nothing except for money and propaganda, which leads to censorship in the end. It is a claim that they often reject, refusing to take any form of responsibility whatsoever. It is just plain arrogance, a thing that leads to idiots

Now, the girls have devised a plan, they will point the Hellfire 8000 in a downwards position, and then they will attempt to use their time watches to avoid the radiation and the rest of the explosion. It is something that must make sense, a thing of relevance that must take some time, but it might not even happen, or so you might think, as it should be carefully constructed, in order to avoid a deadly situation. The entire streets of New York City are completely vacant, with no signs of life. People must have went inside for fear of an invasion of an enemy force, or they could have went to a new country.

With danger being an imminent threat, there is a way to postpone the negative environment. There is a way that will determine the goals of how to interact with the rest of the culture, yet, as people start to fight against the entire leadership, there is a way to determine the reason behind the whole goal. There is something relevant to the rest of the world, as well as the people who try to interact with the position of power. It is something that is meant to help the priority of power. Nothing can stand in its way, as everything is determined to negotiate to a better deal. There is the reason to always think outside the box, and by doing this you can think of new and creative ways to outsmart the enemy. This is by far the best option that you have to eliminate a threat, as well as being determined to interact with your peers. There is something that was meant to be but there is something that should never have taken place. It was the result of misconception, deceit in the real world. It outsmarted everything in its class, as it was determined to make a name for itself. There was a few things relevant to the case, but the rest were irrelevant, so as people might make an agenda out of themselves, it remains a fact that there is always something being hunted in a most despicable way. There are decisions that have to be made quickly and precisely in a very hasty manner, in order to move on with time and to pass the agenda to the next option.

On the rooftop of the building, the girls get ready to point the gun in a downwards position. Since the building is half a mile in the sky, it will be less dangerous than other buildings. The girls will have some time to escape, since the building is so high. It is important to note that this won't be easy, as there are all sorts of problems that can happen. It would be interesting to find out what is happening now, as it could indicate something is in the works for the reason of insanity. For the most part, there is the reason to understand the physical nature of such an occurrence, but there is always a problem with something, since there is a problem with the rest of the world. There is nothing wrong with people, just the ideology they lean against. It is for the most part, a very tricky shot, since there is only one chance to get it right, but that is only if you have limited ammunition, but since there is enough ammunition to destroy the moon, this would be a very interesting chance to see what happens. It is the most damning thing of the focus, as what there seems to be something sort of the rest of the world. There is the chance that something will go wrong, but just think it is a very powerful laser that will cause immense damage to the entire infrastructure system. You will then see that there will be something wrong with the rest of society, as there might be something wrong with the immediate climax of the end of civilization. It must take a chance to notify the difference in leadership, as well as levels. There is the whole world that mentions that there is time to learn, and at this point, you should know how to interact with the system of choice.

There is something that can be said about the rest of life. There is such a reason why a mission could become impossible, yet, there is no way to understand the rest of the civilization. It is something that hides, in the fear of being overthrown, and it is that type that there is the hope to shield the future of the world.

Nothing is more important than the rest of the world. There is nothing better that can maintain the process of peace, but there is the intention of causing great harm to people and to the rest of civilization. It is a choice that must be carefully crafted, in order to avoid any legal ramifications. There is the choice of nothing other than freedom, which must determine the reason to avoid any distress. There is always time to celebrate your freedom, as you never know when it will disappear. There is nothing wrong with society, as it might help you determine the right path for something.

As the right path continues to haunt you, there is also the opinion about something else, the fact that there must be a choice made. With everything in chaos, there is only one choice to be made, to destroy the entire city of New York, with one very powerful gun. It is the only option available, because that is the only way that the Hollywood machine will stop from starting wars within the entire world. Everything else is irrelevant, and it is the goal to destroy the enemy, in order to stop the process of terrorism.

Not much time has passed since the arrival at the top of the building. The girls are carefully positioning the Hellfire 8000 in a mounting unit to point downwards, towards the entire city. It is the only way to defeat the enemy, as it is the best possible way. There must be something done in order to prevent terrorists from taking control of the world, as well as everywhere else. It is the option that this is the best plan yet. It is the best choice to reign in terrorism, in order to eliminate the entire threat, as it might come back to haunt the future of the people. As the girls mount the gun, they must decide where to point it, as if it is pointed in the wrong direction, then there would be something catastrophic.

When mounting the Hellfire 8000, the girls determine that the best and most optimal direction to point the gun is to the south, as that is the most populated area and that is where all of the chaos has happened, yet, the entire city is an abandoned ghost town. There is no one in sight, as they have all fled. There are still dead bodies in the streets. Now is the time to mount the gun, and now is the time to align it. Since the gun has been mounted, it was aligned and pointed to the south. It is now time to run a diagnostic test on all systems of the gun, since there is a slight chance for a malfunction. The test is underway, and all systems will be available in a few minutes. The diagnostic check is complete, and it is safe to use the gun.

Now, the girls must point the gun in a downwards direction, since it is pointing straight forward. The entire mounting system was built by scrap metal found on the top of the building, as well as from the helicopter. It is not that fancy of a system, but apparently, there was some metal found on top of the building because of some unidentified flying objects. These flying objects could have been drones or aerial vehicles that bombed the building with machine guns. It sounds pretty gruesome, but that is normal during a civil war. It is completely within the stated guidelines of the enemy to focus on destruction, in order to prevent from being defeated.

Globally, this incident, the one initiated by the Hollywood machine, was seen as the most prominent, yet unprovoked tactics in history. There was no provocation by anyone or any entity, but the Hollywood machine would say that freedom is provocation, in which in reality, that logic is flawed and shows no understanding of what the meaning of provocation stands for. It is the reason to understand that there is the case to identify the current situation of such an attack, and by doing so there is the ultimate sacrifice to make. As far as anyone could depend on anything, there is nothing that exists for the sheer purpose of hosting hooliganism. These are crazy people who do crazy things, like starting protests for idiotic reasons. Hooliganism is a tool used by some nations in order to remove the idiots from society, but these idiots are just plain crazy. Not everybody who is charged with the act of being a hooligan is one, but the charge is dependent of the prosecutor, so, there might be a political case after all. It is in the case of society that the life of the rest of the people be left for pleasure, leisure, as well as the pursuit of happiness. It is the time to be responsible and to act in accordance with the rest of the world. There must simply be order, and by order, I mean peace, or something that will prevent war from happening. You don't need to establish some government organization, like that proposed by the failed president Woodrow Wilson, or even that of the crazy yet reduced United Nations. These organizations might claim to help the world, but they are not active enough, and even more disturbing, their employees committed crimes against people. It is illogical for anything to exist if people do the opposite of what is right. Nothing is helpful and it will never rise to that level, so that must be logic.

Whatever happens with the people after the invasion by the enemy, there will be considerable action against them by the people of the world. It is a plan to attack anything that is evil, but this plan relies on the site of jurisdiction. If the site does not fall within the proper jurisdiction of that state, then there is no way that the state can attack that enemy. The state where the enemy is located must use their jurisdiction to attack the enemy in order to insure justification.

Since that rant is over and might make sense, it is clearly time to navigate the mount and the gun. The gun has been mounted, and the mounting system has been attached to the building. There was a successful run of a diagnostic test, and it is now time to set the initial target of the weapon. The scope has been set to target in a downwards position, and it has been set to bomb mode, which will have a delayed reaction. Now, it is time to set the weapon to the proper channels, in order to be secured from harm. Everything must be precise, after all, there is a reason to be frightened as it seems to be normal procedure during a bomb blasé. There is simply a case to delay the reaction in order to prevent the initiators from being harmed in such a situation. This is always the case and it shall be proven.

    Ready, okay.

    Sequence is starting now.

    Confirm.

    Shoot.

    Launch.

    The gun has fired by voice activation.

    Bomb initiated.

    Delay in action.

    The bomb has been deployed and will set to a delay of one minute. Meanwhile, the girls have successfully started their time watches, but yet, there is still a reason where it will take them. Half a minute later, the girls arrive in South Africa, for some apparent reason. Now, they are safe from any harm. But back in New York City, it has been a full minute, and the bomb has been detonated, causing a plume of smoke to rise up to the top of the sky. The mission has been successful, and the time watches tell the girls that same information. The blast was so powerful that it destroyed everything in sight. There were no people present, as they either died, escaped, or where kidnapped by the androids to another part of the world, and then where tortured and maimed to death. As a result, there could be the reason of why the girls did not know what to do, well, that was because the original plan failed and because they did not get any information of how to defeat the enemy. It is well known that the Hollywood machine now doesn't exist, because they were all androids, and their only office was located in New York City. All of the members of the Hollywood machine were humans, but they then decided to become androids, just to live for eternity and to not die. They thought they would be immortal, but that was not logical thinking, as real immortals will avoid death and will escape. It is a sort of trait designed to sense evil.

Anyway, with the girls being in South Africa, there is still some thoughts to argue against, but there could be something else that might entertain your delights, but as far as I could tell, there is probably still paperwork to be worked out here. Yet, there is still time to think about the past and future, but there is still something wrong, and that reason might surprise you. Why is it that nothing is back to normal. There could be a lapse in judgement or it could just be something that was never meant to be true. It is interesting that there is a case for survival, and there is something to think about, as there might be the reason to think about the future.

South Africa has been fun, but there is still something else to be done. Something must appear, yet it seems to be taking some time. Then, out of nowhere, a mysterious flash of light appears, and thus, it is the time portal, but there are so many reasons why it must make sense. So now, the girls need to know where they are going, and by the looks of the time watch, it indicates back to 2006 to the first day of school, but there could also be something wrong with this picture. It could be a trap or it could even be an alternate dimension. There could be a chance that this is actually an alternate dimension or there could be something wrong with the picture. There is still the time to think about the rest of relevance, as there is the reason to usurp the power from the enemy. So, as there might be time to answer questions, there are always new reasons to establish the forces of good. It is a good thing that there must be the reason to undergo the narrative of how something is initiated, as there might be the reason of new insanity, the same as the reason for the face of the new global government. As what people tend to say, there is something else to say.

Meanwhile, or so you thought, there might be a serious crisis regarding what has happened. It appears that there is something new in town, a new force of evil that is more malevolent than ever before. It is something that is sort of like an imposing threat of doom. There is a new type of threat on the horizon. It can take the shape and form of anything that it sees fit. It is of course some type of shape shifter. You will never know what has occurred, as there is a strong possibility that no one will ever find out. Before anything bad happens, there is something that you must think about, the same type of political failure that happened decades ago. It is apparent that there is no equality in the rest of the world, but some people are just plain idiots, their society is backwards, and they believe they need to police the world, because they need to stop anything bad from happening. It is the result that is the most disturbing of being the world police, as this marks a very dangerous precedent in the history of the world, and it also breaks international law. There is nothing that can be good about this notion, as it is seriously flawed and needs to be changed. Serious matters need to be taken into constant consideration. There must be a debate about the entire agenda and it must demonstrate the ability to stop a rogue nation from abusing power. There is something to always think about, and as it might be mentioned, there is a case for transparency, which might result in the rest of the world opposing the rogue nation. It is the ability of the power to take a chance with the rest of the world. There

322

must be consequences for this rogue nation, as it has always shown to disobey the sovereign status of other nations, refusing to accept their laws, and constantly abusing their power and authority. The rogue nation must be stopped, and they need to be sanctioned on all sides, in order to stop them from exerting their muscle. But the rogue nation might dispute this, by claiming that they are helping the world to fight corruption and terrorism, and anything else detrimental to the world, well, that is just complete hogwash, because they are violating every international law in existence, by abusing their power. Their jurisdiction does not exist everywhere, and they can only police their territory. It is a sign that is changing, and the rogue nation must be stopped, in order to secure the freedom for people.

Notwithstanding the information, there is no such thing as people that don't harm people, because there are people who do harm others. It is at the very opposite side of the spectrum that there must be a debate about the whole system. As people might care, there is always something to understand, as there is a reason to state the obvious as fact or opinion. There is nothing that will be at the rank of anything, but there is a reason to think about the goal of theories.

Remembering something is critical in society, as it might prove to be part of the reason why there is a fight to protect freedom. This is the fight to stop censorship and to end propaganda. It is a fight that must be at the top of the priority. It must be completed, yet there is something blocking everything, to the point that it leads to nothing. It is at the most the most crazy thing imagined. It is nothing short of an abuse of power. There must be citations, as there is always a time to gather information. There is the goal to end war and to promote peace. It is time to end the surveillance state.

Just as you might think, there is another serious problem, there is the lingering question of what will happen to the girls, well, they arrived safely back in the year 2006 about a minute ago, and are walking the hallways of their school. There is still something wrong, it could be early or it could even be a weekend, but there is an indication on a school clock that it is Monday, which also indicates the temperature and other information. So, if today is Monday, then it must be just too early, well, that would also mean something is wrong, but the clock indicates it is half past nine. So, the girls check the windows of each classroom door and find that it is empty. From there, they walk to the cafeteria, where they find out that nobody is present. The girls then recheck every room to make sure that nothing is out of place, but still, there is no people present. There is a sign that means that there is a problem with the world. This could have been an alternate dimension created by the Hollywood machine in case something happened, or it could just be another type of backup plan. There is nothing else that could happen, unless there is a reason to understand the focus of how to interact with society.

Ploys exist for one reason, to deceive the other parties involved in the situation, and it can either be used for good or evil purposes. This could look like a ploy by the Hollywood machine, but there is no proof yet. There needs to be evidence connecting the Hollywood machine to the situation of everything. It must happen sooner or later, but there must be something to deal with, otherwise, there will be nothing but emptiness. It is quite interesting to think that there is something out there but it is still early to decide what is happening. At the pace that is now set in motion, there could be something else to consider, maybe something from the past or even the future, but there is nothing left in the present. There is something that is imminent, and it must take the form of something that has constant relevance.

There is no proof of anything yet, so there is no reason to be alarmed. Yet, there is still the constant and recent problem of what just happened. So, the girls are exploring the entire school, and they can't find anyone, not even their instructors. It is completely mysterious that something like this is happening, and for it to happen when they got back, well, it could be a sign of another alternate dimension. It could mean that the destruction of New York City caused a rift in time, thus, causing the effect of eliminating everything from society, or it could also mean that this is an alternate dimension that was just created for the girls and that this is their prison, as they were deemed a serious by the rest of society. It could be a simple answer to guess but there are currently no facts present to demonstrate any willingness. There seems to be an absence of anything relevant to the entire system. It is complete nonsense to think something must always exist just to make point.

Within the plain society of the world, there seems to be something that has a plan, a goal to outline the rest of the world, but there seems to be the people of the great divide. For one, the reasons to answer the view of the past is clearly something that is important, but it must be done in a way that has no effect on nature. Everything is in a current state of emotion. There is no turning back, as this will only cause severe damage. There must be something done in order to prevent anything bad from ever going into chaos.

Everything might seem normal, but the girls have been searching for hours, with no results in sight. The girls are in a ghost town of a school that used to have ample amount of sounds through the entire academic year. It is a mystery to find out, but the next thing to go is to venture outside, where they must find something, or else, they will know that something is wrong. So, the girls decide to exit the school, and they exit through the northern entrance. Upon entering the corridor to exit the school, they felt a mysterious breeze crawl up their skirts, since they are not wearing their combat gear anymore, because the mission has been accomplished.

So, the girls finally exit the school, and what they find outside might surprise them. It seems obvious that there is something missing, maybe the entire world has been destroyed, but that would not make sense at all, so it seems that nothing is at the complete theory of how to grasp the situation. Without a doubt, there seems to be something that is not part of history, a place that tries to make an attempt to foil the plot of something that is not relevant to society. There is nothing that you can say or to conclude about what is happening, as it might seem too late, as there is no reason to be afraid. There is no reason to be afraid, as there is the reason to understand the most simplest facts of existence. It seems that there is always a reason for everything, as there might be some time for the ultimate sacrifice. On the site where the dawn sets, there is time to attempt a treaty, something that might seem controversial at first, but there is a reason to negotiate how to indicate when something went wrong. It is the precise measurement that is a part of history. It is the reason why there must be a change to society, as there is a need for reform. If there is something wrong, then there must be the life force of beings. There is the thing of the past, and then there is chaos. There is the authority to determine the correct and whole process to combat the enemy. It is of the focus that there must be reform. For the safety of the rest of the people, there must be reasons to understand anything that is related to each other. It is always a part of life, and it must continue to engage the theory of the whole determination. It is of the most importance that there be a sign to determine the whole process, a sign that will lead to anything. There is something that there must be the reason to understand how everything works. It is just part of the process and how to negotiate the trade of the pact. It is equal. It is determined. There are several consequences to everything, and as it might seem, there needs to be a consensus.

Leading the way is nothing more than an experience. It is the most simple yet elegant thing to do, but there is always the option of how to determine the reasoning behind an old process. There is the thing of the past and the thing of the future. It is resistant to the people of the past. It is hopeful to negotiate with the future. It is nothing more than part of a pact to guide the entire process forward, hoping that it would lead to growth. There is nothing that can escape anything, as it has been here for years. What comes here is the choice of reason, the determination of free will and peace. It is of the point of no return that everything will be lost. It is the time to understand the insanity of everything, to hope that there is a future. There must be time to understand the complete process. It is the season to turn the people into freedom supporters. It is the time to assess the damage, and there must be time to determine the reason to tell the choice of words.

It seems as the people take to the streets that something is happening. People are just plain silly when it comes to certain things. Anything can be mismanaged as well as overlooked. It is something that seems to be a part of the group of people attempting to take a stance. It is the reason why there is not enough time in life. There are reasons why stuff like this happens. This can cause the result of chaos, riots, and start the process of new and unheard of propaganda. It is by choice that the people who find something new must determine the cause for how they will live. It is apparent that there is the reason to understand anything. For the hope of the people, there needs to be a stand, something that makes sense, so that there is a reason to live. It is something that was meant to decide the fate of mankind, the reason to host the type of nuance in the thing of the past. Life must grow in order to make amends. There must be time to understand the future of everything, as it will be related to the thing of the past, so it will relate to the present and the future. There is something to think about, and there will be time to figure out the best way to cope with harm. It is by far the most difficult decision to undertake, since there is only hope for the opposite. There is something that can take place, as it might be determined to hold off something. There has been nothing like it before, and as you might find out, there is just dust and wind, finding a way of the ground, hoping to cause a scare. It is the best choice to take, by deciding on risks.

Right as you might find out, the girls find nothing but a lack of people. There is no one outside. There is just a bunch of burning buildings. Some buildings have just collapsed while others were melted by mysterious forces. It is reason to believe that this isn't over just yet. For some reason, another dimension was created, and it feels like that this dimension was a false hope of accomplishment against the Hollywood machine. This has happened before and there must be a reason for it. A lot of information can be stated to the fact that there is a mysterious interaction, but there remains the simple sign of how the whole thing ever started. As far as I can tell, it is the reason that is meant to form the basis of the reason behind the whole agenda. It is the reason why bad stuff happens, so why must it be reason to understand anything. As what many people believe, before the Faberx Corporation bought out the United States of America and its government, the country itself was a massive surveillance state, with the Hollywood machine controlling part of the government, and it seemed like a nightmare. The banking secrecy act was passed over one and a half decades ago, but that did not even promote banking secrecy, as it promoted the government keeping an eye on your transaction. Back then, the government believed that nothing should be secret, but they do not need to know what amount of money you are making, because that should be kept secret. It was another tactic by the people opposed to freedom, and it was used for political purposes. There was the habit of political parties, and it was created in order to enact a law that supports nothing but illegal and illegitimate laws.

There is no place in society for those pro-surveillance laws, as they disregard privacy. Fortunately, all of those laws opposing privacy were repealed after the Faberx Corporation established the new government, by signing an executive declaration. It was time and time again that freedom was promoted. It was time for a new agenda that eliminated a surveillance state, in order to protect privacy and the rest of your freedom. It was reason to believe something that is securing the border. Something is the same as always, and it was meant to decide who would have won.

Unfortunately, something happened. When the Faberx Corporation bought out the government and the entire country not everybody agreed, and you should already know this, but the Hollywood machine decided to experiment with new technology and they succeeded. It was kept quiet, and nobody ever found out about it, as no one ever said anything. It was a well-kept secret in the Hollywood machine community. Everybody in that specific community remained quiet and they lived on the premises of where they conducted the experiments. No one ever found out, until that day when the instructors of Prep Stone Academy found some mysterious dimension. It was something that was not easy but it was part of curiosity. Everything now, in this current dimension, feels like something bad has happened. After all, the girls are in the right dimension, they are in the year 2006, and they are in school, but the thing that is the most distracting is that there is no one in sight. There is no one here in this dimension. After the girls bombed the city of New York with some very powerful weapon, it became clear that the threat was destroyed. That blast could have destroyed the entire future and it probably altered the present as well as the future. The present at that time is probably the same, so it could be seen as something relevant to the fact that something bad happened. It could be that the future of the world will die off for the rest of eternity. It could seem as there is a new testament in life, something that will shape the world to a new degree. Everything is now different, as it seems like the whole world has been abandoned. There is only one way to fix this, to go back in time, but it is a risk that they will have to take. The girls still have their time watches on.

As the girls continue their journey outside, they know that something isn't right. They try to activate their time watches to open up the portal to New York City, in order to prevent something bad from happening. It is something that might work, but it must be tried. The first attempt worked, and soon, seconds later, a time portal opens. This time, there is nothing wrong, no random setting, and no crazy locations. It seems weird, but in this dimension, the time watches take the girls to the exact time and the exact place where they need to be, and it happens to be minutes before the parade starts. The girls find themselves in the past and they tell themselves to not do anything, that everything is a trap. People keep on saying that talking to yourself in the past or the future will harm the space-time continuum, but this is the only way to solve the problem.

Reluctant at first, the girls from the past hesitate, but they then agree to not do anything and to go back to a place of their origination, or some other decent place. It is something that didn't happen. At the reasoning of the first time it was just a plain incident, but there is some sort of debate that the parade was just a trap. After all, it is no feeling that attempts to solve anything. It is by chance that something needs to happen. There is a choice that must be considered, as there is time to think. The girls in the past return to some mysterious place, and then, the girls from the future disappear into thin air, revealing that everything has been erased. So, this means that there was never any bombing, and no chaos, along with riots in the great city of New York. It means that something bad was prevented from ever happening.

Well, what about the Hollywood machine, well, they were defeated by the Faberx Corporation, but by trained intelligence agents, who tracked their whereabouts for months. The Faberx Corporation had to stop their plan of acquiring the Hollywood machine agents when the girls arrived. The girls were never supposed to show up in New York City. It was the agents of the Faberx Corporation who messed with the time portal, in order to prevent anything bad from happening. The Faberx Corporation in the real dimension actually stopped the agents of the Hollywood machine, but for some reason, some escaped capture. The Faberx Corporation tried to contact people in 2006 to try to find out if anyone was familiar with time travel, but no one answered. Why that specific time, well, they tried to locate one of their agents. The instructors at the school known as Prep Stone Academy were only amateur time travelers, and were not connected to the Faberx Corporation in any form and or manner. The instructors were simply time travel enthusiasts. So, it was just a coincidence that they helped, but the instructors did know and experimented in time travel activities. Part of the problem could be that the instructors are part of the Hollywood machine, but no one knows that for sure. In fact, there is no evidence that exists to support that claim, but how could the instructors know what happen, well, because of observation. For some reason, the past was altered, and an alternate dimension was created, just because of an alleged event. There was said to be a few members of the Hollywood machine who escaped the parade. That means that the agents of the Faberx Corporation failed to acquire at least two enemy agents working for the Hollywood machine. Nothing will ever be perfect, but the agents did capture and imprison all other enemy agents of the Hollywood machine. This means that those two agents planned something, and that for years, an alternate dimension existed.

Well, the chaos has never happened, and you think that the world is back to normal, well, that is still not the case, as the girls are now in Mexico, at a tropical island resort. Since the Faberx agents had to change plans after the girls arrived, that is when something bad happened. For that reason, that is why gunmen showed up. If the girls didn't showed up, then there would be no chaos and riots, and the enemy agents would have been captured. Now, the results of all of this resulted in the girls realizing that they had to go back in time to warn the girls in the past not to do anything, and they did achieve that. After the girls warned the themselves in the past, they all disappeared to a different location, the all-inclusive resort in Mexico on the most pristine beaches you have ever encountered. From the point of disappearance, the agents of Faberx realized that they now had a chance to capture the enemy agents, and they did so secretly with no one watching. The agents of Faberx completed this covert capture mission of the enemy agents after the girls disappeared into thin air. It was a sign of relief, knowing that something bad has been prevented. As for how the instructors knew, well, they just enjoy time traveling, but they have also lived in that era for a short period of time when exploring different dimensions. It is a thing just to enjoy.

Knowingly, there is something to say, and it has to do with the tropical paradise in Mexico. The girls are now safe from everything, and they will soon return to school, as this prevented anything from ever happening. It is still the weekend before the start of the new school year, but then, something might happen. Indeed, something should happen, as if you were stuck in Mexico, you would eventually grow tired of this resort, unless you like to live an upscale life every day of the year, but even people who live that type of lifestyle eventually grow tired, but they get used to it. So, there is a reason that might happen that is in the favor of everything else. It could be considerate that something might happen, but as something starts to develop later on in life, there is a chance that there is a reason to escape.

Moving on from everything else, the girls are enjoying the tropical paradise in Mexico. For one, they just all stripped down naked in order to skinny dip and then to relax in a Turkish bath, which is something you rarely find in modern buildings. It is something like that of a big sauna or hot springs area, but it is entirely closed off, with doors and everything else you can imagine. It is maybe something that you should experience, but it is just pure luxury. You should just hope that nothing ever happens to you, as there might be a detriment to the rest of the entire society.

Meanwhile, as the girls are enjoying their dip in the infinity pool, it is time to contemplate about what will happen next. You already know the confusion that the girls caused the agents of Faberx when they arrived, but that case has eventually been solved, after the girls decided to warn themselves in the past. This gave the agents at Faberx the opportunity to capture the enemy agents of the Hollywood machine, which then, eliminated the entire alternate dimension created altogether. It is something to be proud of, but no one even knew that the agents of Faberx would even be at the parade event. It could mean something good, but we will just leave it at that, but now, there is just something to feel good about. It is the time to think about the future by thinking about the present. The world is crazy.

Crisis averted you say, well, yes, that is what it seems, so you must be glad, but as you move on, you will find out something more. It is something that can be too intriguing, yet, something always happens. To the point of no return, there is no escaping. Nothing can ever escape, as it is a part of history. You must understand everything, as it is a slow process.

Sitting in the pool, the girls fantasize about some sort of dream, but it goes away after an instant. Time is short, so you must dream, but there is other things to accomplish. For one reason, nothing needs to be in order to enhance anything. It is quiet, and the sun rays are glaring their beams of light onto the girls' breasts. It is something sort of like relaxation. It is a fulfilling part of the environment, with everything that you can ever imagine. It is just part of life. It is what people must accomplish, and there are always things to do, as nothing is ever finished, it is constantly growing. It is the time to think about the past and to ward off any evil. It is at the brink of a never-ending assault on freedom. Something has to be done, as there will be nothing to solve if freedom is replaced with propaganda and censorship. It would become nothing but a lack of waste. Everything could happen at once, and it must be solved, so there is the attempt to think of something, as without anything, there is open space.

Enjoying the sunset, the girls feel a tingling sensation below them, but it is the result of the water jets in the infinity pool, yes, this pool also has the capability of massaging your body. It is like happiness and candy, and the girls move their vaginas to one of the jets so that they can be massaged and feel pleasure. It sounds like an orgasm, in which it is, and there is nothing wrong with anything. It is a part of life, and it might happen, but it depends on your lifestyle.

Everything happens so fast, and it is only a matter of time until the inevitable takes shape. It is the most ideal situation when something bad happens, and by this, there is always the mystery case of the reason to happen to the story of the theory, so, as people might say, it is probably too good to be true, and that is exactly what might happen, but there is an occurrence in what counts. There is always an opportunity to take shape, and it must be in the form of proper reasoning. For the time it may be suited for the rest of eternity, there might be some obvious objections to anything involved, so as time takes place to the rest of sanity, it must be good to understand the theory behind anything as it is said to come from deep within the institution of happiness. It is also meant to be the reason why there is such an occurrence. Many times there are serious reasons to institute reforms, but there is a time to take a stand that will lead a revolution to the end of times. It is such a tactic that it will lead to the truth of the matter, and something good will happen. As a matter of fact, there is reason to believe that something might happen soon, as it will relate to the full course of the nature. It is a time that is meant to distinguish the opportunities of freedom, the type of nuances that occur to curb propaganda, and the reason to institute justice. It is the time to reform the idea of reform, the very issue that is stuck with this type of problem. It must be quick and it must be fast, in order to prevent something bad from happening. There is the reason to take no chance. Failure is not an option, and as you might find out, there is a will to guide the people to the rest of the eternity. There is no problem unless there is something wrong. It should be at most, the most serious debate that you have ever attended. It is the time to take the stand against censorship. You must prove yourself to the rest of the world that you will promote freedom. It is of the most importance. There is no such thing as going back, and everything else could be a fallacy because it has always been a fallacy. There is nothing but disgrace to your name, and it will spread until you change your ways. It must be a radical idea to think like something that never makes sense, but it is simply an understatement. There must be complete guidance, for without it, there is always the opportunity to backfire. There is nothing wrong with anything, but you must seek guidance, and as a way to solve anything, there is a way to understand the type of situation you must always encounter. It is always good when change occurs.

Upon your understanding, there is now nothing more to tell you. The girls walk naked to the Turkish baths, and decide not to wear any towels. They are soaking wet. Their bodies are hot and pristine. It is something that you should avoid, as you can't handle their seduction. It is a force that will pull you in, and you won't know what happened, as you were put into a trance. Anyone, they decide to end their time at the Turkish bath, where they put on some clothes, minus any panties or bras, as they might want to rest. It is not that relevant that you should understand, because that is not any part of your business, since it is private.

So, before you know it, the weekend is almost over, and the girls get ready to go back to school, and they see a time portal appear. The time portal will take the girls back to the year 2006 in Winslow, South Dakota, where they will report to their first day of their senior year at the prestigious Prep Stone Academy. It is now Monday, and the time just seems to be right. There is just the reason to think that nothing is wrong, but it is not affordable to any situation.

Arriving at their final destination, the girls notice nothing different. Everything seems normal. It is just a regular old normal day in a small town in South Dakota. People are everywhere, and it seems that nothing bad has ever occurred. It is such a delight that there is no reason to understand what happened. Nothing ever happened, as it was taken care of in time. Everything that went wrong did go wrong, but now that time is over. It is something that would have killed anything, but that is what you probably wanted to hear. You probably wanted to hear that the entire situation was fixed, that the alternate dimension was eliminated. It might sound like that, but there could be a reason why that might be wrong. There is always a reason why something can go horribly wrong, at least what you have been told by certain people. It is a time that makes sense to you. But just as you like it, there seems to be a hidden agenda. You know that you like the idea of time being frozen and that there is an opportunity to change the history of the Earth, as well as the rest of the universe, but there is also a time to think about, the time when there is reason to believe that there is an outcast or some other outlier that doesn't make any sense. It is for that reason that you must determine what actually happened, and it is now time to determine the approach of what you thought happened, but never actually existed. It is now the time to approach everything from the truth, the reality of what actually happened.

Now, truth reveals itself to be the enemy of the reason behind everything. The girls actually never got the chance to defeat the Hollywood machine. The girls never got the chance to do anything. Even though that Teraload and WikiLeaks defeated the Hollywood machine by winning, the part of the girls are part of a different story, because the girls still have three months of training left. Yet, you thought that it was over, but that was never the case. With three months out of the year left for the training, there is surely something in place, but nature has something different in store for the rest of humanity. You thought something good will happen, well, there is a reason why three months are left. Three months remain because one year has not passed. It is the beginning of the ninth month of training, and now, something is about to happen in surprise.

Today is Tuesday, the beginning of the ninth month, but it is just after midnight. A siren rings in the building. Everybody wakes up, and it is revealed that the facility is under attack. What's more interesting is that Rafael Santiago and Allison Andrews are nowhere in sight. The rest of the girls and the other instructors are trapped, making it seem like something happened. It is just the beginning of the crisis. Fire spreads to the entire building, but Rafael and Allison are revealed to be in a safe house within the HEPTAGON, watching below, as the events start to unfold.

At once, Rafael and Allison escape the facility, looking back, and talking to their agents of the Hollywood machine. It is revealed that they are in charge of the entire Hollywood machine, that they are immortal, and that they are having a romantic and sexual affair. The entire place go up in flames, and they start to create another alternate dimension. The agents of the Hollywood machine, along with Rafael and Allison leave the HEPTAGON, now going to a secret facility, where the destruction of the world will take place, in the form of world domination. It was a trap, and it was I, Allison Andrews, along with my sexy beast of a man, Rafael Santiago, who made this all possible. I win.